Georgiana Fullerton

The Life of Elisabeth Lady Falkland

Georgiana Fullerton

The Life of Elisabeth Lady Falkland

ISBN/EAN: 9783743315419

Manufactured in Europe, USA, Canada, Australia, Japa

Cover: Foto ©Raphael Reischuk / pixelio.de

Manufactured and distributed by brebook publishing software
(www.brebook.com)

Georgiana Fullerton

The Life of Elisabeth Lady Falkland

THE LIFE OF
ELISABETH LADY FALKLAND
1585—1639

BY

LADY GEORGIANA FULLERTON

LONDON

BURNS AND OATES
GRANVILLE MANSIONS W
1883

✠

NOLITE ARBITRARI
QUIA PACEM VENERIM MITTERE IN TERRAM
NON VENI PACEM MITTERE
SED GLADIUM
VENI ENIM SEPARARE
HOMINEM ADVERSUS PATREM SUUM
ET FILIAM ADVERSUS MATREM SUAM
ET NURUM ADVERSUS SOCRUM SUAM
ET INIMICI HOMINIS
DOMESTICI EJUS

ex S. Matthæo x. 34.

PREFACE.

THE great attraction of works of fiction consists in the fact that they more or less present to their readers a description of trials, struggles, and emotions which they themselves have experienced. When a biography, without transgressing the limits of strict veracity, fulfils the same conditions, it appeals with far greater power to the heart and mind. Thus Lady Falkland's life can hardly fail to interest the very numerous persons who are going through in our day, hardships resembling those she underwent more than two hundred years ago. A different state of society, and the modern absence of penal restrictions as to religion no doubt modify these trials, but their nature remains the same, and many a wife and mother will find in the history of this convert of the seventeenth century, a resemblance with her own. May this record of her sufferings, and of her invincible perseverance take its place among those " footsteps in the sands of time," the sight of which refreshes the wayfarer on his road, long after the pilgrim of other days has entered eternal rest !

In an historical as well as religious point of view, the biography of the famous Lord Falkland's mother

is worthy of note. The times she lived in, the eminent
persons she was connected with, her remarkable gifts,
and many virtues, unite in making it interesting. She
was not a saint; she had faults more detrimental to herself than to others, but as a generous, courageous, noble-
hearted woman, who fought a good fight, kept the
faith, and continued in it to the end, she may well be
honoured and admired, and her example offered to the
imitation of all who suffer for justice' sake.

A life of Lady Falkland was written shortly after
her death by one of her four daughters, all of whom
became nuns in the Benedictine Convent at Cambray,
in whose archives it was discovered some years ago.
Which of them was the authoress it is impossible to
ascertain, though it appears probable that it was the
work of Anne, the eldest, in religion, Dame Clementina.
Patrick Cary, the youngest brother of these religious
ladies revised that manuscript, and added to it some
notes and comments of his own. It is from this memoir, published in 1861, by the late Richard Simpson,
Esq., and the ample appendices he attached to it, that
the materials of the following biography are principally
drawn. The original life is written with considerable
shrewdness, and a certain amount of force and ability,
but the language is so involved, the names of persons
and places so frequently left out, as well as the dates
of events, that it has been a somewhat difficult task
to disentangle the details and present them in consecu-
tive order and connexion. Many literal extracts from
the original work, have, however, been embodied in
the present narrative. One discrepancy occurs, the

solution of which can only be guessed at. It regards the offering made by Lady Falkland, when still a Protestant, of one of her infant daughters to our Blessed Lady. From the place where it occurs, it would seem that the child thus early consecrated was her third daughter, Mary, but this circumstance is distinctly mentioned later on in reference to Anne, the eldest of the sisters. It may be that Anne's second name was Mary, and that thence arose the confusion. The graphic picture of William Chillingworth's relations with Lady Falkland and her children form not the least remarkable feature in this memoir, exhibiting as it does, the peculiarities of that extraordinary man's character, and the religious condition of England at that period.

G. F.

Ayrfield, Bournemouth :
Feast of St. Cecilia, 1883.

CONTENTS.

PAGE

CHAPTER I.

Childhood and Marriage.

Burford Priory . . . 1
Sir Lawrence Tanfield . 2
Pleads against the Queen . 3
Nervousness in capital
   trials 4
Sudden death of a Judge . 5
Lady Tanfield . . . 6
Childhood of Elisabeth . 6
Her studies at night . . 7
Discovered by her mother. 8
Calvin's Institutes . . 8
Anecdote of the trial of a
   witch 10
Marriage to Sir Henry
   Cary 12

CHAPTER II.

Early married life.

Elisabeth at fifteen . . 13
Her letters to her husband 14
The Dowager Lady Cary . 15
Elisabeth under her charge 16
Her seclusion . . . 17
Her husband prisoner . 17
His return 18
Birth of her eldest son . 18
Her married life . . 19
First religious doubts . 20

PAGE

Absence from Protestant
   services 21
Dr. Neale 21
Her submission to Anglican
   teaching 22
Education of her children. 23
Results on them. . . 24
Her eldest daughter . . 25
Lady Cary's anxieties . 26
Her devotion to her
   husband 27
Indifference to worldly
   matters 28
Traits of character . . 29
Sir Henry Cary made Vis-
   count Falkland . . 30

CHAPTER III.

Lady Falkland in Ireland.

Sir Henry Cary as Comp-
   troller of the Household 31
A mask at Caversham . 32
Generosity to her husband 33
At Dublin 34
Sermon by Usher . . 35
State of Ireland. . . 36
The Protestant Clergy . 37
Enforcement of the Penal
   Laws 38
Lady Falkland's schools . 39

	PAGE
Their failure . . .	40
Rashness in expenditure .	41
Lord Inchiquin and Doctor Hatchett. . . .	44
Lucius Cary in the Fleet Prison	45
Sent abroad . . .	46
At Oxford	46
Lady Falkland returns to England	47

CHAPTER IV.

Return to England and conversion.

Storm on the passage across	48
The plague in London .	49
Lady Home's married life.	50
Her death by accident .	51
Grief of Lady Falkland .	52
Vision of Our Lady . .	53
Lord Conway . . .	53
Misgivings of Lord Falkland. . . .	55
Letter to Lord Conway .	56
Tendencies to Catholicism	57
Dr. Cozens. . . .	58
Disputations at Lord Ormond's house . .	59
Lady Falkland's resolution	60
Her abjuration . . .	62
Imprisoned in her rooms .	62
Interview with Cozens .	63
His failure. . . .	64

CHAPTER V.

Persecution and suffering.

Lady Falkland's allowance stopped	65
Her husband's harshness .	66

	PAGE
He writes to the King .	67
Accusations against priests	68
He urges his wife's banishment	69
Catholics assisting her .	70
She is set at liberty . .	71
Threat of separation. .	72
She answers his letter .	73
Cause of his displeasure .	74
Efforts at reconversion .	75
Conference at Lord Newburgh's	76
Conversion of Bessie Poulter	77
Arrest of Father Dunstan.	78
Generous conduct of Lady Falkland. . . .	79
Letter of the Duchess of Buckingham . . .	80
Letter from Lord Falkland	81

CHAPTER VI.

Correspondence—petitions—retirement from London.

Letter to Secretary Coke .	84
Letter from Lady Tanfield	87
Letter to the King . .	89
Letter to Lord Conway .	9
Lady Falkland's great destitution . . .	94
Faithfulness of Bessie Poulter	96
Mr. Clayton . . .	97
Literary work . . .	98
Lord Falkland to Lord Conway	99
Decision of the Privy Council	10
Lord Falkland to his agent	102
Lady Falkland to Lord Conway	104

PAGE

Another appeal . . . 106
Redress by order of the
Privy Council. . . 109
Lord Falkland to the King 111
Death of Lady Tanfield . 112
The Countess of Bucking-
ham 113

CHAPTER VII.

*Lady Falkland's literary pursuits—
she returns to London—reconciliation with her husband.*

Translation of Cardinal
Perron 115
Compliments to the author 116
Dedication to the Queen . 118
Epistle to the reader . . 120
Lucius Cary . . . 121
His character . . . 122
His marriage . . . 123
Anger of his father . . 124
Anne Cary 125
Pilgrimage to Holywell . 125
Return of Lord Falkland
to England . . . 126
Mediation of the Queen . 127
Reconciliation . . . 128

CHAPTER VIII.

*Lord Falkland's death—The
Miss Carys reside with
their Mother.*

Lady Falkland's children . 130
Accident to her husband . 132
His critical condition . 133
He desires to see a Priest . 135
His peaceful death . . 136
Great sorrow of Lady
Falkland. . . . 137
Her children return to her 138

PAGE

Payment of debts . . 139
Support of her children . 140
Abstinence days . . 141
Consideration for others . 142
Society at her house . . 143
Hopes of the conversion
of her children . . 144
Chillingworth . . . 145
Her motherly patience . 145

CHAPTER IX.

*Conversion of the Miss Carys.
Mr. Chillingworth seeks to
undermine their faith.*

Lady Falkland, and her
daughters . . . 148
Account of Father Cuthbert 150
The Miss Carys received . 151
They refuse to live with
their brother . . . 153
Danger from Chillingworth 154
His history . . . 155
His conversion . . . 156
Laud writes and brings
him back from Douay . 157
Opinions concerning his
return 158
Advice to a Catholic friend 160
Duplicity of Chillingworth 161
Lady Falkland deceived . 162
Snares laid for her
daughters . . . 163
Laud's letter to the King . 164

CHAPTER X.

A traitor in the camp.

The Catholic movement in
England 165
Cunning of Chillingworth 168
His apparent candour . 169

PAGE

Continual deceit . . 171
Direct attacks on the
    Church 172
Crafty proposal . . 173
His falsehood detected . 174

CHAPTER XI.

*Mr. Chillingworth's tergiver-
sations and apostasy.*

Lady Falkland warned . 175
Elisabeth Cary . . . 177
Falsehood of Chillingworth 178
Fictitious interview . . 179
A new religion . . . 181
Father Leander misrepre-
    sented 182
Indignation of Lady
    Falkland . . . 184
Chaperlin and Chilling-
    worth 184
Conference with Father
    Holland 185
Chillingworth loses his
    temper· 186
His final detection . . 187
He resides with Lord
    Falkland . . . 188
Patrick and Placid Cary . 189
The Maid of Honour . 190
Lady Falkland's pecuniary
    straits 191
Her almsgiving . . . 192
Obliged to break up her
    establishment . . . 193
Her daughters with their
    brother 194
Unforeseen results . . 195

CHAPTER XII.

The two Slingsbys.

Conversion of Francis
    Slingsby 197

PAGE

Letter from his father . 198
Newman's visit to Mr.
    English 200
Letter from Lady Slingsby 201
Francis in Ireland . . 202
The Countess of Kildare . 203
Archbishop Usher . . 206
Bishop Bramhall . . 207
Examination before the
    Privy Council . . 209
Lord Castlehaven befriends
    Francis 209
Letters to Father Gerard . 210
Henry Slingsby at Few . 211
Meets Lady Falkland's
    daughters . . . 211
Francis Slingsby recon-
    ciled to his father . 212
His father's tenants . . 214
Discussions as to property 215
The General of the Jesuits 216
Letter from Father Gerard 217
An arduous struggle . . 219
Triumph of grace . . 220
Francis bids farewell to his
    father 221
He enters the noviceship . 224
Renunciation of earthly
    prospects . . . 224
Troubles of Henry Slingsby 225
Death of Francis . . 227

CHAPTER XIII.

*Patrick and Placid Cary's
. escape from Few.*

Change in Lady Falkland's
    manner of life . . 229
Strict economy . . . 230
Her two boys wish to be
    Catholics . . . 231
She writes to Lord Falk-
    land 232

PAGE

Chillingworth   again   at
work   233
His abuse of the Holy
Scriptures   .   .   .   233
His method of argu-
ment   236
Lord Falkland's opin-
ions   237
Lord Falkland's temporary
absence   238
Plan of escape for the
boys   239
Favourable incidents.   .   241
Escape of the boys .   .   243
Their safe arrival   .   .   245
The Privy Council   .   .   245
Threats against Lady
Falkland   .   .   .   247
Chief Justice Bramston   .   248
The boys conveyed to
France   249
Their subsequent life   .   250

PAGE

CHAPTER XIV.

*The last years of Lady
Falkland's life.*

Assistance from Henry
Slingsby   252
Declining health of Lady
Falkland   .   .   .   253
Vocations of her daughters   254
Her last sacrifice   .   .   255
Lady Falkland remembers
her vow   257
Religious life of her daugh-
ters   258
Lady Falkland reduced to
beg   261
Her son provides for her .   262
Preparation for death   .   264
Peaceful end   .   .   .   265
Her writings and transla-
tions   267
Points of character .   .   268

CHAPTER I.

Childhood and marriage.

ELISABETH TANFIELD, the future Lady Falkland, mother of the Royalist hero of that name, was born in 1585, at Burford Priory in Oxfordshire, doubtless one of those old monastic houses confiscated in Henry the Eighth's reign, about half a century before the only child of the wealthy lawyer, Lawrence Tanfield, saw the light within its walls. Some of the former possessors may have been still existing at that time in sad solitude, far from the sanctuary where they had so long chanted the praises of God, or lingering in its vicinity beholding with aching hearts the desecration of their religious home, and the alienation of the fair fields, gardens, and orchards, the produce of which they had been wont to share with the poor. Did some of these aged men, did the Guardian Angels of that house pray for the innocent child, born within its once hallowed precincts? Did they ask for her a better gift, a nobler inheritance than these unblest possessions? It may have been so, for her fate in after life proved very different from that which in her childhood seemed to await her. May it not also have been

B

that the sight of the old abbey, inhabited in other days by God's servants; the stone crosses left here and there on the monastic walls; possibly a stray volume from the monks' library, fallen into her hands when at an early age she became passionately fond of reading, biassed the mind of the young Elisabeth towards the Catholic faith? Subtle are the influences which sometimes prepare the work of grace in a chosen soul. Life-long impressions are often produced by apparently trifling circumstances. Unconscious associations lay as it were the train which a spark of Divine love sets on fire later on. Whether Elisabeth Tanfield mused or not in her childhood on the history of her home in other days, she no doubt often thought of it in her mature years.

It is probable that Burford Priory was purchased by her father, at a somewhat advanced time of life, when his talents had placed him at the head of his profession, and the penniless son of a younger brother had become Sir Lawrence Tanfield, a Judge and Lord Chief Baron, distinctions attributable to the uncompromising rectitude of his character as well as to his eminent abilities. The small patrimony which he ought to have inherited from his father he never possessed. Against the express wishes of her deceased husband, his mother retained the whole of it in her own hands, and eventually divided it amongst her daughters. She gave him indeed an excellent education, and expressed her conviction that with that and his own wits he would be perfectly competent to make his way in the world. The result justified, if not the equity of her conduct, the correctness of her previsions, and as far as this world was concerned, she had no occasion to repent of this act of injustice, for Lawrence never reproached her with it, and never sought to recover any portion of his paternal inheritance, nor would he allow his mother's conduct to be called in question.

In after life, when married to a wife who had great influence over him, and who did not take the same view he did of the subject, this was the only point on which she could not sway him in the least, he would not suffer it even to be approached. From the time that he began studying the law at Lincoln's Inn, he devoted himself to his profession with unremitting industry. No sooner was he able to practise, than his mother left him, as we have said, to shift for himself, and the incident which marked the outset of his career at once showed that she had judged rightly her son's abilities. He was called to the Bar at the early age of èighteen, and the first cause he had to plead was against Queen Elisabeth, her Majesty having for her counsel Mr. Playdon, the most famous lawyer of the day. How young Tanfield came to enter the lists with this forensic giant is thus explained in the Life we quote from.[1]

" His cause was that of a friend and kinsman of his own, who would not have trusted it in the hands

[1] *Lady Falkland, her Life.* A manuscript in the Imperial Archives at Lille.

of so young a man but that it was refused by all
others for the two above-named reasons. But he,
Lawrence Tanfield, had no credit to lose, nor could
he lose any by being overthrown in his beginning by
so learned a man, it being enough honour for him to
have pleaded against him. Thinking the cause
most just, and the man whose it was being his friend,
he as little feared being against the Queen. So well
did he discharge himself that he carried the cause,
and showed so much courage in pleading that
Mr. Playdon, meeting him coming out of the hall,
embracing him said: 'The law is like one day, if you
live, to have a great treasure in you, and England
an excellent judge.'"

Each step in his career confirmed the truth of his
eminent antagonist's prophecy. There was one duty
of his position, when he became a judge, that he
dreaded inexpressibly, and that was sitting on a
cause of life and death. When obliged to do so,
nothing could exceed the minute and close application with which he conducted the case and sifted the
evidence. He used to declare, that he had never
pronounced a sentence of death without feeling "a
cold sweat on his brow and a fit of trembling shaking
his limbs."

An incident which he had witnessed in his youth
seems to have made a strong impression upon
Mr. Tanfield. He was going on the Western Cir-
cuit, and at one of the towns where the assizes were
held, the judge condemned several criminals, and

amongst them a Catholic priest. The executions were to take place on the day after his departure, but he ordered the priest to be hanged before the others on that very day. The following morning, after he had breakfasted, he asked if his orders had been complied with. The answer was in the negative. It was more convenient to the authorities that the executions should all take place at the same time. Upon this the judge swore with a tremendous oath that he would not dine until the priest was executed, and commanded that it should be done at once. He remained in the town until he heard that his mandate had been obeyed, and then mounted his horse, "a quiet animal, who had ever been most gentle as those of judges commonly are," our old-fashioned writer observes, but as soon as he was seated it reared and threw him off. His head struck against a stone, and his brains were dashed out.

We read several instances, in writers of that epoch, of sudden deaths overtaking some of the most violent persecutors, especially when blasphemous expressions had passed their lips. It was not, however, the fact of the man thus hurried to death having been a Catholic and a priest, that particularly shocked Lawrence Tanfield, who seems to have been a thorough Protestant, but the sanguinary violence of the judge, and the impious oath he had uttered. The circumstance of his sudden death following upon it filled him with horror.

He was averse to the persecution of Catholics,

but merely, as far as we can gather from the history before us, from motives of justice and benevolence. His equity was so well known that the dearest of his friends never attempted to bias his judgments, and his disinterestedness was especially remarkable.

Such was Elisabeth Tanfield's father, a man of honour, of virtue, and of great talents, but so exclusively devoted to his profession, that as his grand-daughter quaintly observes: "He did so entirely apply himself to it (the law) and it did so swallow him up, that being excellent in it, he was nothing out of it, and left the care of his own affairs entirely to his wife and servants, not even looking over the evidences when he bought land, a matter," she adds, "so within his own element."

Lady Tanfield, on whom the whole management of the Chief Baron's property devolved, and who was by no means pleased with her husband's indifference to worldly advantages, was daughter of Giles Symmonds, of Clage, in the county of Norfolk, and niece of Sir Henry Lee, Knight of the Garter.

Elisabeth, the only child of Sir Lawrence and his wife, was from her earliest childhood passionately devoted to study. At four years old she could read, and delighted in it, her daughter tells us, "she loved it much." An attempt to teach her French at this age did not succeed, but of her own accord she took it up again not long afterwards, and taught herself whilst she was still a child, not only French but Spanish and Italian also. Latin she acquired a thorough knowledge of in her youth, so that she translated some of Seneca's Epistles, but from want of practice she became less familiar with it in after life, so that when, a few months before her death, she began translating Blosius's works into English, she found herself obliged to consult a Spanish version.

The same thing happened to her with regard to Hebrew, which at one time she perfectly understood. Even after this had ceased to be the case, she could read the Scriptures, with which she was intimately acquainted, in that language. So great was her facility in acquiring this sort of knowledge, that she learnt Transylvanian from a native of that country, but never having occasion to speak it, she soon entirely lost this accomplishment.

It is wonderful to think of the amount of study this young girl must have gone through, and of the persevering application which enabled her to master so many languages at an early age. They proved as many keys to various sources of information, which stored by degrees a mind naturally reflective and acute. The Judge's library was probably well furnished, and his young daughter—who had neither brothers or sisters, or any playmates and companions of her own age—lived in books, and, finding the days too short for this engrossing pursuit, often spent whole nights poring over grammars and histories.

Lady Tanfield at last discovered this practice, and gave strict orders to the servants not to let Elisabeth have candles; but the young lady was self-willed. We find her evincing on this point a fault of cha-racter which often marred, in after life, her many eminent qualities, a kind of reckless impetuosity which often carried her beyond the bounds of prudence.

The love of study had become an absorbing pas-sion—read she would, and as candles were denied her, she bribed the servants and bought some from them for half-a-crown a piece. As she could not pay for these purchases at the time, she ran into debt to these worthless domestics, and when she reached the age of twelve owed them £100 for candles alone, and £200 besides for equally ruinous bargains—probably books and writing materials.

This debt she paid on her wedding-day—a large sum for that period. It was more than those un-principled creditors deserved; but though rash and imprudent, Elisabeth was always honourable and generous in all her dealings.

Her father did not discourage her taste for grave studies, for we find him giving her to read, before she was twelve years of age, Calvin's *Institutes.* If he intended thus to attach her to the teachings of that school, his purpose signally failed. She found in this work such flagrant contradictions, that she was always coming to him—book in hand—to point them out. Half astonished and half amused, he one day exclaimed: "That girl hath the most averse spirit to Calvin!"

It is curious to find this aversion springing up instinctively in the mind of a child turned loose, so to speak, in a library which probably contained the most famous works of philosophy, and no doubt included many relating to the great controversy which was then dividing the Christian world. It is to be presumed that in Judge Tanfield's library the greatest proportion of such works would be on the Protestant side; but to his surprise, the mind of his young daughter naturally, as it were, turned against the Calvinistic tenets he appears himself to have held.

It is easy to understand that Lady Tanfield should have objected to Elisabeth's night-watches, or even thought her devotion to books in the daytime overweening; but we should have expected to find her instructing her child in the feminine art of needle-work. This, however, does not seem to have been the case, for Lady Falkland's biographer mentions that, although she had never been taught by any one to work, she was nevertheless "skilful and curious in it," adding as a comment on this fact, "that those who knew her would never have believed had they not seen it with their own eyes, that she could hold a needle." Whether this incredulity proceeded from an apparent clumsiness in Elisabeth's fingers, or that her tastes and talents were well known to lie in another direction, we are not told.

An anecdote of her childhood is related, which gives a great idea of her precocious intelligence, and at the same time affords a curious instance of the treatment in those days of persons supposed to be witches.

The little Elisabeth, when only ten years of age, was present on one occasion when a poor old woman was brought before her father and accused of having caused the death of two or three persons by her spells. The evidence did not seem very conclusive, but when the Judge asked her what she had to say for herself, she knelt down before him, weeping and trembling, and confessed that it was all true. "Be good to me, sir," she cried, "and I promise to amend." "Did you bewitch such a one to death?" he asked. She answered "Yes." "And how did you do it!" he inquired; upon which one of her accusers hastened to say: "Did you not send your familiar in the shape of a black dog, or a hare, or a cat, and finding him asleep did not they lick his hand, and breathe on him, and step over him; after which he came home sick, and languished away?" Shaking all over and begging pardon, she acknowledged it to be all true, and in the same way pleaded guilty to every act of the same sort laid to her charge.

The by-standers all exclaimed: "What would they have more than her own confession?" The Judge's young daughter, who had been watching attentively what went on, remarked the terror expressed in the poor woman's face, and like a little Daniel came to the rescue. Putting her mouth to her father's ear,

she whispered : " Ask her if she has bewitched to
death Mr. John Symmonds ? "   This was her uncle,
who happened to be present in the room.   The
question was put, and as before, she said, " Yes ;
but she would do so no more, if they would have pity
upon her."   " And how did you do it ? " the Judge
again inquired, upon which she repeated exactly
what her accusers had said in other instances.   Then
all the company laughed, and the Judge asked her
what she meant, and pointing to Mr. Symmonds
said, " Why, the man we are speaking of is standing
before your eyes alive and well."   " Alive sir ! " she
cried ; " I knew him not, and said so only because
you asked me."   " Are you no witch, then? " the
Judge said.   " No ; God knows, I know no more
what belongs to it than the child new born," she
replied.   " And did you never see the devil ? "   " No,
God bless me, never in all my life."   He then inquired into the reasons which had led her to confess
to all those falsehoods.   She said that she had been
threatened with death, if she did not confess, but
assured that mercy would be shown her, if she did.
This was uttered with such simplicity, that she was
immediately believed and acquitted.   The Judge
must have felt proud of the little girl at his elbow.

Thus was Elisabeth's childhood spent.   None of
the ordinary amusements of that age seem to have
fallen to her share.   We see her by her father's side,
interesting herself in his avocations, or poring over
the books in his library ; we fancy her in her chamber,

long after midnight, with pale face and eager countenance, studying, by the light of her dearly bought
tallow candles, the works of the great writers of
France, Spain, and Italy, as well as those of her own
country, and, by a knowledge of the dead languages,
admitted to the enjoyment of the classics, that *terra
incognita* to most of even the best educated women
of our day, but which in the sixteenth and seventeenth centuries was often familiar to those who`
loved study at all, and whose minds were cultivated
beyond the usual average.   Attempts at composition
probably marked that early period of her life, for we
shall soon find her having recourse to such pursuits
under unusually trying circumstances.

This strange, solitary, studious childhood ended
abruptly.   At the age of fifteen, Elisabeth Tanfield
was, in the language of that epoch, disposed of in
marriage by her parents, and bestowed on Sir Henry
Cary, of Aldenham and Berkhampstead, in Hertfordshire, who was at that time Master of the Jewel
House of Queen Elisabeth.   We are told that he
married the Chief Baron's daughter simply because
she was an heiress.   She had no beauty to recommend her beyond a very fair complexion, and her
heart and mind were under lock and key, so to speak,
in his presence.   He does not seem to have the least
cared to become acquainted with the young creature
he made his wedded wife.   She had a dowry that
suited his decayed fortunes, and that was all he
cared for.

CHAPTER II.

Early married life.

IT is difficult to picture to ourselves the state of mind of an ardent, clever, well-read girl of fifteen, when informed that she was to be married to a man she had scarcely seen, and of whom she knew nothing except that her parents considered him a suitable match for her. But what would nowadays be thought an intolerable hardship, supposing indeed that such a stretch of parental authority were possible, was only a matter of course in the seventeenth century. Curiosity, not unmingled with some anxiety, was probably the predominating feeling of Elisabeth when this announcement was made to her. Perhaps she was glad that the husband provided for her was considerably older than herself, that he had spent much of his life at Court and in political and literary society, and travelled a great deal. To one of so active a turn of mind, so devoted almost from her infancy to study, and longing for greater opportunities of self-culture, this may have seemed to afford a better prospect of enjoyment, if not of happiness, than if she had been bestowed, as might easily have been the case, on some fox-hunting squire utterly unaccustomed to hold a pen or open a book. She may have wondered whether, when Sir Henry came to claim her hand, she would inspire or feel any of those emotions which, in eloquent prose or graceful verse, she had seen described in the romances and poems she had read and knew almost by heart. Dreams of mutual affection between her and her betrothed may have passed through her mind, but if so they were soon dissipated. Sir Henry Cary took scarcely any notice of his young bride. She was not pretty, her manners were not attractive, and, as to her mental gifts, he did not take the least trouble to find out anything about them. According to previous arrangement, she was to remain a year with her parents, and only at the end of that time to assume the position and duties of a married woman. Meanwhile he lived at Court or at his father's country place. What impression he made upon her, and whether she regretted this separation, we are not informed. If it was a disappointment to Elisabeth, another still more galling was in store for her. She was desired by her mother to write at stated times to her husband. We can again fancy that she must have been pleased at the prospect of this correspondence, and thought with satisfaction that he would see by her letters, that the shy and silent girl he had disdained to converse with was not wholly without sense and intelligence. If so her youthful vanity, if such it should be called, experienced a crushing blow. Lady

Tanfield was a very illiterate person, as can be seen
by the letters she wrote in after life to her daughter.
She had not the least idea of Elisabeth's power of
mind, and thought it impossible she should know
how to indite suitable letters to the Master of the
Queen's Jewels. So she employed some one, probably
a lady in reduced circumstances or the mistress of
a boarding-school, to compose appropriate epistles
from a newly married young woman to her absent
husband. These commonplace and silly productions
Lady Cary was ordered to copy word for word.
This must indeed have been a severe mortification
to her. Sir Henry, of course, thought the letters
just what he would have expected from a girl in the
school-room, and one of very limited capacity. His
were no doubt as formal and short as possible. He
seems to have been in no hurry to claim his wife
from her parents, for at the end of fifteen months
she was still at Burford Priory, and then he went to
Holland on some diplomatic mission.

His desire was that Elisabeth should remain with
her parents till his return. He wished her to be
"where she would be most content," and "he knew
his own mother well," the biographer we follow
significantly adds. The Dowager Lady Cary seems
to have been a woman of most resolute will. Ever
since her son's marriage she had endeavoured to gain
possession of her daughter-in-law, but as long as he
was in England did not succeed. But as soon as he
was out of the country she moved heaven and earth

to accomplish her purpose. What means she used
is not explained; we are only told that she would
accept no excuses, and that at last the Chief Baron
and his wife were forced to yield the point and con-
sign their daughter to her care.

It was not long before the despotic old lady and
the self-willed young lady fell out. The former
"loved to be humoured," the latter "was not of a
character to apply herself to it." Disagreeable
consequences ensued. Measures were taken to re-
duce Elisabeth to submission. She was treated
harshly, which had not the desired effect. At last
she was placed under restraint and confined to her
room. This did not in the least break her spirit.
She looked provokingly happy. This puzzled her
persecutor, who after a while discovered that this
seclusion was rather agreeable to her, "and that she
entertained herself with her books." This was not
to be permitted, and one day the tyrannical dowager
carried away the whole of Elisabeth's library. Even
then she did not succeed in making her unhappy.
There must have been an amused look in the eyes
of the young prisoner when she bethought herself
of a resource, that not all her tormentor's ingenuity
could deprive her of. She composed verses, and
thus successfully cultivated her talent for poetry.
One of her sisters-in-law, who was very fond of
Elisabeth, stole out of her room one of these early
compositions, and showed it to a friend who printed
it. But the young authoress stopped its publica-

tion. In later life she wrote *The Life of Tamerlane in verse*, which was reckoned the best effort of her pen.

During that period of seclusion, there were only two persons in her mother-in-law's house, besides her own servants, who ever came to see her, and they did so by stealth. One of them was the above-mentioned sister-in-law. They became intimate friends, and in after life Lady Falkland had frequent occasions of requiting her kindness. The other was a gentlewoman who waited on her hard-hearted mother-in-law; probably a sort of *dame de compagnie*. Her attentions she also repaid by the most generous charity. Having left Lady Cary's service this person fell into poverty, but was never forsaken by Elisabeth, who procured her employment and provided for her in her old age.

Whilst his young wife was kept in captivity at home by his imperious mother, Sir Henry Cary was going through a variety of vicissitudes abroad. From Holland he went to France, and was present at the conferences for peace which were held at Boulogne-sur-Mer. These having failed he returned to the Low Countries, and fell into the hands of the enemy. Either at the battle of Neueport or the siege of Ostend, he was taken prisoner by Don Luis de Velasco and carried off to Spain, where he remained until his father sent the sum demanded for his ransom. Ben Johnson in one of his epigrams thus alludes to his mischance :

C

No foe that day
Could conquer thee, but chance who did betray !

Since she had left her own home, Elisabeth's letters to her husband were no longer composed by other people, and he was struck with the very different style in which they were written. He had never doubted the first being her own, and now imagined that these clever and original effusions, which, we are told, "he liked much," were penned by some one else. But having cross-examined her on the subject, he ascertained that they were her own writing, and "becoming better acquainted with his wife, he esteemed her more." It must have been a curious correspondence between that husband and wife, who had parted immediately after their marriage, who knew nothing of each other's characters and minds, and became attached to one another by means of letters exchanged under such singular circumstances. We can infer that she had the delicacy and good feeling not to complain in them of Lady Cary's treatment, for when he was at last liberated and returned to England, we find that great was his displeasure at the manner in which she had been used, and that all this tyranny was soon at an end. They seem, however, to have lived with his mother for some time longer, for it was not till seven years after her marriage that Elisabeth gave birth to her first-born son, Lucius, and it was only when they had many more children, that she and her husband removed to a house of their own. Their household

was small, and their means limited; she showed
great aptitude for domestic management, though she
had but little natural taste for it. Her daughter
tells us, that " she was very careful and diligent in
the disposition of the affairs of her house; and she
herself would work hard, together with her women
and her maids, curious pieces of work, teaching and
directing them all herself. Nor was her care of her
children less assiduous; she nursed them all except
her eldest son, whom her father, Sir Lawrence
Tanfield, took away from her when he was an infant;
that he might live with him entirely from his birth.
She taught three or four of her children. Later on,
when their number increased—she had in all eleven
—having many other things to divert and occupy
her, she confided their education to persons who,
from long experience, she entirely relied on, and she
never changed the servants about them. As long as
they were with her she took care that nothing should
be wanting to them."

But it is not only the outward picture of Lady
Cary's life during these first years of her marriage
which is given to us. We are also initiated into the
perplexities and struggles which began to agitate
her earnest and thoughtful spirit with regard to
religion. Whilst hard at work in the midst of her
household, whilst performing every duty of a wife
and mother, and the mistress of a family, "she
always continued to read much, and at twenty years
of age, through reading, she had grown into much

doubt of her religion." The first occasion of these doubts arose whilst studying Hooker's *Ecclesiastical Policy*. To use her own words, "it had left her hanging in the air." His arguments having brought her so far, she saw not how or where she could stay till she returned to the Church whence they were derived. Whilst these thoughts were working in her mind, a brother of her husband's, Adolphus Cary, returned from Italy "with a good opinion of the Catholic religion." Elisabeth availed herself eagerly of this unexpected opportunity of conversing with so near a relative on a subject which she had probably never up to that time talked of to anybody, and about which she must have had so much to ask of one who had been at the fountain-head of that religion, which, even when disfigured by a foe, fascinates and allures the soul sighing after light and reality, amidst the dim shadows and flickering gleams of heresy. Elisabeth was pleased with her brother-in-law's conversation. He was a great reader of the Fathers, especially of St. Augustine, who, he assured her, which she had apparently not known before, was of the religion of the Church of Rome. Up to that time her reading had been chiefly history and poetry, and writers such as Seneca and Plato. Seneca's epistles she had, it seemed, translated into English before leaving her father's house, as the only translation which her son found after her death was in her grandfather's study. Now, by Mr. Cary's advice, she studied the writings of the Fathers in whatever works she could procure, whether French, Spanish, or Italian. These studies produced the result which they have so often brought about ever since the days of the so-called Reformation. They awakened in her mind the strongest doubts as to the religious teaching she had received, and so far convinced her of its errors and inconsistency, that at two different times she refused for a long time together to go to the Protestant service. The first time that this occurred, she overcame her scruples by persuading herself that the difficulties in the way of a change of religion, and her earnest desire to remain where she was, were sufficient reasons for conforming to the Established Church. It is curious to observe the identical phases of doubt, of mis-giving, resolutions and counter-resolutions, following the same course in the minds of thoughtful persons at that period as in our own.

We find young Lady Cary, after the first stiflings of her dawning convictions, again after a time keep-ing away from the Protestant worship, and only returning to it in consequence of her intimacy with Dr. Neale, Bishop of Durham, and afterwards Arch-bishop of York. This Anglican divine was an emi-nent member of the Established Church. His palace was frequented by the most learned and talented of the Protestant clergy, those out of which were chosen the prelates of the English Church and the King's chaplains. Elisabeth had learnt from the writings of the Fathers and the histories of former times, to have a very great reverence for the episcopal and priestly character, and becoming for the first time acquainted with dignitaries of her own communion, who laid claim to the position and the character of bishops and priests, she felt a great respect for them, and, in her intercourse with them, practised the humility and submission of mind, which her studies had taught her was due to those whom Christ had appointed as His earthly representatives. Like so many in our own day, and particularly the great promoters of the Oxford Movement, she tried to array, in imagination, Protestant ministers with the attributes of Catholic Priests, and to look upon Dr. Neale as a successor of St. Thomas and St. Anselm. Learning and worth they seemed to her to possess, and she submitted herself to their teaching with a genuine docility of heart and humility of spirit. They persuaded her that she might safely remain where she was. The opiate was administered, the light excluded by the same deceptive fallacies which even now keep back so many from the true Church. They never succeeded in convincing her that the Roman Catholic religion was not a better and a more secure one than Anglicanism, but, in the face of the dangers and difficulties which would have attended her conversion, she was glad enough to escape from the conclusion that there was any necessity for such a change. Thus, from the time when doubts first crossed her mind on this all-important subject, she went on for twenty-two years, "flattering herself with good intentions," as her daughter quaintly expressed it. It often happened that she was present, when persons who were considered as heretics by the Protestant Archbishop were examined, and argued in defence of their tenets. Strangers used to wonder that he allowed Lady Cary to assist at these disputations, and expressed fears that what she heard might unsettle her faith. He always said that he would warrant her never being in danger of heresy, so great was her submission to authority, which at that time she believed the Church of England to possess. Lady Cary's most anxious solicitude was about the religious education of her children, and again, like many a mother in our days, she endeavoured to instil Christian principles into their minds without instructing them in Protestant doctrines, and avoiding all catechetical teachings which would have biassed them against the Catholic faith. She inclined them, we are told, according to their age and capacity, to the love and esteem of all moral virtues, and gave them a general knowledge of the truths which are held by all Christians, and that in a manner which her daughter tells us "was apt to have a far greater effect on their minds than things learned by rote and not understood." She would tell them, when they loved any person or anything, that they were to love God much more, as He had made not only that person or that thing, but themselves, and all things else for them ; that they were to love and honour

God more than their father, for He had given them
their father; that the King was His servant, for He
made all Kings and gave them their kingdoms. If
they were good He would give them better things
than any they saw or had on earth, and so for the
rest."

This sort of familiar teaching imparted to these
children a strong sense of what was right and
wrong, of which one of her elder boys, whom she herself taught, gave a singular proof when he was still
extremely young. "She had one day declared with
an oath [1] that she would whip him, but afterwards
forgave him. The child, though he had an excessive
apprehension of this punishment, begged her not to
break her oath. She being much pleased with his
innocent care of her conscience, was resolved not to
do it, but he was so afraid of her forswearing herself
that on his knees, and with tears in his eyes, he
continued to beg her to do it, though all the time
he was trembling with fear. Nor was there any
other way to satisfy the child, but by doing as she
had sworn." Once when she was very ill and
thought herself near her end, Lady Cary wrote a
letter of several sheets, which she committed to the

---

[1] It seems strange that so good a person as Elisabeth Cary should
have used an oath, but it was one of the most inveterate habits of
the times, and common to those of every rank and sex. Moreover,
in common parlance at that time, " I swear I shall do so," would
probably mean no more than now to say, " I declare I'll do it," or
than a person saying in French, " Je vous jure que non," which
would never be reckoned as swearing.

care of her two eldest children, a son and a daughter. It contained all the precepts and moral advice which she wished them to inculcate on their young brothers and sisters, when old enough to understand them. These instructions of a parent, whom she feared to lose, made a deep impression on the mind of that daughter, who, from her infancy, had been the object of her mother's special care. She had taken extraordinary pains to train this beloved child in virtue and piety; and her natural dispositions had rendered the task easy. Of all her children, she was the most dutiful and affectionate; it had been a great trial to Lady Cary to part with her when she was only thirteen. Her father insisted on her marrying Lord Home, and she went to live in the house of her mother-in-law. This marriage was on her part an act of obedience, and the spirit with which she entered on her new duties was in keeping with the education she had received. The young wife was tenderly beloved by all her husband's relatives, and when she died in childbirth, four years only after her marriage, their affliction knew no bounds. Her own mother asked her once what she had done to gain their affection in so extraordinary a degree. She answered with great simplicity that she really did not know of anything she did, unless it was that she had always been careful to observe the rule which she had given her, when first she had left her own home for that of her husband's mother. 'Whenever conscience and reason will permit it, always prefer the will of another to your own,' had been Lady Cary's parting counsel. She probably remembered the conflicts which had arisen under similar circumstances between herself and her mother-in-law, and the miseries which had ensued. Lady Home profited by her experience. Some of the rules laid down for the young wife's guidance would be considered by many people as too strict—but Lady Cary "disapproved of the practice of satisfying oneself with the consciousness of being free from fault, and taking no care to avoid what might have a show or suspicion of uncomeliness or unfitness." She expressed this sentiment in the motto she had inscribed on her daughter's wedding-ring, "Be and seem." It was not only the moral and, as far as her lights went, the religious instruction of her children that Lady Cary attended to; she was tenderly solicitous about everything that concerned them. Her daughter says: "She did not omit to have those that were of an age capable of it taught all that might be fit for them. She always thought it a most unbecoming thing in a mother to make herself her business more than her children, and whilst she cared for herself to neglect them. Her doing was most contrary to this. She who had never in her youth taken delight in her own fineness and dress, took only too much pains about theirs, and carried almost to excess her desire to see them all well attired, and to give them pleasure." She made it a duty to her children, to love their father better than herself. It is said that they all did so except her eldest son, who had not been reared at home. She had taken upon herself all the drudgery of teaching, and the enforcement of discipline, and allowed him the undisturbed enjoyment of their society in play hours. She saw how readily the lesson had been learnt, and never repined at it. It did not lessen her affection and kindness to any of them.

Sir Henry Cary was very absolute, and though his wife had a strong will, she made it subservient to his. The wish to please him had power to make her do things which those who knew her would scarcely have believed possible. Her natural tastes would have disinclined her to the management of her house and every kind of domestic detail, and she would always sooner have had a book or a pen in her hand than a needle. Yet, in compliance with his wishes, she became a careful and skilful housewife and a diligent worker. He was fond of hunting, and wished her to be a good horsewoman. Her fears on horseback had always been intense, yet for years she rode as much and as desperately as if she had taken the greatest delight in it. The seeing him pleased really made her enjoy it as long as she was by his side, though before her marriage, and after her separation from him, she had neither the skill or the courage to sit a horse. " Dressing was all her life a sort of torture to her, yet, whilst she was with her husband, she endured, even to their utmost tediousness, the minutest details regarding it, because such was his will." It is amusing to read how far her submission went, and at the same time her inability to concentrate her thoughts on the subject. "All that she could ever arrive at was to have those about her who could do it well, and then to endure the trouble —for though she was very careful to make sure it should be done, she was not able to attend to it at all, nor to engage her mind in it. Her women were fain to walk round the room after her, pinning on her things and brushing her hair whilst she was thinking seriously on some other business, and it was always her custom to write or to read whilst they curled her hair and dressed her head. It was evident later on that nothing but her husband's wishes could have made her undergo this penance, for when he was angry with her and banished her from his house, she grew perfectly careless of her appearance, and never went out but in plain black frieze or coarse stuff or cloth." As to her own interests in matters of fortune, Lady Cary did not seem capable of considering them. The estate of Berkhampstead, which had been settled upon her at her marriage, was reassumed by the Crown to which it had belonged as formerly part of the property of the Duchy of Cornwall. The remaining portion of her jointure, with a trifling exception, we shall see that she consented to mortgage in order to assist her husband. This made her father so angry that he disinherited her in favour of her two eldest sons. The happy years of her married life were clouded by a deep depression of spirits, before the birth of her third and again of her fourth child. This melancholy amounted almost to insanity. She had not, at least, the perfect use of her reason, and fears were entertained for her life. Her husband, who was a passionately fond father, was extraordinarily anxious about her, whenever she was with child or nursing, and humoured to excess her nervous fancies. Once, for fourteen days together, she ate or drank nothing but a little beer with a tart, and great apprehensions were felt both for her child and herself, which the event did not justify. After that last fit of sadness, she recovered entirely her natural cheerfulness, and it never again forsook her, even in the midst of her greatest trials. She always looked on the best side of everything, and on the good which any event might produce. If she felt disposed to indulge in melancholy thoughts, her remedy was to sleep them off. She had a singular power of falling asleep whenever she tried to do so, and a far more precious gift she possessed, in the power of consoling others and diverting them from their sorrows. Her conversation, we are told, would sometimes disperse a person's grief like a ray of sunshine does a cloud. To those who occasioned her trouble and annoyance, she was often so kind, she proved herself so solicitously their friend, she provided for them so eagerly in their necessities, that strangers and distant acquaintances were often led to suppose that she was the offender, not the offended one.

Generosity in every sense of the word seems to have been her characteristic.

Sir Henry Cary became, in 1618, Comptroller of the Royal Household. He had sold his office of Master of the Jewels a few months before. We are not told whether his wife accompanied him at first to London and to the Court. In 1620 he was raised to the Scotch Peerage, with the title of Viscount Falkland, and in 1622 was appointed Lord Deputy of Ireland. This event had an important bearing on the destiny of his wife, whom we now must call Lady Falkland, and in the next chapter we shall follow her to that country, which must have been at that time, as it is now, full of deep interest to one whose sympathy with the Catholic Church was already so strong.

CHAPTER III.

Lady Falkland in Ireland.

DURING the years which preceded Sir Henry Cary's elevation to the peerage and his appointment of Lord Deputy for Ireland, his duties as Comptroller to the Royal Household had kept him in almost constant attendance at the Palace. His wife managed his own domestic affairs until the death of his father, and the increasing number of her children made it impossible for her to continue to govern her house and educate her family without assistance. She was obliged to engage others to take part in this labour, and the more so that she often came to live at her husband's lodgings at Court. Anne of Denmark had died a few days after Sir Henry Cary's appointment to the post he occupied during the remainder of the reign of James the First. In consequence of the Queen's death, ladies ceased to frequent the Palace. But it was probably during her visits to London at that period, that Lady Cary became acquainted with the friends who showed her so much kindness in the days of her adversity: the future Duchess of Buckingham, the Countesses of Arundel and Denby, Lady Mountgarret, and many others. Her husband, no doubt, introduced her to the wits and literary men with whom he had long consorted, for it is said that even at Oxford, when a mere youth, his chambers were the resort of divines, philosophers, lawyers, historians, and politicians. The name he had acquired there had brought him into notice at the Court, and there he must have been on intimate terms with men of genius who, like Ben Jonson, did not disdain to employ their talents for the amusement of the King and Queen. In 1612, when every effort was used to cheer the failing spirits of Anne of Denmark after the loss of her son, Prince Henry, a mask was performed at Caversham, where she rested on her way to Bath, in which the actors were Lord and Lady Knollys, their four sons, Lord Dorchester, and Sir Henry Cary. So greatly was her Majesty pleased with this performance, that, "forgetting her ill-health, she graciously adorned the place with her personal dancing." In the midst of a courtly, aristocratic, and literary society, Lady Falkland found herself in a new world, a congenial one in some respects, as far as intellect was concerned, but one in which she saw and heard much which must have jarred with her earnest nature and devout turn of mind. Whether during these years she advanced beyond the Bishop of Durham's standard of orthodoxy, we are not told. She is said to have continued "in the same opinion as to religion," but that this opinion included practice in one important respect, we can deduce from the statement, that "she bore great and high reverence for the Blessed Virgin, and that being with child before her departure for Ireland, she offered up her infant, if it were a girl, to bear her name out of devotion, and resolved as much as should be in her power to lead her to be a nun. Lady Falkland was nursing that little Mary when, in August, 1622, she went to Ireland with her husband and her children, leaving behind her the eldest of her daughters, that gentle bride of thirteen, who, on the 22nd of May, had been married in the King's Chamber to Lord Home, "his Majesty having made the match."

Except for the grief of such a separation, this was probably a happy moment in Lady Falkland's life. She had been able by an act of no common generosity to render a great service to her husband. He was in urgent want of a sum of money to meet the expenses of his installation as Lord Deputy of Ireland. The King had allowed him to sell the plate appertaining to his former office, but this was but a small advance towards what he required. His wife, "who never thought of her own interest when his was concerned," consented to have her jointure lands mortgaged in order to supply him with the necessary amount. This was the more generous, because a portion of the fortune settled upon her at her marriage had been since, as we know reassumed by the Crown. And that voluntary surrender of her rights so irritated her father, that he disinherited her in consequence and settled the whole of

D

his estates on her sons—on the eldest, Lucius
Cary in the first instance, and in the event of his
dying without issue, on the second, Lawrence. Not
even the paternal anger, and its effects on her own
prospects, could make Lady Falkland regret what
she had done. Moreover, she conceived great hopes
of doing good in the country where her disinterestedness had enabled her husband to assume the
government. Nor did her sanguine nature allow her
to foresee all the public and private difficulties they
would both have to encounter, or what she was
about to suffer in the midst of an oppressed people,
persecuted for their adherence to a faith to which
she secretly inclined. But only two days after her
arrival in Ireland her eyes were opened on that point.
The Lord Deputy and his family had landed at
Meath on the 6th of September in the evening, and
on Saturday in the afternoon, the Lord Chancellor,
the Marshall, the Lords Justices, many of the
nobility, and all the Privy Council of Ireland met
him half-way between that place and Dublin, and
accompanied him to the Castle. On Sunday morning the ceremony of his installation took place. The
chief officers of state and principal personages of
the Viceregal Court repaired in the morning to the
Church of the Holy Trinity, commonly called Christ
Church, "where being seated in their seats, His
Majesty's sword was laid before them. Then all the
councillors together with the gentlemen pensioners
and the attendants returned back to the Castle, from

whence the Lord Falkland, being by them attended and accompanied by the Lord Viscount William of Athlone riding by his side, they came altogether to Christ's Church, and there being seated, Dr. Usher, Lord Bishop of Meath, made a learned sermon." The text öf that sermon was, " He beareth not the sword in vain." Its spirit and tone was such as greatly to alarm the Catholics. Poor Lady Falkland had to sit and hear, with what patience she could, her husband exhorted and adjured not to tolerate the exercise of the Catholic religion, in a harangue so virulent that it called forth the censure even of the Protestant Primate. If up to that moment she had witnessed with pleasure the pageantry of the semi-regal progress and her husband's entrance into the old and beautiful Irish Cathedral, a depressing heart sickness must have deprived her of all enjoyment during the ceremonies which followed the Protestant Prelate's ghastly sermon. When the sword was delivered into the hands of her lord, could she refrain from thinking of the words of Scripture so hatefully perverted ?

Again, the difficulties as to the religious education of her children increased tenfold in Ireland. All that they saw and heard at the Castle was calculated to arouse the prejudices from which she had so carefully sought to guard them. The contempt showered on recusants, the charges of disaffection to the King and realm, the name of traitor bestowed on' any Catholic who procured the conversion of a

Protestant, their love for their father, who was
driven by the difficulties which surrounded him into
a querulous irritation against the Irish race and
religion, would naturally influence the minds of
young people in spite of her utmost efforts to the
contrary. Lord Falkland's predecessor, Oliver
St. John, recently created Viscount Grandison, had
taken a wise and humane view of the condition of
Ireland, and extended as much toleration as the
laws would permit to Catholic worship. He, as
well as Lord Chichester, the previous Viceroy, had
endeavoured to redress and mitigate the cruel
wrongs of the natives with regard to the possession
of land, and it is probable that if this system had
been fairly tried on an extended scale, a large class
of Irish landowners might have rallied round the
Government. Lord Grandison's projects were good,
but the evil was far gone, and in some respects
irreparable. After the rising of Tyrone in 1608
had been fiercely quelled, millions of acres were
escheated to the Crown, and bestowed by King
James on Protestant colonists from England and
Scotland. That monarch believed that the only
way of extirpating the Catholic religion was by
extending this system throughout the whole country.
Almost every plot of land possessed by natives was
declared to belong to the Crown, and in consequence
whole tribes were driven away from the soil which
had given them birth. To carry out, what would be
called in these days, Lord Grandison's remedial

measures, required a watchful eye and a firm hand. Dublin swarmed with adventurers who had crossed St. George's Channel to repair their broken fortunes. The Celtic population were filled with a justifiable animosity against English speculators. Religious difficulties served to increase and embitter these political and social embarrassments. There was a standing deficit in the Irish Exchequer, and England did little or nothing to supply the want. The Protestant clergy were clamouring for a strict observance of the penal laws, which, under the two last Viceroys, had not been rigorously enforced. The new Lord Deputy, naturally kind-hearted and desirous as he was to fulfil his duties, had not, it appears, clear-sightedness to detect the real sources of evils, such as those which stared him in the face, nor the firmness to adhere to a steady course of action to remedy them. His predecessor had dealt vigorously with the enemies of his administration. The Protestant clamour roused in Ireland reached the throne in England : James had bent before the storm and recalled him. Lord Falkland had no doubt this example before his eyes, and the conflicting statements regarding his government of Ireland probably arose from the fluctuating nature of his policy. On the one hand, Anthony Wood in his *Athenæ* says, "that he deserves to be remembered as an able, a polite, an uncorrupt statesman. His strict though legal administration, in regard to the Irish Papists whom the Court was inclined to favour, raised the loudest clamours against him from that party, but this rather served to elevate than degrade his character, as he afterwards abundantly justified his whole conduct. We have abundant proof of his disinterested loyalty and integrity, as he greatly impaired his patrimony in employments by which others have raised their fortunes." Dr. Leland speaks of him, however, "as having been more distinguished by his rectitude than his abilities. In a government which required vigour and austerity, he was indolent and gentle, courting rather than terrifying the fractious. He was harassed by the intrigues and clamours of the King's Ministers, whom he could not always gratify to the full extent of their wishes. His actions were severely maligned at the Court of England, and his administration in consequence was cautious and embarrassed. Such a Governor was little qualified to awe a numerous and powerful body of recusants." That Lord Falkland did do his best to awe them can, however, be gathered from the fact, that a few months after his arrival in Ireland a proclamation was issued "against the Popish clergy, secular and regular, ordering them under the severest penalties to depart from the kingdom within forty days, after which all persons were prohibited to speak to them." How painful to his wife must have been this line of conduct on his part, we can easily picture to ourselves. How she employed herself amongst that people "for whom she had much affection" we must now relate.

Her's was not a character which could content itself with remaining inactive in the presence of such misery as daily met her eyes. She was debarred from spiritual works of mercy amongst the Irish poor, both as a Protestant and as the wife of the Viceroy, but plans for their temporal welfare she set herself with ardour to contrive. And first, in order as she hoped to communicate more freely with them, she began to study their language in an Irish Bible, but from want of teachers and of books failed in the attempt to master it. Then, "for the benefit and commodity of that nation, she set upon a great design." Like so many persons in the present day, who take refuge from an oppressive sense of the insufficiency of the religion they profess in an un-unbounded devotion to good works, which relieves their consciences and leaves no time for thought, she conceived vast plans, and threw herself heart and soul into a work her daughter thus describes: "It was to bring up the use of all trades in that country, which is fain to be beholden to others for the smallest commodities. To this end she procured some of each kind to come from places where those trades are exercised, as several sorts of linen and woollen weavers, dyers, all kinds of spinners and knitters, lace makers, and many other trades. And for this purpose, she took of beggar children (with which this country swarms) more than eight score 'prentices, refusing none above seven years old, and taking some less. These were disposed to their several masters and mistresses, to learn those trades they were thought most fit for ; the least amongst them being set to something, as making points, buttons or lace, or some other things ; they were parted in their several rooms and houses, where they exercised their trades, many such rooms being filled with little boys and girls, sitting all round at work, besides those that were bigger, for trades needing more understanding and strength. She brought it to that pass that they made broadcloth so fine and good of Irish wool, spun and dyed and weaved and dressed there, that her Lord, being Deputy, wore it. Yet it came to nothing. She had great losses by fire and water; her work-house, with all the materials and much cloth that was in it, was burnt. Her fretting mills were carried away, and many of her things destroyed." After she became a Catholic, Lady Falkland ascribed these misfortunes and the failure of her well-meant efforts to the fact, that the children employed in her factories were taken to the Protestant church. She had, indeed, reason to thank Providence for the non-success of her plans, for it saved her from the responsibility of having endangered the faith of these Irish children whilst aiming to promote their temporal welfare. But her daughter goes on to tell us that there were other reasons, which would in themselves account for the unsatisfactory result of her schemes. " She was better at contriving than at executing. She undertook too much at once. Having but little choice as to those she employed, she often engaged unskilful, or, as they sometimes turned out, dishonest persons. Though rather prone to suspect people, she was very easily taken in (cozened), and having no order and method about money matters, or memory for accounts, she was subject to paying the same thing over and over again. Some one confessed to her once that he had made her pay the same bill as much as five times in five days. Nor did she like to be undeceived by those who saw she was cheated, being apt to suppose that it was out of dislike of her projects and to divert her from them that they did so. When her mind was set violently upon anything, which it always was when it bore a semblance of good, she could not bring herself to believe that she was cheated, and this over-eagerness, even when she had means at her command, involved her in embarrassments. Sooner than forego some object she had set her mind upon, she would pawn or sell anything she had, even an article she would have need of an hour after. The same vehemence prompted her into making great promises to those who assisted her in her undertakings, and expressing a disproportionate gratitude on these occasions, which led to great expectations not easy to fulfil when she came afterwards to consider of them."

Lord Falkland seems to have acted, with regard to his wife's benevolent schemes in the same vaccillating manner with which he conducted the government of Ireland. "He seemed often displeased with them, but though he might easily have stopped her works, he led her to believe that it was the manner in which they were carried on, not the work in itself, which he disliked, and that manner she saw not how to amend." She was always under the impression that whilst he desired to disengage his own responsibility in the matter, he wished her not to leave them off. And at a later time she discovered this to have been truly the case, for letters of his fell into her hands, in which he highly praised that for which he had often chidden her, and affirmed that, "had it been well prosecuted, the work would have been of exceeding benefit to Ireland."

It is rather difficult to reconcile what is said in this part of Lady Falkland's life, with the statement in a previous chapter as to her ability in domestic management, and "her capabilities for what she would apply to." Perhaps these last words afford a key to these contradictions. Her acute intellect and strong will were probably bent, in the early days of her married life, on the accomplishment of her home duties, and stimulated by a passionate desire to gain her husband's affections. Just as she rode desperately to please him, though a coward at heart, she no doubt worked hard at accounts, and conquered the bias of her nature in order to do as he wished. And now that his position was altered, an equally intense desire to make his administration popular in Ireland, and at the same time her own inordinate zeal for good works, may have led her to give the reins to a naturally reckless habit of expenditure and a head-strong self-will in pursuing her objects. She strug-gled to keep up her industrial schools as long as she remained in Ireland; but soon after her return to England in 1625, they ceased to exist.

Of Lady Falkland's religious state of mind during her stay in Ireland very little is said. She became acquainted with Lord Inchiquin, "an exceeding good Catholic, whom she highly esteemed for his wit, learning, and judgment, though he was only about nine-and-twenty years of age when he died. Her lord did the same, admiring him much as a man of so sincere and upright a conscience, that he seemed to look on whatever was not lawful as not possible." It is added that "he did somewhat shake her sup-posed security in esteeming it lawful to continue as she was." Her mind was evidently deeply engaged in the all-important question which had troubled her almost from her childhood. Whenever she met with any one who had changed his religion, her great desire was to discover, if possible, the origin of such a change. One of her husband's chaplains, Dr. Hachett, then a Protestant dean, had once been a Jesuit. She observed that in his sermons he never spoke against Catholicism, but only exhorted his hearers to a good life. She could not rest till she had asked him, and in the most urgent manner en-treated him to tell her what had led to his becoming a Protestant. He said that "indeed being a Jesuit, and desiring to be sent to Rome, which place had

for that Society in every way greater advantages
than all others, his desire was refused, and his
Superiors sent him, on the contrary, to Scotland,
his own country, but of all others most disadvan-
tageous and incommodious to those of their Order,
and that he, being most unwilling to go thither, out
of the desire he had to find some way how to avoid
so hard an obedience, began to look into the Protestant religion, and, as she knew, satisfied himself."
With this answer she also remained satisfied. We
find her giving the name of Patrick to the eldest of
the two sons to whom she gave birth in Ireland.
She commended them both from their infancy to the
great Apostle of that country, and always believed
he had taken them under his protection. She lived
to see them both Catholics. Her eldest son—the
only one of her children who, in spite of her efforts
to the contrary, loved her better than his father—
must have caused his parents some uneasiness at one
moment of his life. He, as well as his brothers,
had been educated at the Viceregal Court since
Lord Falkland had been deputy, and afterwards at
Trinity College, but "under the care and vigilance
of such governors and tutors, that they learned all
those exercises and languages better than most do
in more celebrated places, insomuch that when
Lucius came to England at the age of eighteen, he
was not only master of the Latin tongue, and had
read all the poets and other of the best authors with
notable judgment for that age, but he understood

and spoke French as well as if he had been many years in France."

It must have been soon after his arrival from Ireland that this accomplished young man, who is, however, described in the *Biographia Britannica* as being at that time "a wild youth," committed some indiscretion which led to his being imprisoned in the Fleet. Lord Clarendon, in his famous character of Lord Falkland, makes no mention of this early event in the history of his friend; but from his father's petition to King James, there can be no doubt of the fact. It is a curious specimen of the style of the times.

"I had a sonne, until I lost him, in your Highness' displeasure, where I cannot seek him, because I have not will to find him there. Men say, there is a wild young man now prisoner in the Fleet, for measuring his actions by his own private sense. But now that for the same your Majesty's hand hath appeared in his punishment, he bows and humbles himself before, and to it. Whether he be mine or not, I can discern by no light, but that of your Royal clemency, for only in your forgiveness can I own him for mine. Forgiveness is the glory of the supremest powers, and this the operation, that when it is extended in the greatest measure, it converts the greatest offenders into the greatest lovers, and so it makes purchase of the heart, an especial privilege peculiar and due to Sovereign Princes. If now your Majesty will **vouchsafe,** out of your own benignity to become a second nature, and restore that unto me ·which the first gave me, and vanity deprived me of, I shall keep my reckoning of the full number of my sons with comfort, and render the tribute of my most humble thankfulness, else my weak old memory must forget one." [1]

This appeal was no doubt successful, for Lucius was sent to to travel abroad, "under the tutelage and protection of a discreet person, who wrought in him a great reformation of life and manners." The future Lord Falkland had ever, we are told, a great respect and veneration for this tutor, whose name is not mentioned. Considering how strongly Liberal, to use the language of the present day, were the opinions of the Royalist hero at the outset of his career, it is not unreasonable to suppose that the wildness attributed to him in early youth was of a political rather than a moral character, and that it was for "exercising his private sense" in such respects that he incurred the Royal displeasure.

When he returned from abroad, Lucius Cary came into possession of the fortune bequeathed to him by his grandfather, the Chief Baron Tanfield. He then chiefly resided at Oxford, where, like his father before him, he became the centre of a society of wits and men of learning.

It was about the same time that Lady Falkland left Dublin never to return there. We can only guess at the reasons for this departure. It may

[1] *Biographia Britannica,* v. iii. p. 290.

have been caused by her partiality, not sufficiently concealed, for a religion which her husband hated more and more as the chief source of his difficulties in the government of the Irish ; or it may have been, as would seem indicated by some of his and her letters, that she went to London for the purpose of representing his necessities to the English Ministers, and pressing his suits through her personal influence with some of them. The wish to see her daughter, Lady Home, from whom she had been separated for three years, may also have influenced her. She took with her the eldest of her unmarried girls and her younger children, leaving the rest with her husband, "who was so tenderly careful of them," one of these daughters writes, "that he could supply the part of both father and mother." Lord Falkland's disposition was evidently amiable, and his love of his children intense. His wife he probably admired more than he loved. Her peculiarities and faults may often have been trying to him, and her virtues also. The combination of great merits with troublesome little defects is often a peculiar source of irritation in domestic life. This may account for the strange fact that so kind-hearted a man, under the influence of angry feelings and a misdirected affection for his children, should have proved so cruel an enemy to his wife as he showed himself after her conversion.

CHAPTER IV.

Return to England and conversion.

WE can only guess at the cause of Lady Falkland's departure from Ireland in 1625. It may have been occasioned by her undisguised inclination towards a religion, which her husband hated more and more as one of his chief difficulties in the government of Ireland, or it may have been that she went to London to represent his pecuniary difficulties to the English Ministers, and use her influence to that effect with Lord Conway and others, with whom it appears she was on friendly terms. The wish to see her daughter, Lady Home, from whom she had been separated three years, and who was expecting her confinement, may also have contributed to hasten this return. Had she been superstitious, the circumstances which attended her departure might have been looked upon as an evil omen. A violent storm drove back to the Irish coast the vessel she sailed in, and placed in danger her own and her children's lives. She was sitting on the hatches, with her infant on her knees, when an immense wave submerged them both. The child had a narrow escape, for it remained breathless and motionless for more than a quarter of an hour. At last they arrived in London, but found the plague raging there. Lady Falkland determined to take her children at once to Lady Tanfield's house in Oxfordshire. Lady Home, who had hastened to London to meet her mother, was to accompany her to Burford Priory. But before her departure Lady Falkland had the happiness of kissing the hands of the royal bride, Henrietta Maria, the beautiful young Queen of fifteen years of age, whose marriage with Charles the First was rejoicing the hearts of his Catholic subjects. They founded great hopes on her well-known attachment to her faith and her influence over her enamoured husband. Though these expectations proved in a great measure fallacious, she did no doubt render many good offices to her co-religionists, and in the case of individuals, and even of priests, obtained in their favour, on several occasions, exemptions from the action of the penal laws.

As, during the first years of her married life, Henrietta Maria unwisely set her face against speaking, or even trying to learn the English language, and French was not generally spoken by the English nobility, she was probably pleased to find one lady amongst those presented to her who was thoroughly conversant with it and acquainted with French literature. But the King and Queen, as well as others, were abandoning the plague-stricken city. The Court removed to Windsor, thence to Hampton Court, and pursued by the pestilence, retreated to

E

Beaulieu in Hampshire. Meanwhile Lady Falkland
travelled to Burford Priory, the home of her childhood, little dreaming of the affliction which was
about to sadden the first days of her return to her
native land.

Lady Home seems to have been one of those young
creatures, beloved by all who knew them, and looked
upon even by strangers with interest and admiration.
Her husband and his family were devoted to her, yet
her life amongst them had not been "without
occasions for the exercise of patience and of a high
obedience which was rendered where it was due."
She must have steered her course with great prudence
and sense during the three years of her married life,
not to have offended or estranged the rigid Scotch
Puritans amongst whom her lot was cast when
almost a child, and yet to have retained "her good
inclination for the Catholic religion which she had
received from her mother, who alone had ever spoken
of it favourably in her hearing." She had imbibed
that partiality from her infant years: she had seen
her mother, on what promised to be her death-bed,
giving tokens of it, and the impression this made
upon her was ineffaceable. Just before their departure from London, Lady Falkland had the consolation
of hearing her daughter say to a visitor who was .
speaking strongly against Catholics, "You know
nothing of them but what the Scotch ministers say,
and that is what nobody in their senses can believe."

It was a happy party which started for Burford

Priory at the beginning of July, leaving behind them the infected city, and travelling by short stages in the fashion of the time along green lanes and pleasant commons, on their way to the old home, which they had none of them visited for three years. Lady Home's situation, and the joy they all felt in having her with them, made her companions carefully solicitous for her safety and comfort. She was a precious treasure, confided to them by an absent husband and loving relatives—the flower of the flock in her own family, the pride and joy of her mother's heart. A gentleman attached to Lady Falkland's service for years, and who had known all her children as babies, made Lady Home his particular charge. When they had to dismount and walk, which was not an unusual occurrence, he always undertook to lift her over the rough parts of the road, and the brooklets which intersected it. On one occasion, towards the end of the journey, the coach in which they travelled had to cross a rapid stream, and the ladies and children to walk along a narrow bridge, consisting only of a plank. Lady Home's faithful attendant insisted on carrying her in his arms. Half way across his foot slipt and he fell into the water, "but," as the old-fashioned narrative relates, "taking only heed of her, he cast himself so along in the stream, that she fell upright with her feet on his breast, and she, seeing them all troubled with fear for her, and he especially, who had so long served her father and mother, grievously afflicted at it, she would not acknowledge

feeling any hurt or being frightened, but at the end
of the journey the same night, fell sick, and within
a week died, being first delivered, almost three
months before her time, of a daughter, who lived
three hours, and was christened. Had it lived, her
mother was resolved to have nursed her grandchild
with her own, not yet weaned. Her daughter died
in her arms." Every circumstance connected with
the loss of this beloved child was calculated, as far
as this world went, to heighten the grief of Lady
Falkland. After a long separation, she had found
her as virtuous as she was charming, and as affectionate as ever, and in thought and opinion still
adhering to all she had taught her. She had been
permitted to join her by a husband and a family who
looked upon that young wife as their most precious
possession. She was taking her to the house of her
own mother, who had always been harshly disposed
towards herself, but who would be softened and won
over by her granddaughter's irresistible attractions.
But all such hopes were at an end. The over-zeal
of a poor old man had brought about the destruction
of all the happiness centred in that fragile existence.
It was a bitter chalice for the bereaved mother, but
she did not give way to violent and inordinate grief.
She had learnt to see God's hand in every event
which befell her, and derived consolation, not only
in the knowledge of her daughter's purity and inno-
cence of heart and life, her diligent performance of
every moral duty, but also from her instinctive love

of the Catholic religion, her unconsciousness—for
no one had ever informed her of it—of the obligation she was under of embracing it, and the readiness
with which she faced death.   It was anxiety for her
infant's safety, not her own, which had been permanent in her thoughts during her hour of trial.
One circumstance attending the death-bed of her
child, Lady Falkland loved to think upon.   She was
convinced that the Blessed Virgin had appeared to
her.   Being perfectly awake, and in her senses,
Lady Home affirmed that a bright woman, crowned
and clothed in white stood by her side. If this was not
a real vision, it showed at least, what images were
predominant in her soul during the last conscious
moments of existence.   An early and holy death
outside the visible fold of the Catholic Church, may
be justly ascribed to God's foreknowledge and mercy
It was in that light that, in after years, Lady Home's
mother looked upon her peaceful end.   Had she
lived, the day must have arrived, when she would
have been obliged to follow, either her own example,
and enter on the way of sorrow she herself had to
tread, or have resisted grace and endangered her
salvation.   Mysteries of mercy are often hidden in
the abrupt endings of lives precious beyond others,
but which are not permitted to run their course on
earth.

On her return to London from Burford Priory,
Lady Falkland's first care was to forward her husband's interests and set him right with the Ministers

of the Crown.   Towards the end of July we find her
thus employed, and Lord Falkland writing as follows
to Lord Conway.

My very good Lord,—

By all my wife's letters I understand my obligations
to your lordship to be very many, and she takes upon
her to have received so manifold and noble demonstrations of your favour to herself, that she begins to conceive herself some able body in Court, by your
countenance to do me courtesies, as if she had the
wits as well as the will.   She makes it appear she hath
done me some good offices in removing some infusions
which my adversaries here have made unto you, to my
great disadvantage, and hath settled your lordship in a
good opinion of my affection to your service and your
person.   It was high time, for many evil consequences
from the contrary have befallen me since that infusion
was first made, which I fear will not be removed in
haste.   And I must thank her much for her careful pains
in it, though it was but an act of duty in her to see me
righted when she knew me wronged.   But I am much
bound to your lordship for giving her leave to perform
that duty, and to let me feel its effects.   And I beseech
your lordship still to continue that favour to us both,
giving her good counsel and good countenance within
a new world and Court, at such a distance from her
husband, which a poor weak woman stands in the
greatest need of to despatch her suits, if she have any
that are reasonable, and giving expedition to any she
haply may solicit for me. . . .

That Lord Falkland should have had fears and misgivings, such as he expresses in his next Letter, as to his wife's living in London and at the Court, uncounselled and unprotected, is not to be wondered at. He knew her to be impetuous and imprudent; her generosity, her easy belief in the virtues of others, and great inexperience, made her likely to be imposed upon, and, as he evidently dreaded, liable to fall into mistakes prejudicial to his interests, which she was so anxious to forward. He was also, no doubt aware that, from the first moment of her arrival in London, she had sought the society of persons likely to encourage her in Anglo-Catholic practices, which he suspected of close affinity with those of the Church of Rome, but he was so deeply involved in pecuniary difficulties that he could not, or would not, furnish means for her residence elsewhere. What he desired was that, instead of living at her mother's house in town, she should live with her at Burford Priory. But Lady Tanfield, as her daughter well knew, was by no means inclined permanently to receive her and her children. They had never got on well together, and she strenuously opposed her son-in-law's determination to burthen her with the support of his family. He, on the other hand, was bent upon it, and wrote thus to Lord Conway:

I am glad your lordship doth approve my wife's good affection to her husband, which was a point I never doubted, but for her abilities in the agency of affairs, as I had never a great opinion of them, so I was never desirous to employ them even had she had them, for I conceive women to be no fit solicitors in State affairs, for though it sometimes happens that they have good wits, it then commonly falls out that they have over busy natures withal. For my part, I should take much more comfort to hear that she were quietly retired to her mother's into the country, than that she had obtained a great suit in the Court. Your lordship knows I once before besought you to give her good counsel in the absence of her husband, in that great distance from him and in so great a Court, a new course to her. Better counsel you cannot give her than to retire to her mother's, and abide there until the doubtful times do blow over, and the daily expected war in Ireland be ended, for in time of war what should a woman do here? And when a peace shall be concluded, I may be likely to sue his Majesty for leave to retire and live with her. . . . If your lordship will try your skill to persuade her with content to that retreat, I shall be bound to you for it and be happy in it if you prevail. I must confess she hath not been wanting to represent your lordship's respects to me in fair forms, and you yourself hath often given me assurance of your own noble inclination to maintain the dignity of my place; yet give me leave to say, freely and truly, that I neither see or hear of anything but diminutions. All authorities under me are growing with the eclipse of mine, which will appear in the end, to the dishonour and the disservice of his Majesty, not mine.

It is evident that Lord Falkland's public and private annoyances worked on his nerves in a manner which made him hardly just to his wife. Between his insistence that she should live with her mother and the latter's ungracious refusals to receive her, poor Lady Falkland found herself in an embarrassing position. It is probable that her own desires led her to remain in London. The very reasons which contributed to make Lord Falkland anxious to seclude her in Oxfordshire, must have weighed with her in a contrary sense. She was no doubt glad to remain within the reach of churches where, to use the phraseology now in use, Church principles were carried out. The society of Henrietta Maria's Catholic French ladies and her chaplains, and the friendship of the Laudian ladies of the Court, must in every way have been congenial to her feelings and her tastes. She was again in constant communication with the Bishop of Durham, and practising the High Church religion with which she was trying to content herself, though "with less satisfaction daily." Her house was frequented by divines of the High Anglican type, whom she still hoped were real priests, and she endeavoured hard "to do like Catholics and to draw as near to them as she could." We find her going through exactly the same process through which Puseyites did, and now Ritualists strive to beguile themselves into the belief, that the English Establishment can be so modelled and shaped in imitation of the Catholic Church, as to afford rest to the souls of those who would fain be Catholics, but who will not make the sacrifices involved in a change of religion.

Dr. Cozens, a Prebandary of Durham, and one of the King's chaplains, was the oracle, the private Pope of many High Anglicans of that period. At the request of the Countess of Denby, the Duke of Buckingham's sister, he published a book entitled *A Collection of Private Devotions; or the Hours of Prayer.* Collier, in his *Church History*, says " that this lady was somewhat unsettled in her religion, and warping towards Popery, and that these Devotions were drawn up to recommend further the Church of England to her esteem and preserve her in that communion," by means, no doubt, of as near an approach to Catholic forms as was possible in the Anglican Establishment. He adds that " some moderate persons were shocked with it, as drawing too near the superstitions of Rome; at least they suspected it to be a preparation to further advances." The Puritans attacked it with virulence.

Lady Falkland, who was an intimate friend of Lady Denby's, was probably one of the pious ladies whom this manual was to arrest in their progress towards the true Church. It may have produced some temporary effect of that sort on her mind, for she made up her mind to go to confession and to choose Dr. Cozens as her confessor. This was going beyond the teaching of his book, and it took him rather by surprise. " He excused himself from hearing her for the present, not being used to hear confessions, but he said that he would take time to prepare himself for it by studying casuists in the country, whither he was going for that purpose to spend six months. But before that time was elapsed," (Lady Falkland's daughter remarks,) " she had made, God be thanked, a confession more to the purpose."

Since her return to London, Lady Falkland had made acquaintance with Lord Ormond, a zealous Catholic, whose house she soon began to frequent. There, for the first time, she conversed with Catholic priests, first with Father Casket, a Franciscan, and then with two Benedictine priests, who went by the names of black Father Dunstan and white Father Dunstan. They were probably thus distinguished in reference to their complexions. Disputations were held at Lord Ormond's house, in which these Fathers demonstrated the insecurity of the position held by herself and her friends, and the unlawfulness of their remaining as they were. Dr. Cozens's absence had evidently left his disciples a dangerous liberty, which in Lady Falkland's case led to decisive results. She was completely convinced by what she then heard of what she had long been inclined to believe, and would at once have been reconciled, as it was then called, if Lady Denby had not professed herself equally impressed, and intreated her to wait until they had listened to one more discussion, and then they would both together be received into the Church.

For little less than half a year the same thing went on. Whether from indecision, or nervous apprehension of what was then an act of no common heroism, involving as it did danger and suffering, or a preconceived plan for preventing her friend from separating herself from the Protestant Church, which she was not herself prepared to renounce, Lady Denby kept deluding her with the oft-repeated assurance, that only a little more argument, a little more time, were requisite to bring her to the point. At last, perceiving that she never resolved to do what she promised, Lady Falkland determined to wait no longer for her, and began to prepare herself in right earnest for her own abjuration. She intended to be received into the Church by white Father Dunstan as he was called, the first Benedictine she had ever known. Throughout the whole of her Catholic life she had the greatest devotion to that Order, partly becase it was by means of those Fathers that her conversion had been brought about, and partly on account of her love of learning and study, for which it had always been famous.

One eventful morning, Lady Falkland went to the palace where Lady Denby lodged, and announced to her that not another day would she delay the act they both had in view. If she chose at once to be reconciled to the Catholic Church, well and good, but otherwise nothing would prevent her from carrying out her intention. As usual, Lady Denby began to plead for further time, and to use every argument she could think of to support her request. But Lady Falkland was not to be moved. She told her that she neither could nor would put off again what she felt to be her absolute duty towards God and His Church. Her friend, seeing she could not prevail, exclaimed: "Well, I have you now in the Court, and here I will keep you. You shall lie in my chamber, and shall not go forth." Lady Falkland was amazed at these words; she did not feel quite sure what they meant, but thought it best not to betray any anxiety, and to remain quietly where she was. Lady Denby reiterated her assurances that some other time she would join her in doing what they had both designed, and evidently thought that she had dissuaded her from immediate action, or at any rate did not suppose she would go away at once. So she went to speak to some one within her apartments, begging her to wait for her return. Lady Falkland, when she was left alone, began to suspect what was indeed the case, that her friend had gone to seek the assistance of some one who would persuade, if not compel her, to give up her intention. There was no time to lose, she darted from the room, left the palace, and with all possible speed made her way to Lord Ormond's house.

It had been her intention to spend a few days in recollection and prayer before she was actually received into the Church, but not knowing how far she might be forcibly hindered from effecting her purpose, she was now afraid to risk the least delay.

Father Dunstan was at Lord Ormond's when she arrived there, so she asked him to let her make at once her abjuration. The most secret place that could be thought of was an empty stable. There was accomplished the act which ended her long spiritual struggles, which set her feet on the rock of ages, which satisfied every yearning of her heart, every aspiration of her soul. And in the self-same hour began the long course of trial, poverty and suffering, which continued more or less to the end of her days.

Rising from her knees, she walked back with a firm step to the palace, went straight into Lady Denby's room, and said: "I will stay with you now as long as you please, for all is done." Much troubled at this, Lady Denby hastened to her brother, the Duke of Buckingham, and informed him of what had happened. The Duke carried the news to the King, who was highly displeased. Every effort was made to induce Lady Falkland to retract while there was time. But neither the royal displeasure nor any arguments or threats moved her in the least. At last she was allowed to go home, but was soon followed by Secretary Cook with an order from his Majesty that she should remain confined in her house during the King's pleasure. For six weeks she was thus a prisoner in her own rooms, her household being wholly Protestant, and no Catholic venturing to come near her. On the second day of her seclusion, she had a visitor in the person of

Dr. Cozens, who had no doubt been hastily summoned to London in order to reclaim the truant who, during his absence, had escaped from his little fold into the wide pastures of the Catholic Church. The one object of the poor prebendary had been to retain within the limits of the Establishment, even at the cost of many a concession which savoured of Popery, a chosen circle of disciples, and especially of noble ladies, whose allegiance to the Anglican Church was sadly shaken. His despair at finding that the cleverest and best-informed of these ladies had abandoned this courtly circle of devotees, and given so fatal an example to her friends, appears to have been intense. He is said to have been a man "of an extremely passionate nature," which tallies with the description given of his interview with Lady Falkland on the day after her conversion.

"He came to visit her, and having heard from her all that had been done, fell into so great and violent a trouble, that casting himself on the ground, he would not rise or eat from morning till night, weeping even to roaring." He used the very same arguments to make her return to the Anglican Church, which are now so often employed to detain in it persons anxious to be received into the Catholic Church; the disgrace she was bringing on the party who were striving to uphold Catholic doctrines and practices, the discouragement given to those who accepted High Church teaching, the fears which would be roused by her desertion, and the triumph it would afford to Puritans.

But he could gain nothing from one whose eyes were now fully opened to that unreality which in the seventeenth, as in the nineteenth century, characterized every effort to revive Catholicism in a schismatic body. Lady Falkland complied with only one of his requests. She fasted with him throughout the whole of that day—but as this led to no result such as he desired, he at last went away, and never came near her again.

CHAPTER V.

Persecution and suffering.

THE first result of Lady Falkland's conversion, as far as worldly matters went, was the action taken by Mr. Welstead, her husband's agent, who, without waiting for his orders, at once stopped her allowance. This, her daughter tells us, reduced her to extremity, for she was never much beforehand with her income. Her eldest daughter was a maid of honour, and lived at the Court, but her younger children and the servants who took care of them, she was obliged to send for their dinners and suppers to the houses of her friends. She was determined not to part with them until compelled to do so. It was not long, however, before Hitchcock, her head servant, received orders to take them all away from her house, and every servant in it also, except a young woman named Bessie Poulter, whom she had brought up from a child. She was then a Protestant, but positively refused to leave her mistress. Not only did all the other members of her household depart with her children, but everything in the house that was moveable in the way of provisions was taken away. She was left without coals, wine, or beer, without

F

money wherewith to buy the necessaries of life, and in solitary confinement, with her one faithful attendant.   Lord Falkland evidently approved of the measures his agent had taken to starve his wife into submission; and Hitchcock must have acted under strict orders from his master, for he seems to have been well disposed towards Lady Falkland, who had shortly before showed him great kindness, interceding for him with Lord Conway, to afford him time to pay his debts by making him a nominal member of his household, and thus securing him from arrest. It is satisfactory to know that, as she afterwards ascertained, he spoke of her, in his letters to Lord Falkland, with great respect and esteem, and did not join in the accusations which some of her other servants brought against her, in order to increase his irritation.   Changing her religion, he did, indeed, conceive to be a great offence, but in every other regard he defended and praised her.   She was more obliged to him, we are told, for this forbearance, than displeased with the strict manner in which he had obeyed his master's orders.   Lord Falkland's grief and anger when he received the, to him, most bitter news of her conversion was, as might have been expected, excessive.   We can judge of it by the letter he addressed to the King on the 8th of December, 1626.   He must have been carried away beyond the limits of prudence in writing with such bitterness on the subject to his Sovereign, who had just married a Catholic Princess, and who, though often irritated against her French chaplains and attendants, was known to bear no personal ill will to his Catholic subjects. The Lord Deputy's allusion to the protection afforded to his daughter related, no doubt, to Anne Cary, the maid of honour, who had evidently been removed to the Court when her mother's abjuration was made known :

May it please your Sacred Majesty,—The same packet which brought me word, to my great grief, of her apostacy, whom now I may say I have long unhappily called wife, did to my comfort assure me that your Majesty had vouchsafed, out of your most benign clemency, to take my innocent child, her daughter, for better deliverance from the peril of that most leprous infection, whereof her years made her more capable than the rest, into the protection of your own royal care, and under your own roof, which the Almighty God of Heaven will recompense unto your Majesty. So I humbly beseech Him, in the multiplication of His best blessings upon your sacred person, with infinite prosperities in a long life and reign.

As there is great mercy in this salvation and distinction, [between Lady Falkland and her daughter] so is there no less mercy in that justice which shall duly punish all those who have been instruments of her prevarication, for an example of terror to others. Of them I have informed my Lord of Canterbury's grace, because I hold it most proper to his Metropolitan office to attend to the execution thereof. And this I implore, not to satisfy an incensed indignation desirous of re-

revenge, but to discharge my loyal and grateful duty, bound as I am to be careful of your Majesty's preservation, for how can your throne be long established, and your sacred person safe in it, whilst these locusts of Rome, whose doctrines are full of horrid treasons, as many of their lives are of horrid impieties, be permitted to be at liberty, compassing all your dominions, and with impunity endeavouring to alienate your subjects' affections from you?

He then goes on to say, that " a kingdom divided against itself cannot stand," and that if the hearts of any of his Majesty's subjects are filled with the love of the Pope, no place can be left for the love of the King. And where there is no love, there can be no obedience but what is exacted by fear, which begets hatred, hatred conspiracy, and that danger.

This letter seems to have been intended to convey to Charles the First a hint that he was disposed to act too favourably towards Catholics, for it goes on to say:

Some of these priests, as I am informed, expect to receive speedy preferment in her Majesty's household. If this should succeed, it will encourage others to be bolder, when they shall perceive their fellows' iniquities crowned with such a reward, but your Majesty's known incomparable goodness frees me from that fear.

We have already seen that almost from the first moment of Lady Falkland's return to England, her husband's object had been to compel her to live at her mother's country-house, and at her expense. Lady Tanfield's resistance, and perhaps his wife's increasing favour at Court, had made him drop for a time this, his favourite project. Now, however, it seemed a favourable opportunity to bring the King's authority to bear on Lady Tanfield as well as her daughter, and to relieve him from her support.

As for the apostate herself, [he writes] since I was not so happy as to obtain from the first her confinement at her mother's, which possibly might have prevented this falling away, I do now humbly beseech your Majesty that she may be now committed thither, with commandment to her mother to receive her, to keep her safe and free from any communication by word or letter with any of that profession. Haply when she shall no more hear the charms of these enchanters, she may recover out of these distractions whereinto they have put her, it being a principal way of theirs first to make apprehensive spirits mad with despair, that they may gain them to hope for no salvation but in their Church, and then keep them foolish to hold them. This is the only way for her recovery and reclamation, which, if it may be obtained by your Majesty's pious and prudent directions, and I cannot yet despair of it, your glory will be infinite. I beseech the God of Heaven to make your felicities even as the sands of the sea for number, and for time, as long as the sun and moon endureth. Your sacred Majesty's most loyal and much afflicted subject and servant,

H. FALKLAND.

Meanwhile, the poor convert underwent such want during her confinement to her house, that she had often not a bit of food to put in her mouth. This was altogether so strange a position for one who had never known the least approach to poverty, that she was ashamed, and anxious to conceal it. She would not allow the companion of her captivity to starve, and therefore sent her for her meals to Lord Ormond's house, but strictly forbade her to mention her own necessities. Bessie Poulter obeyed her orders, but privately took from the table and put into a handkerchief pieces of pie-crust or bread-and-butter, which she brought home with her. Sometimes for days together Lady Falkland had nothing else to eat. Every one, even her best friends, seemed to have forgotten her. At last her maid, unable to endure the sight of her mistress reduced to such extremities, informed Lord Ormond of her position, who then, during the remaining time of her confinement, daily sent her dishes from his house. Used as she was to much society, and fond of conversation, Lady Falkland felt very desolate during this complete seclusion. The first person who ventured to call upon her was a Catholic gentleman, Mr. Chaperlin. The joy and comfort his visit gave her were unspeakable. He made her a present of a Catholic prayer book the first she had ever possessed. We can well fancy the delight with which this gift must have been received, nor can we wonder that her gratitude to this good man was so great, that as long as she lived "she scarcely ever went to her prayers without saying an Hail Mary for him."

After Mr. Chaperlin had visited her, some others followed his example. A Catholic cousin of Lady Falkland's, Lady Manors, when she discovered the state she was in, mentioned it to Lady Carlisle, who spoke of it to the King, adding, that being a prisoner, she could do nothing to remedy her condition. That no one had appealed to him before, turned out to be the cause of her prolonged confinement, which had now lasted more than six weeks. Charles the First had either been purposely misunderstood by those who were anxious to deal harshly with a Catholic convert, or else he had given an order, in a moment of irritation, which had afterwards escaped his memory. As soon as the state of the case was laid before him, he wondered at hearing that Lady Falkland was still a prisoner, declared that this was far from his intention, and regretted that he had not been earlier informed of it. He immediately gave her leave "to go abroad at her pleasure."

It was, perhaps, the knowledge of the King's clemency towards his wife, and of her release from thraldom, which led to Lord Falkland's writing to Secretary Coke, on the 29th of December, 1626, the following letter:

Right Honourable Sir,—My agent hath acquainted me what pains you have taken with my apostate wife to have stopped her course, and with what favour you

have furthered my humble suit to his Majesty to have
her instantly restrained into the custody of her mother,
which is the only way of hope to have her reclaimed,
for otherwise there is none. Without the punishment,
and that exemplary, of her seducers, they will take so
much encouragement to prosecute such attempts with
boldness everywhere, that in a short time we shall have
similar unhappy divisions made in all the families of
this kingdom as is now the case with mine, to the
hazard of great and manifest dangers. I must render
you, sir, my very humble thanks for what you have
already done, and beseech the continuance thereof until
I obtain the effect of my desire, which is to put her in
the way of a possibility of recovery, or of acquitting
myself of my duty to the uttermost in seeking it. If I
cannot prevail by the assistance of his Majesty's just
power, I must resort to a separation *à mensa et thoro*,
which I intend to do if I despair of her recovery.

In this letter was inclosed an extract from the
one Lord Falkland had received from his wife in
answer to a previous missive which had been shown
to the King. He says in reference to that extract:

How much it concerns his Majesty in his honour and
in his wisdom, to prevent the evils which the progression
of these lapses and their examples threaten to his person
and state, doth appear by this inclosed abstract out of a
letter of her's to me, which came to my hands the 25th
day of this month, and was partly an answer to mine,
a copy of which I am informed your honour read to his

Majesty, and whereof many copies, I hear, are spread by her among the Papists, whereby it is manifest how very unsafe it is for me to nourish that serpent any longer in my bosom that deals so treasonably with me.

I know your honour will acquaint his Majesty with the inclosed abstract, which I did not think agreeable with my duty to conceal from his knowledge, of whose honour I am as tender as I am careful and studious of his service.

Your honour's affectionate friend, ready to serve you,

FALKLAND.

The extract from Lady Falkland's letter evidently refers to two accusations which her husband must have brought up against her, one being that she fed Jesuits and priests, as well as conversed with them, and the other, that she publicly professed the Catholic religion. She says: "You charge me with feeding Jesuits and priests; for Jesuits, to my knowledge, I never saw the face of one in my life, nor intend to do so. For priests, it is true I have conversed with some of them, else I could not have been what, for no death I will deny myself to be. As to feeding them, it is possible some one may have sometimes dined or supped here, but if there were a bit the more, or if I ever appointed anything, but only sat down to what was provided, I will be subject to your displeasure. *And since it pleased his Majesty to make me, whether I would or no, declare myself Catholic, which was on Tuesday last a month*, not one of that function has ever entered the house; so careful as I am."

It is difficult to perceive in this passage anything that supports Lord Falkland's assertion that it clearly touched the King's honour, and that he was bound not to conceal it from him. It appears more likely that he wished to excite his displeasure against Lady Falkland, who had thrown on his Majesty the responsibility of her open profession of the Catholic faith. She had intended out of consideration for her husband, to keep her conversion a secret. It was Lady Denby who had hurried on the disclosure by revealing at once to the Duke of Buckingham, and through him to the King, what she had no right to divulge. Lady Falkland may have indeed been glad on her own account, that the King insisted on a positive answer to the charge made against her. It relieved her from the burthen of secresy, and as her daughter says, "she always rejoiced much to make confession of her faith." Had she, however, been able to practise her religion secretly, it would have probably made an immense difference in her husband's view of the matter, even had she thought it her duty to inform him of her abjuration. It was not her religious opinions he objected to so much, violent as his language was, as the effect which her act was likely to have on his own prospects and position. She had been lately gaining in the opinion of the King and Queen, and many influential persons in the Government and the Court. She had proved more likely to advance his interests than he had at first expected. The public announcement of her conversion blighted these fair hopes, and his anger was proportionate to his disappointment. She had justified herself at the King's expense as it were, and unable to reproach his Majesty directly, he reverted to the underhand means of conveying to him what his wife had written, and probably hoped that the annoyance this might give would forward his own object, by causing her to be consigned as a prisoner to her mother's reluctant care.

Now that Lady Falkland was set at liberty, she began again to frequent her old acquaintances, who seem to have treated her kindly, but to have renewed their efforts to shake her allegiance to the Church of Rome. The King himself sent her a paper, written by one of the Protestant Bishops, purporting to prove that even were the Catholic Church true, yet it was lawful to remain in the communion of the Church of England. Father Prim, a Benedictine, with whom she had become acquainted since her conversion, sent this document to Father Leander, Prior of Douay,[1] who answered it so fully and satisfactorily, that when the Bishop who had drawn it up read this reply, he sent some one to Lady Falkland desiring her not to publish it. Anxious not to give further offence she complied with this injunction.

Letters had poured upon her during the latter days of her imprisonment, and after she was re-

---

[1] Father Leander's family name was John Jones. He was connected with the old family of the Scudamores, in Herefordshire, was elected Prior of Douay in 1621, and died in London in 1635.

leased, personal remonstrances were not wanting to persuade her, that she was disgracing her husband, ruining him and her children, and placing an insuperable bar between them and herself, for it was equally certain, she was told, that he would never allow them to live with her or live with her himself. She was reminded of all the favour shown to her by the King before her change of religion, and of the still greater opportunities she would have of advancing her husband's fortunes, if she now returned to her allegiance to the English Church. These arguments were continually pressed upon her, and some of her relations and friends expressed a desire, that a disputation should take place in her presence between a Protestant divine and a Catholic priest. This was accordingly arranged, and a conference held at the house of Lord Newburgh, her sister-in-law's husband. His chaplain, Dr. Wheatley, and Black Father Dunstan, of the Benedictine Order, met there for this purpose. It seems strange that a priest should have been able, at that time, to come to a Protestant house and argue in support of his religion. These inconsistencies are always to be met with in the history of all persecutions. They are easily accounted for in the reign of Charles the First, by the different spirit which animated the Court and the great majority of the King's subjects. Lord Newburgh evidently belonged to the extreme High Church party, and though the Anglican clergy of the school of Laud

were almost as violently opposed to the true Church
as the Puritans, some of the laymen of that sect
favoured Catholics to a certain point. The dispute
in question took place, and was reported and printed
by Dr. Wheatley in so unfair a manner, that, when
he requested Dr. Long, a Protestant clergyman who
had been present at it, to sign that report, the latter
declared that nothing would induce him to set his
pen to so untrue a document, and that if *the other
gentleman* drew up a more accurate statement, he
would be obliged to authenticate it. This did not
restrain Dr. Wheatly from publishing his own
version, and owing probably to the dangers and
difficulties of a priest's position, Father Dunstan's
never saw the light.

Meanwhile, Lady Falkland had the satisfaction of
procuring the conversion of the young person who
had clung to her so faithfully during her imprisonment. For some time Bessie Poulter had refused
to see or speak to a priest. She seriously believed
that all Catholic clergymen were witches, having
heard the Scotch ministers, when she was in Lady
Home's service, declare this in the pulpit. But at
last she consented to listen to Father Dunstan's
explanations, and was received into the Church.
Some time afterwards he was denounced by
Hitchcock, the servant who had taken away Lady
Falkland's children, was arrested in her house, and
thrown into prison. Strange to say, this same man,
on his death-bed some years later, entreated his

former mistress to send him a priest, who did not, however, arrive in time. Hitchcock died expressing great regret that he could not make a formal abjuration, and recommending his wife to become a Catholic. His devotion to his master appears to have been the motive of his conduct towards Father Dunstan. He fancied that Lord Falkland would highly approve of what he had done, for he knew that the conversion of Bessie Poulter had added to his displeasure. Whether, even in the midst of all his anger, he had a dislike to brutal persecution, or that he was annoyed at the attention which the arrest must have directed on his wife's proceedings, it certainly appears that he was by no means pleased with his servant's action. As it so often happens, in domestic trials arising from religious differences between husbands and wives, they would not have been so acute and prolonged, in Lord and Lady Falkland's case, had they been left to themselves; but every kind of falsehood was used in order to exasperate him and misrepresent her. Some of his friends wrote to him, that she placed impediments in the way of his affairs at Court, and did him ill offices with those in power. His servants informed him, that, whilst she complained of the wretched poverty in which he left her, she could find money to spend on priests and Papists. He believed nothing she said, and her defects in past days and natural faults of character told against her in his mind, now so warped and bittterly prejudiced. Her friends the Duchess of Buckingham, Lady Denby, and Lord Newburgh, wrote earnestly to him in her defence, but in vain. One man especially, who had long been in his service, destroyed the effect of all such letters, by those in which he continually fanned the flame of his anger. She, on her side, was evidently most anxious to avoid everything that might displease or injure him, and was ready to yield every point in which her religion was not concerned. Thus we are told "that after she was a Catholic though he would neither speak to her nor see her, that she forbore things ordinarily done by all and which she did much delight in, from having heard from some one that he seemed to dislike it, and, if she had the least apprehension it would not please him, she would not do the least thing, though her distress for money was such, that she had either to beg or borrow, without any knowledge as to how or when she could repay, or to starve. About this time, some of her friends having represented to his Majesty's Council how proper and necessary it was that her husband should provide her with means of existence, they obtained in her favour an order by which he was commanded to allow her £500 a year, but she never would make use of it, and would not even mention it to him, knowing well how irritated he would be at being compelled to do this against his will. Her position was most embarrassing, for her friends blamed her for not availing herself of the Council's order, and naturally enough were in consequence less disposed to lend her assistance. She tried to excuse herself, and to place the most favourable construction on Lord Falkland's conduct, by saying, that she was convinced that he would have done of his own accord what the Council commanded, had it been in his power, but that she knew in what difficulties he was, and on that account could not bring herself to press him on the subject. She did not tell them of her dread of making him angry, for her object was to screen him from their animadversions. But how to exist was the question. It seems that in March, 1627, Lord Falkland had well-nigh obtained what he so much desired—a Royal order commanding his wife to go and live at her mother's, for we find a letter from the Duchess of Buckingham to Lord Conway which implies as much :

My Lord,—I have to entreat a favour from you in behalf of the poor distressed Lady Falkland, for I protest her case is very lamentable. I desire that you will speak to the King, that those letters which he signed to be sent to Lady Tanfield, ordering her to keep her daughter a prisoner, may be stayed, for she is very willing to go and live with her mother *if she will receive her*, and that is all, I am told, that her lord desires. Therefore I entreat you to move the King for her, and if need be to get my lord to join with you, that she may have leave to come back again if her mother will not receive her, and that these letters may not be delivered at all. This desiring you to get it done as speedily as you can, and I shall take it as a favour done to your loving friend,

K. BUCKINGHAM.

This feminine mediation, which Lord Falkland alludes to in the following letter to Lord Conway, was apparently successful, for on the 4th of April he writes in a very bad humour:

My very good lord,—The 18th of last month I presented your lordship with my humble thanks for the directions which, jointly with Mr. Secretary Coke, you sent my wife's mother and her unhappy self to cohabit together, and that by his Majesty's commandment. But since, by a packet arrived here on the first of this month, I understand, to my great vexation of mind, that there is a pause obtained for the execution thereof, and liberty propounded for her to live where she best likes. I am confident it is but by her great importunity, mixed with some feminine wily pretences, and assisted by feminine mediation, that this stop hath been obtained, but I hope it shall not have power to prevail to make it a conclusion. Were she not under that obloquy she now hath brought upon herself by her odious defection, fuller of malice than of conscience, yet surely her residency ought to be according to her husband's election, not her own. So *our* religion teacheth. And if *her* new religion teacheth contrary doctrine, in that as in other things abominable, let me first obtain an utter and absolute divorce, that I may be separated from all interest in her person and ways,

G

so that dishonour and confusion of face, with ruin of fortune, may not thereby assail and overwhelm me, and I shall then be contented to give up my claim of superiority, and being made free, leave her free.

But being the wife of one of a more considerable quality than a common person, by all rules of policy hath made her a delinquent, and so his Majesty declared by his proceedings with her at the beginning of her defection. There is no hope of her being reclaimed but one. Where she now remains she is confirmed in her obstinacy, and cannot be let alone without dishonour to his Majesty, and, above all offence to God, and scandal of the truth.

To conclude, my lord, if she prevail in her iniquitous request, and I fail in my just, reasonable, and humble petitions, do but think with how little comfort I am here pursuing his Majesty's service, whilst overborne with such shame and oppressed with so much grief, and what cause I shall have to complain and declaim against such hard measure. I beseech your lordship, as you will have to answer at the great Tribunal for the well employing of your present powers, to urge seriously for the speedy accomplishment of his Majesty's directions, and therein the reasonable satisfaction of him that remains your faithful servant,

H. FALKLAND.

This letter procured a renewal of the King's order to Lady Falkland to repair to her mother's house. Those she wrote to Lord Conway, Lady Tanfield's to herself, which she forwarded to him in support of her assertion that her mother refused to receive her, and her petition to the King, explain her painful position, and express in a pathetic manner the peculiar hardships to which she was subjected. The next chapter will contain them.

CHAPTER. VI

Correspondence—petitions—retirement from London.

LADY FALKLAND having received from Lord Conway and Mr. Secretary Coke the royal order, which well-nigh drove her to despair, wrote to the latter the following letter :—

My Lord,—I received yesterday an expression of his Majesty's pleasure, which commands me to my mother's in the nature of a prisoner. I hope, if I am constrained to go there, that his Majesty will be pleased to allow me fit means for my degree, for I have now nothing from anybody. I have committed no fault that I know of, and if I had, sure I believe the King would take some other way for my punishment than so unusual a one as to starve me to death. My mother hath expressed to me that if ever I should come down to her, which she believes his Majesty will never force me to do, she will not give me the least relief now or leave me anything at her death. Having freely given up a fair jointure to help my lord for his provision into Ireland, for which kindness of mine to him my father disinherited me, and for no other cause, as he justified at his death, I have now nothing to hope for but her favour at her death, which I hope his Majesty will not drive me to forfeit. I therefore entreat that until my mother expresses in some way that she is willing I should come to her, your lordship will be pleased, in compassion of a woman distressed without just cause, to move his Majesty for me. If it pleases him I should remove from London, it is my most earnest desire, if only my lord will give me necessary means to feed and clothe me, for nothing keeps me here but sharp necessity. Therefore, if that may be allowed, I beseech your lordship to move his Majesty to confine me, if I needs must be confined, into Essex, where, in a little house near my sister-in-law, Barret, I may pass my time quietly, and have the comfort of her company, which I think will please us both. So I should not trouble London with residing in it, which is the only reason your letter gives for the command. I beseech you to speak with the Duchess and the Countess of Buckingham about me, and rather to believe what those noble ladies and my brother and sister (in law) Barret, with whom I daily converse, say, than those pestilent servants of my lord's, who seek to make advantage of my misery and know nothing of me, because they never see me, though they feign to do so to work their own base ends. If your lordship be pleased to discourse about me with my brother (in law) Barret and my sister, they can, and I know will, speak truly.

I intend not in what I have said to lay the least imputation on my Lord Deputy, whose servants' informations to him have begotten my misery, and I desir no better testimony for me than all my lord's own kindred which are now in town.

If I have done amiss in anything but the supposed fault of changing my religion, I will be content to suffer in the highest degree. I have neither meat, drink, or clothes, or money wherewith to purchase them, and I lie in a lodging which I have no means to pay for. I received a message from you by word of mouth in which you wondered I had removed my lodging and lived where, as you have heard, two priests also lived. I was before at my mother's house, from whence she sent to have me removed, because she is coming thither herself, in order to solicit the King that she may not against law be forced to receive me. Since then I have had to remove thrice until I could find a lodging fit for me. I think your lordship must mean the second of those three, from whence I only removed because there were other lodgers in it. This house where I now am I have all to myself. And now my lord, do show your pity yet more than formerly, and you shall gain honour by it, and do a deed of charity by the consent of all religions. Help me out of London I beseech you, but into Essex, not to Burford and not confined at all, so shall I be bound ever to acknowledge myself your lordship's

Much obliged servant,

E. Falkland.

Lady Tanfield's letter to her daughter was inclosed in the preceding one; it is a curious specimen of the illiterate spelling of the period, and very different in style from Lady Falkland's. The orthography of this singular composition has been altered in order to make it intelligible.

Bess,[1]—I perceive by your last letters, by the carrier, that I shall never have hope to have any comfort from you. My desire was I doubt not but pleasing to God, to have you to live with your husband and to live in that religion wherein you were bred, even the same wherein by God's grace I will live and die, as did your dear father; but, Bess, you respected neither him, that most good man, nor me, for if you had, you could never have erred nor fallen into that mischief wherein you are now. You pretend that your displeasing of your husband is, that you do not come to me; to me he cannot command you. I will not accept of you, and if by any extraordinary device he could compel you, you shall find the worst of it, and any such extremities could not last, for I cannot nor willingly will not endure them. Wherefore, I pray you, Bess, no more of these threatenings, for so I take them from you. I am not to give any account why I came not to London, though it is too well known, my ailings stayed me. They say I should not have forced you from my house there; it is my house but for a short time, and your father commanded me to leave it. If it had not been for your being there I had sooner rid myself of it, but still hoping you had meant as you said, that you would be gone into Ireland, I kept it in my hands and paid a dear rent for it, which I could no longer endure. For my part, you may live where you please. If in Essex, then you shall have some such poor stuff from London as I can spare, and if you should live at Cote, there is yet some stuff that may

---

[1] In the original *Bess* is always spelt *Bes*.

serve your turn. I would be glad to know your resolution on this or the other; but I would have been better pleased if you had your lord's consent, but how it is between you two I know not; it is like to be evil enough if you once petition against him. What can that breed but malice and hatred on both sides, and is more likely to be the means of having him called home than would be your living there with him; but, Bess, all your reasons are grounded on your own will and your faultinesss. I praise my God I never did that thing to offend my father, my mother, nor my dear, my most dear husband, your most loving father, for which I find now my conscience clear; and I wish with my soul that you had followed the example of your heart-grieved mother, but your heart is too hard to give me any content, when only your wilful ways forbid all your children comforts, breeding, or any means hereafter to live, for now I see, I see with a heavy soul, an utter ruin and overthrow of you all. Though I shall leave off writing to you, and desire not to hear from you, yet I will with humble prayers to my Almighty God and Saviour, pray Him to put grace into your heart, that your mind may be changed from this ungodly life you now live in to the blessing of Him, Who sees all hearts and their good meanings and their deserts. Nothing can be hid from Him; to Whom I shall ever again never cease to pray, with my nearest devotions, as well for you as for your discomforted poor mother. .

E. TANFIELD.

Burford, May 6, 1627.

At the same time that Lady Falkland sent Lord Conway (then lately become Lord Keltullagh) this undeniable proof, that her mother would fight to the last against admitting her under her roof, she wrote the following petition to the King :—

May it please your Majesty.—I have been so little accustomed hitherto to the framing of petitions, and have so little help to assist me in anything, that I am driven to express myself in this manner, though the humility of my heart would willingly have presented itself in a lowlier form, if any such there be. Though I am secure, how clear I am from the least disobedience to your Majesty, yet having lately received a command, dated long since, wherein your secretaries have expressed your royal pleasure to be, that I should go down to Burford, to my mother, I am forced to address myself this way to your Majesty. For I am forbidden immediate access to you, and I desire to avoid the semblance of what I so much hate, which is disobedience, I know your Majesty intends to command no impossibilities, and this is accidently no less, my mother being gone to the Bath, and intending to come up, before she sees her own house again, to kneel before your royal feet, and crave the freedom of a subject, that neither she or I may be proceeded against without the form of law. Upon my lord's going into Ireland I was drawn, by seeing his difficulties, to offer my jointure into his hands, that he might sell or mortgage it for his supply, which accordingly was done; and that being gone from me, I have nothing to trust to hereafter but my mother's bounty at her death ; for my father disinherited me, only because I had resigned my jointure; so if I offend her, God knows what may become of me, if my lord, which God forbid, should die. She vows if ever I come to her, either of mine own accord, or by command, for she is confident such a command cannot be procured from your Majesty, if I do my best to hinder it, that she will never, neither in her life nor at her death, either give me anything, or take any care of me. Therefore I most humbly importune your Majesty to call back a command so prejudicial to me, since to obey it will be the means to deprive me of all livelihood hereafter. Yet that should not hinder me, for I would hazard any temporal good to show my zeal to do your Majesty service, but that this is besides impossible, because of my mother's absence from her own house. I am here in so miserable a state that to starve is one of my least fears; because if I should do so, and not be guilty of my own destruction, it would be the end of all my afflictions. I speak it not to tax my lord, who, if he were a stranger to me, I must out of truth, confess, that I think his judgment and disposition to be such, that I, who have marked him much, cannot say I ever knew him fail in the perfection of either, except with regard to his believing too much the information of his servants against me, who, for their own interest, seek to estrange his affections from me. I am now in so pitiful a case as to have neither meat or money, nor means to come by either. So that though, even in your Majesty's opinion, I have committed no faults worthy of death, if you do not compassionate me, I am like to suffer that, or worse. I heard from a person of quality, that your Majesty was pleased to believe that I altered my profession of religion upon some Court hopes, but I beseech you, how wicked soever you may deem me, for it would be wicked to make religion a ladder to climb by, yet, judge me not so foolish as to understand so little the state of this time, as to think promotion likely to come that way. And as it is expressed in the command I received, that its chief reason is the unfitness I should live in London, I desire to retire myself where I may only serve God, and to that end, if my lord would allow me means competent in any indifferent body's judgment, I would take a little house in Essex, near a sister of my lord's and a dear friend of mine, Lady Barret, one in whose conversation I have ever placed a great part of my earthly felicity, and though her religion mainly differs from mine, yet I know she loves me. This is no vast ambition, yet this is all I aim at. I desire nothing but a quiet life, and to re-obtain my lord's favour, which I have done nothing to lose, but what I could not with a safe conscience leave undone. If your Majesty, in your care of your meanest subject, will be pleased to make this conclusion for me, I must say that your mercy to me in this particular, will be as great as I have ever conceived it to be in general. This can be in no way prejudicial to my lord, your faithful servant; that your Majesty continues your royal favour to him, is to me an infinite contentment, and I see no effect of this favour, even where it makes against me, that does not rejoice me much; so just is it in you to esteem so loyal, so diligent, so sincere a servant, who, upon my soul, doth perpetually neglect himself and his own affairs, rather than in any one point omit what may tend to your Majesty's honour and profit.   What I beseech you to do, is to order one of your secretaries to send for my lord's agent, and to command him, until there is time for my lord to understand how things are, and send his directions, to supply me weekly with as much as may be by your Majesty, or any one that you may please to appoint, what is thought necessary to support me with victuals, house-rent, and apparel.   I had rather sustain any misery than petition to be supplied contrary to my lord's will, to which I have and will submit myself as far as I can, until conscience obliges me not to suffer myself to perish, and I hope that it will not offend him if I have recourse to the fountain of clemency, which is your Majesty.   My wants are pressing—I have not means for one meal.   Either let your Majesty be pleased to take order in it yourself, or refer it to any two of your Privy Council, that I may not sink under such penury as I am now in.   I beseech God to bless your Majesty with all His blessings, both here and hereafter, and I daresay you have not on earth one, of any belief, that is more loyally affected to you than

Your Majesty's most humble obedient

Subject and servant,

E. FALKLAND.

Lady Falkland added to this appeal the following earnest request to Lord Conway, that he would give it to the King in the presence of some of her influential friends :—

My Lord,—I must beseech you to do me the great favour, with all the speed you can, to present this unworthy paper into his Majesty's hands, and to importune him to read it, for it concerns no less than to save me from starving. If it be possible, I beseech you to deliver it when my Lord Steward and my Lord Chamberlain are by, in whose good wishes I have much confidence. If you will oblige me thus much I will faithfully pray for you. If you can, I pray you, let the Duke of Buckingham be also present, for I know he will second so just and necessary a request. Though it were not good manners in me, yet I beseech your lordship to remind his Majesty, that if I had been suffered to go at once to my lord in Ireland as I intended to do, all this had not happened, therefore, I hope he will not let me perish for want of food. I have left my humble petitionary letter to his Majesty open, which I beseech you first to read and then cause it to be sealed before you deliver it. If you second it strongly, I dare be bound you shall receive extraordinary thanks from all the three great ladies of my Lord of Buckingham's family, beside your reward from God Almighty for doing so charitable an act. Expedition is also my suit, for delay may destroy me. I remain,

Your Lordship's faithful servant,

E. FALKLAND.

But like most petitioners, poor Lady Falkland had to learn, that expedition is a boon seldom to be obtained from those in authority, and in her case there were no doubt peculiar difficulties in bringing to a solution the matter in hand. It does not appear that her appeal was given into the King's hands, though Lord Conway informed him of its contents.

The command to her to repair to Burford was evidently not insisted upon. This would indeed have been impossible in the face of Lady Tanfield's letter and her absence from home. But the minister wrote to the Lord Deputy a statement of his wife's condition, and her application for means of existence. This drew from Lord Falkland an angry reply, written on the 26th May, 1627. But it will be well, before we transcribe that letter, to give some account of the place where his wife resided, and the extremities she was reduced to, whilst he and the officers of the Crown were debating over the point at issue, one, as she truly says, of life and death to her.

Humanly speaking, nothing could be more distressing than Lady Falkland's position at the moment when, as a last resource, she had made her appeal to the King. She was living on the charity of her friends, both Catholic and Protestant. Her husband allowed her nothing. Her mother turned her out of her house in London, where she had lived since her return from Ireland. Both bitterly reproached her for her change of religion, and told her that her misfortunes were owing to herself, and that she deserved all she suffered. Propositions were made to her regarding places of residence, such, for instance, as Cote (or Coates),

one of Lady Tanfield's country houses in Oxfordshire, but as they were unaccompanied by any offer
of support from her, or even the means of repairing
thither, nothing came of these proposals.

Lord Falkland was beset by urgent money difficulties. Lady Tanfield was avaricious; each strove
to compel the other to provide for the maintenance
of the wife and daughter who had grievously
offended them both, and who in the meantime was
forced to beg or to starve. In order to trespass as
little as possible on the generosity of her friends,
she took a cottage, or rather a tenement, on the
banks of the Thames, in a small town ten miles
from London, and lived there alone with Bessie
Poulter, her devoted and now Catholic maid. This
cottage was in so ruinous a state that there was
constant danger of its falling on their heads. They
had no other furniture than a flock bed on the bare
ground, which was borrowed from a poor woman in
the town, an old hamper which served for a table,
and a wooden stool. When we call to mind that
Lady Falkland had been an heiress, that she had
spent the preceding years of her life at the Vice-
Regal Court in Dublin, and since her return to
England, had frequented the Court and lived
amongst persons of the highest rank and fortune;
that she was by nature fond (her daughter says so)
of comfort and good eating, of spending money, of
society and conversation; that she was spurned by
a husband she truly loved, and who in many respects

was worthy of her affection; separated from her children, whom she passionately loved—we can then estimate how strong was the supernatural grace which enabled her to endure these sorrows and hardships so cheerfully, that, in after days, she was heard to declare, that never had she or her companion been more contented and merry than at that time.

Bessie Poulter had made sacrifices as well as her mistress. We are told "that she might easily have procured a service more to her commodity, if she would have left her lady, being *so handsome* at everything she did that many a one would have been glad to entertain such a servant." Her fidelity to Lady Falkland was rewarded by a vocation to the religious life. She became later on a nun in the English Teresian convent at Antwerp. It must be owned that in the cottage by the banks of the Thames, she had served a good apprenticeship to that austere religious order, with regard to comfort and food. As the only seat in the house was a stool, it is to be supposed that Bessie must have, like the Carmelite nuns, sat on the floor, and her diet was also akin to theirs. During the whole of Lent, their fare was fish of the cheapest description, and bread soaked in the water in which it was boiled. This last delicacy Lady Falkland lived upon, leaving the fish to her maid. It so happened, that, before and since that time, the latter always had an insurmountable aversion to food of this sort, but then it did not trouble her in the least. She looked upon this as one of those minor mercies God sometimes grants to simple souls, who look to Him in small things as in great. Bessie Poulter used to relate that Lady Falkland was very absent, and so engrossed by her thoughts that she was apt to forget everything but what occupied her mind at the moment. Her head was, as usual, full of plans, and fancying she had messages to send, she would call out for some one to come to her, and receiving no answer, exclaim: "Who is there? Why do not any of my people come to me?" Then suddenly remembering, or being reminded by her sole attendant of the state of the case, they would both laugh heartily. Matters, however, were becoming anxious. The little money Lady Falkland had brought with them was well nigh exhausted, and the entire solitude in which she was left becoming daily more depressing. At that juncture God sent her an excellent friend in the person of a Mr. Clayton, who, before he became acquainted with her, had already lent her money, and continued to do so "up to the greater part of what he had." His character is described in a few words. "He was one of those very few who, contenting themselves with what they possess, kept wholly free from desires and pretences, so that even though he had but little, it almost seemed as if all his acquaintances were obliged to him, and he to no one, for he made use of one friend only to do another a pleasure." He had not only

H

assisted Lady Falkland himself, but he informed of her position, her friend, Lady Banbury, and some others, who supplied her pressing necessities. We have evidence of the interest Mr. Clayton took in the literary work with which Lady Falkland beguiled her solitude at that time, even as she had done in early days in the house of her mother-in-law. Now that her whole heart and soul were devoted to the Catholic Church, it was on religious subjects that she employed her pen. In another chapter we will speak of her labours in this respect, and of the encouragement and assistance she received in this respect from Mr. Clayton.

Lord Falkland, in the meantime, under the pressure of his own pecuniary embarrassments, was becoming daily more irritable. He was beyond measure annoyed at not obtaining from the King the order he had so persistently solicited for his wife's banishment to the country, and a peremptory command to Lady Tanfield to harbour her daughter. Lord Conway had written to him, by order of the King, giving him an account of Lady Falkland's position, and her appeal to his Majesty. His answer to that letter was fierce and bitter. That her recklessness in spending money, and embarking in imprudent speculations, gave some colour to his accusations, that "the wealth of the Indies could not supply her needs," cannot perhaps be denied, but these defects on her side did not justify him in leaving her without means of existence.

My very good Lord,—Your letter of the 26th of May, received the 13th of June last, hath made choice of my unhappy wife for the sole subject of it. It takes notice of a letter of hers, come to your lordship's hands, to be delivered to his Majesty, and recites several suggestions, whereof some are true, and some are false; the first, which are true, being only urged to incline the belief of those that are not so, and best serve the turn she aims at, for she, being replete with serpentine subtlety, and that conjoined with Romish hypocrisy, what semblance can she not put on, and what oblique ways will she not walk in, hardly discoverable?

Those servants whom she would endeavour to blemish with the style of unfaithful, because they will not become useful to her deceitful and sinister purposes, I do maintain and aver to be honest. If she complains of wants, I do believe it to be true that she sustains them, for by her courses it appears that she affects them, and they consequently pursue her. That she is not relieved by me in those wants is most true, and that for a double reason; first, because of the impossibility for my estate to afford that, which the wealth of both the Indies could not supply, if she had them; next, being what she is (a Catholic), and living where and as I would not have her, I will not allow her a penny as long as she is such, and where she is. Neither do I think your lordship, or any lord of the Privy Council there, would do otherwise, were you so unhappy as I, to be so matched, and I hope you will all do by me as you would be done by.

That her father disinherited her, for her obedience to

me, is much misrepresented by her; he foresaw in her
that bad disposition she has since manifested to the
world, which made him do what he did against her and
against me on her account.   If her jointure is sold, it is
she that has had the benefit of the sale, and she has spent
the treble of its value out of my purse.   I never saw a
penny out of her father's, but my part of her first petty
portion paid at her marriage.   If her mother does
refuse to receive her, and conjures her to stay away,
it is herself who has sued for these rejections, to have
the better colour to remain where she is and as she is,
in despite of me, by the power of her Popish friends,
who must themselves maintain her, if by force or arti-
fice they hold her.   But his Majesty is to them all
superior, and if it please him he can constrain her to
go to her mother, her mother to receive her, and her
mediators to be silent.   The honour of our religion,
and of his Majesty in the interest of his deputy, who
has become notorious over all the Christian world, for
this defection of his wife's and her contestation with
him, against duty and the law matrimonial, notwith-
standing her specious pretences, doth require that he
should remove her, and settle her with her mother,
where she shall receive such allowance from me as is
fit for her, but nothing for her Popelings that depend
upon her to devour her, and, through her, desire to do
the like by me.

If this may not be obtained, which I conceive in
honour and justice cannot be denied, then let there be
a fair and legal separation, and I will consent to such
an allowance as my estate can afford, and leave her

free to live how and where she lists. If this be not reason, then is reason not understood by your lordship's most humble servant,

H. FALKLAND.

In spite of this indignant remonstrance, the King determined to refer Lady Falkland's case to a committee of the Privy Council. The decision was, that, provided she consented to withdraw to Coates, the house her mother had agreed to lend her, and separated herself from a woman "whom her husband conceived to be a principal cause of her seducement, she should be allowed out of her husband's estate £500 a year, and as she was known to be in great want, that she should be supplied with immediate means." The woman referred to must evidently have been Bessie Poulter, though, as we have seen, her conversion did not take place until some time after her mistress's. The object of Lord Falkland evidently was to cut off his wife from all opportunities of practising her religion, and in this the Privy Council seem to have been willing to second him, although they disapproved of his conduct to her in other respects.

From the letter Lord Falkland wrote to his agent at this juncture, and Lord Conway's to the same gentleman on the 20th of July, we cannot but infer that the Lord Deputy's one object was to avoid disbursing anything for his wife's support, and that he was rather annoyed than otherwise at her acceptance of the terms prescribed, seeing that it compelled him to make her an allowance.

It is hardly conceivable that a man of education and refinement, and possessed no doubt of some amiable qualities, should have been led by passion and prejudice to use the brutal and disgraceful language which occurs in the following letter to his agent. How little Lady Falkland deserved it, even though she had faults, no doubt very trying to him, is proved by the fact, that a few years afterwards he was sincerely reconciled to her.

I have read my wife's letter to you. I conceive it was but a bait to catch you—I mean her importunate protestations to be ready and desirous to go to Coats, her mother's house. You have well avoided the possibility of being deceived, by urging Mr. Chancellor of the Exchequer to sound the bottom of her intention, which either was feigned, or else she had it secretly from him, that it was not possible for her any longer to withstand his Majesty's pleasure, for I am confident I shall never more discern any conformity in her to my will, but where she is constrained by force of necessity, which is force.

When she shall be ready to go you must convey her, if her mother do not, who has furnished that house for her I am told, and there, I doubt not, she will defray her, until I hear she is settled there, with what number of servants, and what their names, conditions, and religions, and then I will take order for such allowance as I will make her to be ordered and disposed by her mother, unto whose hands I will send it duly, but never to her own.

For the £50 she calls upon you to pay to my Lady of Buckingham, pay it not for two reasons. First, because I do not believe it to be due, but a pretence for to deceive me of so much, and I had rather she should now cheat others or herself, than me any more: and as to my caring not to have her live on charity, assure her I care not whether such a *prodigal impostor*[1] as I know her to be, is constrained to eat husks with pigs or to live on alms. As to her protestation to be ready to conform herself to my will, where her conscience might not be touched, I only wish she had a will to fulfil any duty, or a conscience to be touched; then she would no longer walk in that oblique perverseness, dishonour, and ruin, to her own shame, and my hurt. Tell her all this, that she may not suppose that she is misunderstood by your master.

If the agent delivered these messages to Lady Falkland, there is reason to admire the forgiving spirit and persistent affection which she never ceased to evince towards a husband who could speak of her in such terms. The King and his Ministers seem to have become by this time somewhat weary of the Lord Deputy's delays in complying with his part of the arrangement, and on the 20th of July, Lord Conway writes from St. Albans to his agent:

[1] These words are written thus in the original letter: " Perdigall imposture."

Sir,—You know so particularly all passages concerning my Lord Deputy's desires, and his lady's solicitations about her going into the country, that I will not mention anything of what is past. She seems now to doubt of being conveniently accommodated for her journey to Coats, and provided for when there. His Majesty hath referred it to the Lord Treasurer and the Chancellor of the Exchequer to advise and direct what shall be fitting in this case, to whose advice and direction you will do well to accommodate yourself, for the preventing of any further complaints or importunities to his Majesty.

In the meantime Lady Falkland was only saved from starvation by the charity of her friends. Rendered desperate by interminable delays, and goaded by pressing necessities, she addressed Lord Conway with some warmth. He did not resent her vehemence, for he wrote on the back of one of her letters, "*In memoriam.* Doubtless must she not be neglected."

My Lord,—That Lord Conway is a gentleman, a soldier, and a courtier makes well for me, since all such have inclinations and obligations to succour distressed ladies. I must be free with your lordship. I found you at first most noble towards me, and of late, so much altered, that I believe you must have received misinformation concerning me. I speak not to tax you, but I confess I am so jealous of the loss of my friends, that I cannot chance but question the grounds of this change. If it please you to let me know if you have heard anything to distaste you, I doubt not that I shall be able to answer it in a way that shall fully satisfy you. I have informed all my friends how favourable I have found your lordship, and I am sure you will not alter towards me without just cause. Mr. Wild is my enemy in this business, yet I wish him well, because I know it is not from enmity to me, but from friendship to my lord, and I therefore rather desire his good than his hurt. I must now beseech you to keep me from the uttermost misery. Mr. Chancellor has chosen his best, to let the order to be drawn [for her allowance out of her husband's estate] which, when it is done, will be sent to your lordship to be signed; but this cannot be suddenly performed, and in the meantime, I shall be unable to subsist. The gentlewoman in whose house I lie,[2] hath £20 due to her for rent, and is as loth to remove me as I am to be removed, but, alas! her necessities are so extreme, that if she has not money instantly, I must lie in the street, and truly, my lord, I have not means for one day's food.

Lady Falkland goes on to propose that a certain sum due to her husband should be paid to her by the King's command. " If it be not done," she adds, " I must starve. His Majesty hath taken so much pity on me by his gracious order for my maintenance, that I humbly beseech him to use his authority to give me means to live, till I can have

---

[2] From this it appears that Lady Falkland had left the river-side cottage and was again in lodgings in London.

the benefit of the gracious justice he intends me." Lord Conway began by accepting favourably the proposal submitted to him, but afterwards wrote that the sum of money in question "was an imbroiled matter, and that he feared that if it was transferred to her it would multiply the Lord Deputy's discontents. That his Majesty would take into consideration some other way for her which he would solicit, and not fail to send her word when it was effected." Lady Falkland wrote in reply :—

My Lord,—My necessities press me more than I can tell your lordship. I have got nothing, and I protest that it is not possible for me, except I should press further on my friends (which I will never do), to exist any longer. I am fain to be relieved by those that are in distress themselves, and hereafter, I will rather choose to suffer than undo my friends for me. I beseech your lordship now show the difference between a gentleman and none, in never leaving until you find means to get me my rights. No one is more loth to have my Lord Deputy discontented than I am, but alas! when the question is whether he is to be displeased, or I am to starve, will it admit of a dispute? If what I proposed cannot be done, find out, I beseech you, some other way, that his Majesty may not, against his intention, be made the overthrow of his poorest subject. In preventing my ruin you will do the King a fair service, my Lord Deputy an ill-understood kindness, to me an act of charity, and to yourself, in this, the best office, since you shall please God in helping the oppressed. I cannot follow you otherwise than by letter, both by want of a road, and besides, because I am forbidden the Court, which, if it were not so, I would not yet trouble you, but in cases of necessity. I beseech you, my Lord, be my solicitor, for I have none other, either to you or the King.

This appeal induced Lord Conway to write to the Chancellor of the Exchequer, commanding him, in the King's name, "to take a course, that from some source or other Lady Falkland's necessities may be supplied, and her maintenance provided for, according to former directions." Her next letter shows that at last some redress had been afforded her, for she says :—

I have such infinite thanks to give you, that nothing but acknowledging that all I have and shall have, is from your favour, can express it. I will never leave off trying to do your lordship service, and all my friends shall know how effectual a friend you have been to me.

But if her pecuniary position was slightly improved, another trial was grieving her to the heart.

In the same letter in which Lady Falkland thanked Lord Conway for the assistance he had afforded her, with regard to the means of support she was in such pressing need of, we find her appealing to him most earnestly in behalf of a poor gentleman who had been arrested at her house, "whom," she says, "would never have lain in

prison, but because he kept her from starving."
This was Father Dunstan, the Benedictine. She
reminds Lord Conway that " My Lady of Buckingham had likewise spoken to him on the subject,"
and adds, " You shall see he is well reputed, even
amongst Protestants, for he hath procured Mr. Williams and Mr. Ward, two of the best goldsmiths in
Cheapside, to be his bail, and I dare be bound
there was never better bail offered for any Catholic."
And she concludes thus : " You have already made
me your servant, add this favour [the befriending of
Father Dunstan] and you will make me your slave ;
you will never have to be ashamed of any favour
done to your faithful servant, E. FALKLAND."

What was the result of the joint intercession of
Lady Falkland and Lady Buckingham in behalf of
the imprisoned priest does not appear. We have
already seen that the Lord Deputy was displeased
with his servant .Hitchcock for procuring the arrest
of Father Dunstan. It is difficult, however, to
reconcile this statement with his violent language
against all those concerned in his wife's conversion.
Be that as it may, his feelings towards the latter
were by no means softened, and great was his annoyance when he learnt, strangely enough through one of
his servants, not by any official communication, that
the following order had been issued by a Commitee
of the Privy Council, on the 4th of October, 1627 :

Referees—Lord Treasurer,' Lord Steward, Lord

Chamberlain, Lord Conway, Lord Grandison, the Chancellor of the Exchequer.

Whereas upon the humble petition of Elisabeth, Vice-Countess of Falkland, wife unto Henry, Viscount Falkland, now Lord Deputy of Ireland, made unto his Majesty for competent maintenance, to be allowed unto herself and a fit number of servants, his Majesty has been graciously pleased to refer and commit the consideration and ordering thereof to us of his Majesty's Most Honourable Privy Council, whose names are hereunder written, with full power and authority to determine of her said maintenance, and all the circumstances thereto appertaining. We, the lords, appointed by his Majesty to be Commissioners concerning this cause, after good and mature deliberation, do finally order and set down as followeth: namely, that the said Lord Deputy shall provide: meat, drink, and all necessaries for the said lady, his wife, and nine servants to attend her, and all this fitting her quality, at the mansion house, called Cote (otherwise Coats), in Oxon; that the said servants' wages shall be paid, that there shall be furniture and horses kept for her, whereby to take the air, or otherwise to employ upon necessary occasions. That she shall have wearing-clothes and wearing-linen, and all other necessary habiliments provided for her by the said lord, her husband, and £100 per annum paid unto her, over and above for her private expenses. And in case the said Lord Deputy shall not perform this our said order, then he shall allow her £500 yearly, whereof one quarter shall always be paid beforehand. And that the said Lord Deputy shall pay such debts as are expressed in the schedule hereunto annexed, amounting unto above £272, which said debt hath accrued for meat, drink, and clothes for the said lady, his wife, since he took his children out of her custody.[8] And if the said Lord Deputy shall appoint any servant to provide such necessaries for the said lady, as before specified, then the said servant shall behave himself as a dutiful servant ought to do, to his lady and mistress; and if he shall fail to do so, upon just complaint made unto us by the said lady, his mistress, he shall be forthwith removed, and another substituted in his place, such a one as we shall think fit. And we do further order that the said lady shall make her ordinary abode at Coats, except it do plainly appear unto us, the said lords, that the place is unmeet, by reason of the unwholesomeness of the air, and in such case, that some other place shall by us, the said lords, be appointed. And if there shall be any other difference arise then, that it be put to our arbitrament and to be determined by us.

This document shows how completely the Council took Lady-Falkland's part, and that she had it in her power to force him to do her justice, but she evidently had an insuperable reluctance thus to act,

---

[8] To the Countess of Buckingham £50; to the Lady Hastings, £50; to Mrs. Banber, £35; to Mr. James Clayton, £30; to Sir George Petre, £12; to Mrs. Platt, £16; to Lady Mountgarret, £10; to Mrs. Harrington, £7; to Mrs. Caddeman, £10; to Mrs. Penruddoch, £6; to Lady Manners, £8; to Lewis, a chandler, £15; to my man Gibson, £9; to the baker, £4 10s.; to the brewer, £3 12s.; to the butcher, £6 13s. 6d.

and we find Lord Falkland writing to the King, January 27, 1628, as if only a desire on the subject, and not an express command had been issued by his Majesty.

May it please your sacred Majesty.

I understand by my servant Maude, that it is your royal pleasure that I enlarge my proposed allowance to my unhappy wife. Though I have no other means to do it withal, than out of my entertainments, which I more painfully labour for than any one else whomsoever in your Majesty's employment, and find them so scant that they will hardly support the honour of your table, now that all other perquisites allowed my predecessors are taken from it, yet I am contented to make her allowance during my being your deputy, up to £300 a year, which will suffice to keep her, not only from starving, but free from want, if it be managed well and carefully dispensed. For other expenses, I am confident your Majesty will not constrain me to provide for her, whose ways are so disallowable, and humour so vast, that the Indies will no more suffice her vanity than the meanest limited portion.

This shall be duly paid her at two usual seasons; only I beseech your Majesty, for your own ease and honour, that she may be forbidden upon a penalty, to come within ten miles of your Court, or the city of London. All your kingdom else is spacious enough, and may be free for her. This will secure your Majesty from the clamorous trouble of her importunities, and, in some measure, silence the scandal and shame now,

by her means, brought upon the most loyal and labori-
ous of your sacred Majesty's vassals and servants,

H. FALKLAND.

Neither Charles the First nor the Lords of the
Council held the same opinion of his wife as the
Lord Deputy did at that time; and his proposal in
this last letter was not even taken into consideration.
On the contrary, not long afterwards the King confirmed and ratified the order already given, and
"willed and required the Lords of his Council immediately to grant all such warrants from the Board
for the defalcation of so much of the Lord Deputy's
entertainment in Ireland, as shall be meet for the
speedy and punctual performance of the same
order, so that the Lady Falkland may have it paid
to her here."

It is not clear how far Lord Falkland ever did
comply with the conditions imposed upon him by
the King and his Council, or whether his wife availed
herself even then of the order, that her allowance
should be deducted from "his entertainments." It
may be that her forbearance in that respect smoothed
the way to their approaching reconciliation. Her
mother died about that time, which accounts for her
not having taken up her residence at Coats, which,
as well as Burford Priory, then became the property
of her son Lucius. It is mentioned that when he
returned to England, and was placed in possession
of his fortune, he took measures to improve his
mother's position. She was, no doubt, anxious to

remain in London, where the practice of her religion must have been far easier than it could have been in the country ; and where she was within reach of Catholic friends, more or less openly professing their religion. Catherine, Countess of Buckingham, so often mentioned in the foregoing correspondence, was the daughter and heiress of the Earl of Rutland, and, up to the moment that the King's friend and favourite sought her hand, a fervent Catholic. Buckingham was bent on marrying her. She had set herself resolutely against his suit, and professed a dislike to his character, and a horror of his immoral conduct. But, unfortunately for her, Williams, the future Lord Keeper, was at that time incumbent of the parish of Belvoir. He was clever and ambitious, and Buckingham's favour was the stepping-stone he had his eye upon as the means of his advancement. He spared no efforts to bring about his marriage with Lady Catherine Manners, and worked unremittingly to persuade her that her suitor had been misrepresented and unjustly attacked. The Earl's good looks, and the charm of his manner probably wrought more powerfully still than Williams's arguments. The Catholic girl was persuaded to conform, outwardly, at least, to the Protestant religion, and was married to Buckingham in Williams's church.

We find her in subsequent years an intimate friend of Lady Falkland's, "very unsettled in religion," interceding for an imprisoned Catholic priest, and so much herself a Catholic, that when Lord

I

Falkland refused to pay the money she had lent his wife, he seems to have included her amongst those who, having helped to seduce, were bound to support her. There must have been at that time several Anglican ladies on the brink of conversion. Lady Falkland, the only one amongst them who had courageously acted up to her convictions, still kept up her intimacy with her former friends, and it was perhaps on that account also, that, when at liberty to do so, she took up her permanent abode in London.

At the risk of wearying our readers we have given at some length the particulars of the painful transactions relative to her maintenance, which ensued on her conversion. On the whole, her share in them exhibits favourably the nobleness of her character. To the end of her life she was more or less in money difficulties, as she had been almost from her infancy. The earlier years of her married life, after her husband's return to England, appear to have been the sole exception to the rule—if, indeed, her good management of his affairs at that time included economy with regard to her own means. This habit of careless spending, unfortunately, gave a handle to her enemies, and a sort of excuse for her husband's harsh conduct. But her generous nature is so visible in her letters, and in the manner in which she felt and spoke about those who were most unkind to her, that we thought it advisable not to suppress or considerably abridge, either her own letters or the documents relating to this correspondence.

CHAPTER VII.

Lady Falkland's literary pursuits—she returns to London—her reconciliation with her husband.

WE must now revert to the time when, in her solitude and poverty Lady Falkland resumed those literary pursuits which were so congenial to her tastes. The late King James the First had written an answer to one of Cardinal Perron's controversial works, which had drawn from his Eminence an able rejoinder. English Catholics anxiously desired to possess this reply in their own language. Lady Falkland had already begun to translate the writings of the great French divine, when her attention was drawn to the volume in question. She at once set about what was to her a delightful labour, and completed her task in thirty days. Her enthusiastic friend and admirer, Mr. Clayton, celebrated this feat in the following poem, *In laudem nobilissimæ Heroinæ quæ has Eminentissimi Cardinalis disputationes Anglice reddidit :—*

> One woman, in a month, so large a book
> In such a full emphatic style to turn,
> Isn't it all one, as when a spacious brook
> Flows in a moment from a little burn ?

Or isn't it rather to exceed the moon
  In swift performance of so long a race,
To end so great and hard a work as soon
  As Cynthia does her various galliard trace?

Or is she not that miracle of arts,
  The true Elixir, that by only touch
To any metals, worth of gold imparts?
  For me, I think, she values thrice as much,
A wondrous quintessence of woman kind
In whom alone, what else in all we find.

The following lines, attributed to Father Leander, are still more laudatory, both of the writer to whom they are addressed, and of learned ladies in general. The initials appended to them are F. L. D. S. M. :—

Believe me, readers, they are much deluded
  Who think that learning's not for ladies fit,
  For wisdom with their sex as well doth suit
As orient pearle, in golden chase included;
  'Twill make their husbands, if they have true eyes,
  Wise beauty, beauteous wisdome, deerly prize.

Who doth not prayse th' Empresse Eudoxia's fame,
  That made old Homer tell our Gospell's story?
  Or noble Proba, Rome's immortall glory
That taught sweet Virgil sing our Saviour's name?
  Or gracious Elpis, sage Boetius' love,
  Whose sacred hymnes holy Church doth approve?

But will you see in one brave ladie's mind
  These three great gracious ladies full compriz'd,
  Their worth, their witte, their vertue equaliz'd;
Look on this work, and you shall plainly find
  Eudoxia, Proba, Elpis yield in all
  To this translatresse of our Cardinall.

Another complimentary address to "the most noble translator" is extant. The authorship unknown.

Α κοκακ.

I would commend your labours, and I finde
That they were finish'd with such ease of minde,
As in some sense the praise I give must fall
Under the title of mechanicall,
When those who reade it come to understand
The paines, you tooke were onely of your hand,
Which though it did in swiftnesse overgoe
All other thoughts, yet to your owne was slow.
As the sunne beames no sooner do appeare,
But they make all that which stands in their light cleere,
Your bright soule did but once reflect upon
This curious piece, and it was clear'd and done.
But that a woman's hand alone should raise
So vast a monument in thirty days,
Breeds envie and amazement in our sex,
Of which the most o'er weening witts, might vex
Themselves thrice so much time and with farre lesse
Grace to their workmanshipp or true successe.
Why should I not speak truth without offence?
Behold this mirror of French eloquence
Which shee before the English view doth place,
Fill'd with the whole originall truth and grace,
.That the most curious author would avow
It were his own, well pleas'd, if he liv'd now.

. . . .

And though we in a common proverb say
That Rome was not built all up in one day,
Yet could we see a citty great as Rome
In all her splendour in one minute come
To such perfection, wee might more expresse
Our wonders, and not make the glory lesse.
So I conclude with modest truth, and dare
All their free censures who can but compare,
And whosoere shall try may spend his age
Ere in your whole work hee shall mend one page.

Of this work, so extolled by Lady Falkland's pious
friends, laboured at with such earnest diligence, and
doomed to merciless suppression at the hands of
Dr. Abbot, the bigotted Archbishop of Canterbury,

who seized the edition printed in the Low Countries
on its entrance into England, and made a bonfire of
it, only a few copies reached "the translatresse of
our Cardinal." It had been dedicated by her to
Queen Henrietta Maria, under the title of "Reply
of the most illustrious Cardinal of Perron to the
answer of the most excellent King of Great Britain,
translated into English by Elisabeth Viscountess
Falkland," whose prose was very superior to her
admirers' poetry. The dedication was as follows :—

Your Majesty,—May please to be informed that I
have in this dedication delivered to you that right, that
I durst not withhold from you. Had I given it into
any other protection I had done your Majesty a palp-
able injury. You are a daughter of France, and therefore fittest to own his worke, who was in his time, an
ornament of your country. You are the Queen of
England, and therefore fittest to patronize the making
him an Englishman, that was before so famous a
Frenchman. You are King James his sonn's wife, and
therefore, since the misfortune of our times, hath made
it a presumption to give the inheritance of this worke
(that was sent to the Father in French) to the sonne in
English, whose proper right it is, you are fittest to
receive it for him, who are such a parte of him, as none
can make you two other than one. And for the honour
of my sex, let me say it, you are a woman, though far
above other women, therefore fittest to protect a
woman's worke, if a plaine translation, wherein there is
nothing aimed at, but rightlie to expresse the author's

intention, may be called ˉa work; and last (to crowne
your other additions), you are a Catholick, and a zealous
one, and therefore fittest to receive the dedication of a
Catholick work. And besides all this, which doth
appropriate it to you, your Majesty is she, to whom I
professe myselfe,

A most faithfull subject, and a

Most humble servant.

But the Queen's name did not avail to save from
ruthless destruction the ill-fated volumes, nor are
we told that she ever received a copy of it, though
probably Lady Falkland found means to convey
to her Majesty one of those which had escaped
Dr. Abbot's vigilance.

Lady Falkland's Epistle to the Reader is also a
specimen of the best English of that epoch, and of
her own forcible style :

Reader,—Thou shalt here receive a translation well
intended, wherein the translator could have no end
but to inform thee aright. To look for glory from
translation, is beneath my intention; and if I had
aimed at that, I would not have chosen so late a writer.
But here I saw so much of antiquity as would fitly
serve the purpose. I desire to have no more guessed
at of me, but that I am a Catholic, and a woman; the
first serves for mine honour, and the second for my
excuse; since, if the work be but meanly done, it is no
wonder, for my sex can raise no great expectation of
anything that shall come from me. Yet it were a great
folly in me, if I would expose to the view of the world

a work of this kind, except I judged it to want nothing fit for a translation. Therefore, I will confess, I think it well done, and so I confessed sufficiently in printing it. If it gain no applause, he that wrote it fair hath lost more labour than I have done; for I dare avouch it hath been four times as long in transcribing as it was in translating. I will not make use of that worn form of saying I printed it against my will, moved by the importunity of friends ; I was moved to it by my belief that it might make those English that understand not French, whereof there are many, even in our universities, read Perron—and when that is done, I have my end. The rest I leave to God's pleasure.

Later on, Lady Falkland translated the whole of Cardinal Perron's controversial writings ; but, probably deterred by the fate of her first publication, she did not get her work printed. In an admonition to the courteous reader which prefaced "the reply," apologies are made for the numerous misspellings and mistakes, proceeding from the printers having been Walloons, and the extreme difficulty of getting English books correctly printed abroad.

About the same time, namely, her residence in the cottage on the banks of the Thames, Lady Falkland wrote in verse the lives of St. Mary Magdalene, St. Agnes the martyr, and St. Elisabeth of Portugal. Numerous also were the hymns she composed in honour of our Blessed Lady, whose name she took in Confirmation when she received that Sacrament from the hand of the Bishop of

Chalcedon, at what precise time we are not told, but as in 1630, information was given to the Government, that "Bishop Smith of Chalcedon lived in the French Ambassador's house, in the chamber over Lady Falkland's, besides divers Jesuits more," it is likely to have been in that year. She had probably lodged at the French Embassy for this very purpose.

We have already said that Lady Falkland's position had been somewhat improved by Lady Tanfield's death, which placed her eldest son Lucius in possession of his grandfather's property, and enabled him to relieve in some degree his mother's necessities. After his return to England from the Low Countries, where he had gone to seek a military command, which he however did not obtain, Lucius Cary resided chiefly at Burford where Lord Clarendon says, that all the men of note and learning from Oxford flocked, "and there found a university in a less volume." So much did he resemble his mother in literary tastes and ability and extensive information. They seem to have been on good terms together. He did not evince any resentment at her change of religion, and, when he met Catholic ecclesiastics at her house, treated them with respect and courtesy. So much so, a Protestant historian remarks, that it made her entertain strong hopes of his conversion, which were apparently never realized. The writer of Lady Falkland's life, from which this history is chiefly derived, in speaking of her mother's death, about the commencement of the revolutionary troubles, says, "that had she lived longer she would have suffered the most insupportable affliction she had ever had, in the death of two of her sons, killed in the wars, without any sign of hope that they had died Catholics—one being Lucius, Lord Falkland, who fell in the battle of Newbury, and Lawrence Cary, who was slain in the so called Battle of Swords in Ireland." To this passage, however, is affixed the following note, probably added by the reviewer of the work, Patrick Cary: "God be thanked, there are great hopes they both died Catholics." Whether this surmise had any foundation, we have no means of ascertaining.

Whilst Lucius Cary resembled his mother in talents and in tastes, his character differed widely from hers in other respects. Gentleness, courtesy, prudence, and reserve seem to have been distinguishing qualities in the future Lord Falkand. He had none of her rash impetuosity, of her overweening eagerness, though his gifts of eloquence and repartee were evidently derived from her. Two instances of his ready wit, which did him good service at different epochs of his life, are on record. When as a very young man he became a candidate for a seat in Parliament, an old gentleman said to him, in a sneering manner, "Sir, methinks you have not yet sown your wild oats." Lucius Cary replied, "Then I will sow them in the House of Commons, and I warrant you, Sir, there will be geese enough there to pick them up." This ready answer forwarded, it is said, his election. A more important object was gained by that quickness at retort, when at the time of the Civil War,. Henry Morten, who was himself, Antony à Wood tells us, an incomparable wit for repartee, was obnoxious for having been one of the late King's judges, and in great danger to have suffered as others did, if Lord Falkland had not saved him by saying, "Gentlemen, you talk here of making a sacrifice. It is said in the old law, that all sacrifices are to be without spot or blemish, and now, you are going to make an old rotten rascal a sacrifice!" His wit took the house and saved Morten's life.

We shall have occasion to speak later of Lady Falkland's famous son, in connection with circumstances of her own life, which brought them into collision in a painful manner, but which even then, do not seem to have altogether estranged them from one another. He was the one of her children, as we have already said, who as a child loved her best—the only one who preferred her to their father. By the latter he was unkindly treated after arriving at man's estate, in consequence of his refusal to marry a rich heiress, to whose wealth Lord Falkland had looked for the re-establishment of the family fortune. Already had he entered into negotiations with the young lady's parents, when Lucius announced his intention of marrying Lettice, the daughter of Sir Richard Morison, of Tooley Park, Leicestershire. The anger and grief of his father were extreme. Money difficulties were the bane of Lord Falkland's existence, and drove him, in spite of his naturally affectionate disposition, to act unkindly towards his son as well as his wife. He absolutely refused his consent to the marriage, and after it had taken place, would not be reconciled to Lucius, who vainly offered to make arrangements with his father, for the relief of his embarrassments. They could not supply what the marriage which he had planned would have effected, and it was only some years afterwards, that Lady Falkland, after he had become reconciled to her, brought about a better state of feeling between him and his son. Her daughter-in-law is spoken of by a contemporary writer, " as the most devout, pious, and virtuous woman of the time she lived in, and adding to her unspeakable piety, a great command of her pen." There was probably much sympathy between them in spite of difference of religion, and Lucius's choice of a portionless and excellent wife, no doubt met with the approval of his warm-hearted and generous mother.

Up to the year 1630, we have no details as to Lady Falkland's life, nor does it seem clear where she resided, though it most probably was in London. The only one of her children she ever saw at that time, was her eldest daughter, who was Maid of Honour to the Queen. This young lady, who in after life became a devout and exemplary nun, appears to have been in her early youth "much given to vain attire and dressing, in which she spent each day many hours." We may easily imagine that a young girl at Court, who attached no doubt great importance to the opinions of the fine ladies and men of the world she consorted with, should have chafed at the needy appearance, worn out clothes and mean way of living of her mother, whom, she was constantly told, had disgraced her family and reduced herself to abject poverty by her change of religion. But in spite of this, she seems to have been always attached to her persecuted parent. We know this from the testimony of one of her sisters, who says, that "having been less parted from her than the rest, she retained always more memory of what she owed her, was best loved by her than all her other children and loved her better in return than any of them, until they became Catholics." She adds, that when Anne went back to Ireland for a while, a year after her mother's conversion, she was very zealous in her defence of her.

In 1629, Lady Falkland accompanied by the Rev. Father Everard Dunstan, whether the black or white Religious of that name is not said, made a pilgrimage to St. Winefrid's Well, together with fourteen or fifteen hundred lay persons, including Lord William Howard, the Earl of Shrewsbury, Sir William Norris, Sir Cuthbert Clifton and others, besides about a hundred and fifty priests, who all

met there on the Feast of the Saint, the 3rd of
November of that year. It is impossible not to
think with regret, that what was accomplished there,
in the face of persecution and with all the difficulties
then attending a journey, seems beyond possibility
now that a few hours of railway travelling suffice to
bring Pilgrims to Holywell from every part of the
United Kingdom.

In May, 1630, Lord Falkland was recalled from
Dublin. His wife's conversion had not sweetened
his temper towards the Irish Catholics, and the
ministers of Charles the First had often warned him
of "apprehensions of danger if any reformation in
religion should be attempted there." At last his
rule became unbearable, and his friends state, that
"by the clamour of the Irish and the prevailing
power of his Popish enemies, he was removed in
disgrace." His affairs at the close of his vice-
royalty seem to have been in a very bad condition.
He would not see his wife on his return to England,
and Lady Falkland was again reduced to such
extremities, that she addressed the Lords of the
Privy Council, praying, that if her lord were not
pleased to take her into the communion of his life
and fortunes, and to treat her as a loving husband
ought to treat his wife, that she might obtain the
effectual performance of the orders already made by
his Majesty for her relief. She then mentioned the
stringent reasons which obliged her to renew this
application. "For if this order be not confirmed,"

she said, "she would deceive and undo divers of her friends who had sustained her alive, by lending her their moneys, with expectation to recover them again by virtue of the said orders." Then, always in fear of widening the breach between her husband and herself, she added, " As for her personal appearance at the Council, (which would have involved publicity) she desired it might be spared, because she was unwilling to appear in any place to oppose her lord, or to appoint any person to that purpose, thinking it unmeet to confront him."

In consequence of this application, "his Majesty was graciously pleased to take into consideration the Lady Falkland's poor estate, whereof he had by other means been informed, and to order that four of the Lords of the Council should call before them the parties, and settle between them, if possible, some good accord for Lady Falkland's maintenance."

The prospect of such a meeting and for such a purpose must have been equally trying to both parties. After all the painful passages in their mutual relations during five years, to stand for the first time face to face in the presence of strangers, and in person plead the wrongs which each had suffered, or believed they had sustained, at the hands of the other, would have been a terrible ordeal.

This order of the King's may have been the means, however, of bringing about a happy result. Henrietta Maria, who from first to last, showed the greatest kindness and generosity towards Lady Falkland, now undertook to mediate between her and her husband, and we cannot wonder that as a Queen, and the most loveable and attractive of women, her interposition proved effectual. Their reconciliation was complete. On Lady Falkland's side there had never been any change in her feelings towards one she had ever loved, in spite of all his ill-treatment. We shall soon find that he also at last did her justice, and gave the highest proof that it was anger, and not a bad opinion of his wife, which dictated his savage language regarding her.

From motives of expediency, amounting almost to necessity, Lord and Lady Falkland agreed that for the present she should continue to inhabit her lodgings, which were convenient for the furtherance of her suits at court, and her many plans for the restoration of their fortunes, and also for the practice of her religion, whilst he resided at his brother-in-law's, Lord Newburgh's house, but from this time forward their friendly relations towards one another were uninterruptedly maintained. She took the greatest care not to give him offence, as indeed had been the case from the moment of his arrival in England, even before he would see her. "She had been more careful in some things to live in rather a better fashion than she had done for some time past, and yet to avoid as far as she could to have her wants relieved by others, knowing that it would displease him. Yet, as she was not allowed anything by Lord Falkland, she was forced in her most pressing necessities to have recourse to the King, who always befriended her, but even when in extreme want she would not now do it without her lord's leave, and till she knew he did not apprehend that it would be any hindrance to him in his own solicitations, and had his assurance that he was well content and desirous she should do it."

CHAPTER VIII.

Lord Falkland's death—the Miss Carys reside with their Mother.

LORD and Lady Falkland's children, with the exception of Anne, the Maid of Honour, who resided at the Court, were, in the meantime, quartered at the houses of various relations and friends. Now, for the first time. for five years, their mother began occasionally to see them. Her daughter describes the manner in which she sought to win their affection. " She showed herself most kind, seeking by all means possible to gain some influence with them, which in no other way was she likely to do but by pleasing them, for they esteemed any respect they paid her as a voluntary act, or at most, a necessary civility, but not much as a duty, though any notable breach of it would have much displeased their father, who in his greatest anger against her, yet wished his children to show respect to their mother. Most of them having been parted from her so early, and receiving from him the care of both father and mother, they paid to him the love and reverence which should have been due to both, leaving her but a small part. Now that they saw her, but only when they chose, they would have taken it as a great injury if she had seemed to claim authority over them. She, therefore, did apply herself much to procure for them whatsoever might please them, and make them willing to be with her, yet, never durst she speak of religion, further than desiring some of them to add to their prayers the asking of God the knowledge of the truth, for had she done otherwise, she would but have made them weary of her. Still she spoke of it often before them as not of set purpose."

Two years after his return to England, Lord Falkland recalled his children home, and with them took up his abode at his country house in Hertfordshire and then, for the first time since her conversion, his wife also spent some weeks under his roof. This was during the course of the summer of 1633. He then expressed a wish that she should permanently reside with him, and went so far as to design a place for her chapel, and for her priests to live in. It seemed then, as if a happy change in her life was about to take place. But though her visit to Berkhampstead was a providential occurrence, and a great consolation to her throughout her remaining days, this short interval of domestic happiness with the husband of her youth, was but a brief ray of sunshine in her chequered career.

Towards the end of August of the same year, Lord Falkland was summoned to wait on the King, who was just returned from Scotland, and, with a large party of courtiers, shooting at Theobald's Park. During his attendance on his Majesty, the ex-Viceroy of Ireland fell from a stand and broke his leg. The King, approaching him, he made an attempt to rise and stand up, but fell again, and broke the injured limb in a worse place and manner than before. Charles the First sent for his own doctor and surgeon then in waiting, and commanded them not to leave Lord Falkland on any account till he was well. He was carried into a lodge in the Royal Park, and the first thing he desired was, that his wife should be sent for. She came instantly from London, a distance of about twenty miles, in such haste, that she neither went to bed nor slept that night, and from the moment of her arrival, remained with him day and night, never once taking off her clothes. What sleep she got was in the daytime, sitting on a chair in his room, or lying on the ground on a pallet, which he asked should be brought in for her. Some few of his friends visited him on his couch of suffering—his sister, Lady Newburgh, and her husband, and his daughter Anne amongst others, but no one remained to nurse him to the last except his wife, and his servants. The surgeon who had undertaken the case, attempted to set his leg, but failed to do so, and the wound gangrened. Dr. Thyarne and M. Aubert, the Queen's doctor and surgeon, were then called in, and also a hospital surgeon of great experience.

They consulted together, and agreed that the leg

was to be cut off above the knee. Lady Falkland
was very anxious that M. Aubert should perform the
operation, but the patient himself was persuaded to
choose the other surgeon. He showed wonderful
self-control and patience under his sufferings, and
whilst his leg was being cut off, did not give the
least sign of pain. This had likewise been the case
at the time of his accident. To all those who spoke
to him just after it had happened, he spoke with
unvarying civility and courtesy, and whenever his
wound was dressed, he maintained the same composure, only once when the surgeon was probing it
to find how far the gangrene had reached, he frowned
and cried, " Oh ! softly." Lady Falkland never left
his side during the operation, and at the very moment it was going on, her three daughters from
home, and their two younger brothers from school,
who had been sent for to see their father, arrived.
They had not heard of his critical condition, and
when they were told that the surgeons were in the
act of cutting off his leg, one of the girls gave a
piercing shriek. Lord Falkland heard it, and recognized her voice. He told some one in the room to go
and comfort her, and as soon as he was laid in his
bed again, he sent for his children, smiled when they
came in, spoke words of comfort and of encouragement, and then after giving them his blessing,
he sent them back to the home whither he was
never to return. How strange it is to think that
this dying man, so patient and so tender to all

around him, was the same person whose fierce and unkind letters we transcribed in a previous chapter. The only way to account for it may be that his passionate affection for his children, and his delusions as to the Catholic religion had exasperated him almost to madness against his wife, whom he then thought had ruined their fortunes, and would perhaps, as he thought, imperil their souls, in case she drew them to follow her example. His residence at Lord Newburgh's house, who seems to have been well disposed towards Catholics, and his personal intercourse with Lady Falkland, had, no doubt, changed in many respects his impressions as to her religion. To what a degree this was the case, we can gather from the following details of his last days.

Before his leg was cut off he did not think himself in any danger of death; still on the morning previous to the operation he received the Sacrament in the Protestant form. But soon it became evident that the operation had not proved effectual, and that the wound was more likely to gangrene again than to be cured. He was too weak for another operation to be attempted, so the physicians only staunched the blood with a powder, without, however, letting him know of his danger. The next morning the bleeding recommenced, and the same remedy was applied. This happened again at seven o'clock in the evening, and then it was some time before medical aid could be procured. At last a doctor and two surgeons came, but they told him at once there was no hope, and without attempting anything more allowed him to bleed to death. Lord Falkland was not agitated by the announcement of his approaching end, though he did not at all expect it, and was surprised that they did not try any further means to save him. But turning to his wife, he began to give her his last directions with regard to his children and servants, and what he wished to be said to the King and to his friends. The surgeons, his attendants, and his chaplain were in the room. On that account he spoke to her in French, "which he did very badly, and inquired about some business matters of hers." Then, after a pause, he said, "Votre homme est il ici?"[1] She supposed that he was asking for her own footman, and answered that he was there. He said that he did not mean him, and then she understood that it was her priest he was alluding to. She had not taken measures to have one at hand, for it had never crossed her mind that there was the slightest chance of his wishing to see a Catholic clergyman. She knew of none nearer to them than in London, and was obliged to tell him so. He then asked her, always in French, " If there were no way but legal?" Upon which she knelt by his bed, and as well as she possibly could, instructed him how best to prepare himself for death in the absence of exterior means. She did not venture to suggest, that he should declare his desire to become

---

[1] " Is your man here?"

a Catholic before the bystanders, not thinking it necessary, and fearing that it would be too great an effort, to so loving and anxious a father, to do what would prejudice his friends against his children. He said no more, but seemed to hearken to all she told him. More than three hours elapsed which he spent for the most part, in complete silence, especially towards the end, and all the time she was praying by him, or speaking to him. When he was very near death, one of the surgeons asked him to declare that he died a Protestant, for else it would be reported, as his wife was there, and speaking so much to him, that he had died a Papist. He turned his head away without speaking, and the man continued three or four times "to bawl into his ear words to the same effect." At last Lord Falkland said to him, "Pray do not interrupt my silent meditation." Two of his Protestant servants who were present, testified afterwards that he had refused to say he died a Protestant. Shortly afterwards, without agony or struggle, and seeming perfectly sensible, he breathed his last at the age of fifty-seven.

After his death, a copy of his wife's translation of Perron's work, which she had given him, was found in his closet, with marginal notes in his handwriting. Thus had that hardly-used woman her reward. Almost all the fruits of Lady Falkland's holy industry had been confiscated by her enemies, but that one volume, which found its way into her husband's hands, produced a result which made her remaining life, with all its trials, sweet and peaceful. It had led to a friendship between him and Mr. Clayton, with whom he often spoke of religion, " for he knew him to be learned, judicious, and most sincere," and at the eleventh hour, grace was apparently given to him to make that last prayer, that last act of faith on which Eternity depends.

Lady Falkland wept over the death of her husband with great sorrow, "for she truly loved him much," but did not give way to violent expressions of grief; her daughter tells us that she was never wont to do so in any of her trials. She had much consolation also in the signs he had given of faith and repentance in his last hours, and the hopes she built upon it, that, had he lived, he would have been reconciled to the Church, and that his soul had found mercy with God. It was however a life-long source of regret to her, that she had not, in case of his possibly wishing to see a priest, had one near at hand.

The one object of her thoughts as soon as she rose from her prayers by his remains, was how to secure that her children should live with her. To see them and obtain their assent to it, before any hindrances arose from others, she felt to be of the first importance. She had no coach of her own, and sent to Lord Tichburn's house to borrow one, and when it came, she conveyed in it, and accompanied, the dead body of her husband to his own house, which was nine miles off, where she arrived at three o'clock in the morning. Her children gathered round her, anxiously inquiring about their father. In order to prepare them for the sad news, she began by telling them that he was much worse, and then added past hope; but seeing that they were pained and disturbed at the thought that she had left him in his last agony, she had to confess he was dead, and then sought in the midst of her own deep grief to soothe and comfort them. When the first ebullitions of sorrow were over, and they could listen to her calmly, she spoke to them of their father's wish that they should live with her, and tried all she could think of to incline them to agree to it, and ended by begging them to give her a promise, that they would not leave her to reside with other friends, whatever persuasions might be used with them to that effect. They consented to her wishes, chiefly influenced by a sense of the faithful devotion she had shown to their beloved father, beyond all other friends. Some of them were old enough to know how hard had been his treatment of her, and were no doubt touched by the forgiving spirit and deep love she had evinced towards him. His expressed will on the subject was also conclusive, and from that day they clung to their mother with unwavering determination. It was a strong reliance on the aid of Providence which enabled Lady Falkland unhesitatingly, gratefully, and joyfully to undertake the support of so large a family without any clear idea whence it was to arise. A small remainder of her jointure, which fell to her by her husband's death, she instantly assigned to the payment of her debts. Out of £200 a year, which was all she had from her father and mother, she set aside £100 to pay off by degrees the most considerable as well as the kindest of her creditors, Mr. Clayton. With the sum proceeding from the sale of the furniture of her husband's house, she paid a debt of his. She had, we are told, "a violent desire to pay them all, though, even if she had been able to do so, she was by no means bound to it." But she never ceased to hope she would one day achieve it. From this instance of her extremely sanguine habits of mind, one of the most striking features in her character, her daughter takes occasion to say, "But this difference one always found in her hopes—when they were built on human policy and industries, they infallibly deceived her, even when they seemed grounded on probability; whereas in such things as more immediately related to the service of God, and as to which she placed her confidence only in Him, she experienced without fail His mercy to her beyond her hopes, though they might appear to be little less than impossibilities."

Such was the case with regard to what was, humanly speaking, an act of the highest imprudence. With £100 a year (even though that sum was of course a larger income then than at the present time) to maintain her four daughters and two young sons, was too rash an undertaking even in the opinion of her own friends, who said she should not

expose her children to live "at such uncertainties."
Those who had assisted her when she first became
a Catholic, she had ceased to have recourse to, from
the fear of displeasing her husband, and now was
equally bound to abstain from it, as her grown-up
daughters would not for a moment have endured to
remain with her, had they known, that she was
indebted for pecuniary aid to any stranger of lower
rank than the King and Queen. And indeed few
there were who would have helped her, so great was
the blame she had drawn on herself by undertaking
so unnecessary a charge, as they considered it.

She acted in simple faith. Her object in seeking
to have her children with her was not her own
gratification, but "that they might have more
occasion to come to the knowledge of the truth and
better means to follow it," trusting in God wholly
for the rest, both as regarded their conversion and
means to maintain them. In order to make them
willing to live with her, she had promised not to
speak to them of religion until they themselves
desired it. They made sure that they would never
desire it. She felt that to speak to them of what
they had no mind to hear would only avert them
from her religion. So doing thus much and praying
most earnestly in their behalf, was all she thought
lay in her power, and never doubted God would
effect the rest. Nor was she deceived in her confidence, either as regarded their conversion, or means
to discharge her debts incurred in their support.

She seems to have consulted Father Benet Price, her confessor, as to the lawfulness of having meat served at her table on fasting days, not only for infirm Catholics, but also for her children, with a view to their remaining where they were likely to be converted, which they would certainly not have done if this had been denied to them. As to the infirm Catholics he made no difficulty, and thought it might be allowed in the case of Protestants where there was a likelihood of conversion, but he demurred with regard to her children, whom he did not consider at all likely to be converted. But she did not feel herself bound to take his word as to the last point—for she knew that they would never have remained with her otherwise. " The latitude she allowed herself on this subject did not in the least proceed," her daughter goes on to say, "from any disregard of the ordinances of the Church, whose precepts," she tells us, "were so heartily loved by her and so joyfully obeyed, that they had full power to check in an instant her strongest appetites. Sometimes, having risen early and been abroad all the morning for her business, finding herself at noon in the house of a Protestant friend, she would be with importunity made to stay, and if this should happen on a fast day, out of her natural absence of mind and seeing no sign to remind her of it, would sit down hungry to table and be ready to put meat into her mouth. Her eldest daughter would then stop her, telling her of the fast, and she rejoiced so truly to have escaped the unwilling breach of the precept, that there seemed no place in her for even a first movement of reluctance. With most hearty thanks she would desire her to continue to do so, and really loved her the better for having assisted her to observe the laws of the Church, though the said daughter, then a Protestant, had no other end in it than to laugh at seeing her so suddenly stopped in her haste. Had there been fish to be had or her mother less hungry, she would have been like to let her alone." Lady Falkland's absence of mind and liability to distractions often exposed her to this risk, which made her very unwilling to dine or sup in company. After her reconciliation with her husband, she used often to do it for his sake, and he, in order to set her mind at rest on the subject, always reminded her of her fasts when they occurred on days when they dined or supped in company.

During the first Lent after her husband's death, and when she had to provide meat for the sick in her house and her Protestant children, she fasted rigorously herself, living almost entirely, except on Sundays, on milk porridge without butter, and cakes made of flour, water, and salt, baked on the hearth. She was the only person at her table who observed Lent ; the Catholics who took their meals at her house almost every day being kept from it by infirmity. Yet she was careful always to have fish provided (not for herself, for she would seldom take heed of what was for herself only), but for the chance

that any stranger who was a Catholic should come in,
and also in case her children would eat it instead of
meat, which when any of them did, "she was most
glad." And to encourage it "she would endeavour
to get for them what they loved most of that kind,
to invite them to it, using all the means she durst
venture on to draw them to forbear from flesh."

After her husband's death Lady Falkland never
went to masques nor plays, not even at Court, though
she was passionately fond of theatrical amusements ;
or to any public entertainment of any kind, though
she was often at Court and other places for purposes
of business. Avoiding herself dining and supping
out, she tried in every possible way to induce her
children also to stay at home at those times, for it
was only at her table that they had opportunities of
hearing conversation about religion. During the
first winter after Lord Falkland's death, her two
eldest sons, Lucius, who had succeeded to his
father's title, and Lawrence Cary, were often staying with her, and many of their friends, Oxford men,
frequented her house. She was exceedingly fond of
society, and delighted in having friends at her table.
She wished them to feel themselves as much at
home there as herself, and secured as far as she
could that nothing tedious or troublesome should
interfere with their enjoyment, or check the freedom
of conversation. Still, if it became a question of
inviting any one whose company was not agreeable
to her, but whom she had known in better circum-

stances, and now really wanted a dinner, no inconvenience to herself stood in the way of her hospitality.

To return, however, to her great object, the conversion of her children, she found that the best means of forwarding it was to gather together " persons whose discourse was frequently of religion, though mixed with other topics ; able men, capable of making any conversation pleasant, and who drew her daughters' attention to the subjects she desired them to consider." What they heard on these occasions began imperceptibly to make some impression on their minds, though as yet they gave no outward sign of it. It inclined them to reflexion, even though at the time they did not seem to mark it much. Their eyes were gradually opened to the manifold inconsistencies of Protestantism. They could not but observe that some of them took in argument a part against their own side. Their eldest brother, for instance, was so entirely Catholic at that time in his opinions, that he would affirm " that he knew nothing but what the Church told him," alleging in defence of remaining as he was, that though things seemed to him to be thus clear on the side of the Church of Rome, and that in discussion he always disputed in defence of it, yet he would not take upon himself to resolve on anything so important as a change of religion until he was forty years of age. Poor Lord Falkland did not then foresee that he would not live to be thirty-five. This " good inclination," as his sister terms it, towards the Catholic faith, which he had possessed for some years, resulted from his conversations with his mother and the company he met at her house, and it continued for some little time after the period we are speaking of. But not long afterwards he fell in with a man whose influence over him proved disastrous, though he was by way of being secretly a Catholic, and as such encouraged by Lady Falkland to frequent her house. Mr. Chillingworth, for it is of him we are speaking, made Lord Falkland acquainted with the writings of Socinius, which gave a new and false bias to his religious opinions. We shall see later how deceptive and dangerous a part this man played with regard to Lady Falkland's daughters. But at first his conversation, and the line adopted by their brother, tended to remove their prejudices against Catholicism. On the other hand they heard very good earnest Protestants disagree amongst themselves, laugh at one another's arguments, and often break off in jest what was begun seriously, being honest or judicious enough to do so rather than to defend their cause by saying seriously false or ridiculous things. They also remarked more and more as time went on, that those who were seriously touched in conscience with a desire to find out the truth, ended by embracing Catholicism, unless detained, as was too often the case, by worldly considerations.

The following tribute to Lady Falkland's patience and humility in the pursuit of her one aim and hope,

K

the conversion of her children, we will transcribe with only a few verbal alterations.   It is a striking memorial of the love and faith of a devoted mother, and one which will come home to the heart of more than one parent in our own days.   Her daughter writes :

What she did undergo to keep them with her, both for them and from them, may well give cause to acknowledge that she was their mother in faith as well as in nature.   There were other reasons now besides her desire or their promise, that made them stay with her, such as the desire to have their own wills absolutely (which none but so patient a mother would have been likely to grant them), and the idea that her house was the natural place for them to live in, without having the least obligation to any one.   Even when with the greatest care and solicitude she did procure them all they wished for, or that she thought would please them, depriving herself secretly of things most necessary, in order to furnish them at an instant's notice with the trifles they asked for, if the least thing was not had for them on a sudden, just when they wanted it, not taking heed of what she had done, but only of what was unavoidably denied them, would threaten her, especially the two eldest, that they would be gone, and wonder she should offer to keep them when she had not the means to do it.   They reckoned her extraordinary care but the part of a mother, and scarcely thought that as children they had any duty towards her.   And though she spared not, as has been said, any care or pains to keep them in all things as they did expect, and which they knew well they should not have had in any other place, yet they seemed to think her greatly beholden to them for staying. And on small occasions in which it seemed to them she did amiss, and withal vexed them (for else they had not been so zealous), they would reproach and taunt her with saying her religion gave her leave to do anything. This touched her very nearly, for as she most highly esteemed the benefit of being a child of the Catholic Church, she was likewise most sensible of the great ingratitude of giving disedification in it, thereby casting a reproach on the same Church, and confessing she had done ill, would with tears ask pardon for the scandal she had given them.

Nine months elapsed during which Lady Falkland suffered this ill-usage from her daughters, and met with no encouragement from others. Even Catholics seem to have "taxed her much in conscience" for burthening herself to no purpose, and condescending to her children's fancies, especially with regard to having meat dressed for them on abstinence days. But nothing could shake her faith, and as it happened, God was preparing to reward her long suffering and confidence in Him sooner than she had even ventured to hope.

CHAPTER IX.

*Conversion of the Miss Carys—Mr. Chillingworth
seeks to undermine their faith.*

OUT of Lady Falkland's four daughters, only one,
Anne the eldest, had given the least sign of approach
towards the Catholic faith.   On the contrary, they
showed themselves more adverse to it, if possible,
than usual, at the time when, nevertheless, they
were really beginning to waver on the subject.
This is not unfrequently the case, when doubts
distract the minds of those who are conscious that
some one is anxiously watching for some token of a
change in their opinions.   They probably noticed
such a change in their eldest sister, the best beloved
child of her mother, and, afraid of being led on by
her example, stiffened themselves, so to speak, in
their apparently strong Protestantism.   But grace
was nevertheless working in their hearts.   The
touching humility, the secret prayers, the gentle
patience of their long-suffering mother, no doubt
unconsciously influenced them, but the instrument
of their conversion was a saintly priest, a religious,
called Father Cuthbert, whose secular name was
Breton.   He was often at Lady Falkland's house,

and Lucy, Mary, and Elisabeth Cary, though they did not speak to him, watched this holy man, listened to his conversation with others, were impressed by his virtues, and at last ventured to ask him questions. As one of these sisters says: "His humble sanctity allayed the fear they had to manifest their simplicities, which they would never have been able to do to any one, however holy, that had not appeared to them, as he did, not to belong to the world at all. And his prayers," she adds, "greatly assisted in the work of their conversion." The same writer gives the following sketch of the life of this saintly priest :

He had been a monk from the age of sixteen or seventeen, and a very exemplary one; at the age of five and twenty he was sent to England for his health. Two or three times he was recalled to his religious house in France before the time in question; and gladly would he have returned there, for like St. Anselm, he used to say that he felt like an owl when away from his monastery, but by God's Providence he was always detained, and prevented from leaving England, and led there so edifying a life that it drew esteem and praise from the most earnest Protestants. They sometimes complained that they were deceived by the sanctity of his life, not that they did not think it real and did not believe him to be most sincere, but because they were sure that other Catholic priests were not like him. And no doubt this idea of his holiness and truthfulness gave an authority to his words. Yet he did no extraordinary outward things, being very sickly, and wishing to recover his health, out of his great longing to return to his monastery, yet when the remedies he took had a contrary effect, he seemed fully as contented as if he had obtained what he sought. What he most observed was much abstraction and recollection, and the ordinary things he did seemed to receive a grace from within, and to proceed and be ordered and directed by no common interior spirit.

About three years before he died he had a dangerous sickness, and showed a great sense of fear, though with resignation and hope, and often encouraged himself by the memory of St. Hilarion on the same occasion, and frequently repeated that saying of St. Paul, *Nihil conscius sum, sed in hoc non justificatus sum*. He ever desired those who came to see him to pray he might die in a state of grace. But at the beginning of his last illness, which was consumption, a change occurred in this regard. He passed from a state of holy fear to that height of charity which expels fear. Judging his life would not be long, or further serviceable to his congregation, he desired at least to die in the service of God and it, and to that end besought his Superior to impose on him the charge of assisting the sick of the plague, which was then in London. This being denied him, he from that time gave up all study but that of the Bible, the works of Blosius, and his rule, the spirit of which he daily more and more highly admired, and directed the rest of his life entirely to the ordering of his soul, which he ever much attended to, but now did wholly and solely think of. And when his end was near, he did eminently desire death, but most resignedly. Before, he had feared sudden death, now he coveted that by which he might most speedily pass to God, which with a great but humble confidence he hoped to do, cheerfully promising his prayers and help in the next world to those that asked him. And in the continual exercise of love and resignation, having most devoutly received all the sacraments, and with a great love of holy poverty, desiring that not the least of the little things he had should be disposed of but by the will of his Superior, after a strong agony of three hours, his senses and devotion continuing to the last, he died happily by the grace of God.

The Miss Carys had made up their minds to become Catholics, but still their mother knew nothing of their resolution. They had left off going to the Protestant Church, and their friends were beginning to suspect the true state of the case. They had, in fact, as good as acknowledged it to them. Lady Falkland had, perhaps, conceived a glimmer of hope on the subject, and remained quite silent, " for fear of hindering what she most desired," but conversant with her mother's character, our authoress, as a writer of that day would have called her, hastens to add that, " it is more like she knew nothing of it, for what she did know she hardly could conceal." At last the matter could no longer be kept from those it rejoiced or those it grieved, and the happy mother learnt that her prayers were answered.

As might have been expected, the young ladies' open profession of their religious convictions, even though they had not yet been received into the Church, produced a great commotion amongst their relations and friends. Their uncle, Lord Newburgh, who had always been very good to them, and "very careful of them out of regard to their father's memory," was much agitated by the unwelcome news. He appears to have been an Anglican of the Laudian school, but less bitter against Catholics than the generality of that sect. He had always been kind to Lady Falkland whilst she was suffering persecution, and did not object to see and converse with priests, but with a mistaken zeal for his nieces' welfare, was most desirous to hinder them from an act of so great worldly folly as reconciliation with the Church of Rome. Thus minded he went to the King, and obtained from his Majesty an order to Lady Falkland, through Mr. Secretary Coke, commanding her to send her daughters forthwith out of London to their brother.

Lady Falkland had no better friend at Court than the King himself, so she carried herself her answer to his Majesty, "deeming it her best and most secure way to seek either justice or mercy immediately from him." Having obtained "an audience, she humbly represented to Charles the First how hard a dealing it would be to take her children from her, she desiring to have them with her, and they desiring not to leave their mother; and seeing that they were of an age to have a choice in the matter, the youngest of them being twelve, and none of them having done anything to forfeit their natural liberty ; that it would, moreover, be exceedingly hard on her son, who had not committed any fault to lay such a punishment on him as the maintenance of four sisters without asking his consent, and against their own will." Upon this the King gave her leave to keep them till she heard his further pleasure.

His Majesty consulted Lord Falkland on the subject, whose answer was, that he was not willing to have his sisters live with him against their own will, making his house a prison to them, and himself their gaoler. Naturally enough he resisted this compulsory offer, and, at that time at least, did not probably consider it a great misfortune that they chose to be Catholics.

These negociations had the effect of hastening the actual reconciliation, as it was then called, of the Miss Carys. When they were asked if they would leave their mother and live with their brother, they all answered in the negative. But fearing that compulsion might follow on their refusal, and that they would be removed to some place where they would have no means of accomplishing their resolution, and thinking on the other hand, that when once belonging to the Church, and strengthened by the grace of the Sacraments, they would have greater power to resist persecution, every one of them sought at once to be received. The urgency of the case enabled them to get over their fear of confession, which seems to have been their greatest difficulty.

There were not wanting timid Catholics who tried to dissuade Lady Falkland and Father Cuthbert from allowing them to take this step so suddenly, as they called it. These cautious friends assured her that their relations would never rest till they got possession of them, and that if that happened they were certain to fall away. But " she, who had such confidence when there was not the least sign of hope, was not to be frightened out of it now." Father Cuthbert knew well that these girls had not been influenced by any awe of their mother, or swayed by the wish to please her. He had seen all that had passed, and did not doubt that the hand of God was in this change.

Lord Falkland's remonstrances had apparently succeeded in averting compulsory measures with regard to the young converts after ,as well as before, their reception into the Church. They were suffered to remain under their mother's roof ; but it so happened that in her house a greater danger to their faith arose than the most dire persecution could have caused.

There was a man who under false colours had obtained free access to it, and, from the time they became Catholics, did everything in his power to disturb their consciences and shake their faith, although up to that moment he had promoted their conversion. This was no other than that strange being William Chillingworth, whose religious history remains to this day an enigma. In order to understand the part he played in Lady Falkland's family, it may be well to recall to the memory of our readers the outlines of his life, whom Protestants more or less suspected of having been always a Papist at heart, and most Catholics believed to have never been one at all.

William Chillingworth, son of Mr. William Chillingworth, Mayor of Oxford, and born in that city in 1602, was admitted a scholar of Trinity College in 1618. Two years afterwards he took the Bachelor of Arts degree, and in 1620 became Master of Arts. He is said to have been "no drudge at his studies, but, being a man of great parts, that he would do much in a little time." It was his habit to walk in the College grove and meditate, but when he met with any of the other scholars, he entered into conversation and disputed with them in order to acquire a habit and facility in arguing. This was chiefly on points of divinity, although he did not confine his studies to such subjects, for he applied himself with great success to mathematics and acquired some reputation as a poet.

At that time the chief subjects of conversation and argument at the University turned on the controversy between the Church of England and the Church of Rome. Several Catholic ecclesiastics lived in or near Oxford, and some of the young scholars embraced that faith and sought admission into English Seminaries " beyond sea." Amongst the former was the celebrated John Fisher, S.J., a holy and eminent man and a learned controversialist. He became acquainted with William Chillingworth, and they had many discussions with regard to points controverted between the two Churches, but more particularly on the necessity of an infallible, living Judge in matters of faith. Father Fisher's arguments convinced the young Anglican student of the need of such an authority, and this conviction once arrived at, of course led him to see that nowhere was it to be found but in the Church of Rome. He accordingly forsook the one by law established, and with great eagerness and enthusiasm embraced the Catholic religion. He wrote on this occasion to his friend, Mr. Sheldon, who afterwards became Archbishop of Canterbury, and asked him seriously to consider the following questions.

First. Whether it be not evident from Scripture, the Fathers, and reason, from the goodness of God and the necessities of mankind, that there must be some one Church infallible in matters of faith ? Secondly. Whether there be any other society of men in the world, besides the Church of Rome, that either can upon good warrant, or indeed at all, challenge to itself the privilege of Infallibility in matters of faith ? [He concludes his letter with these words]: When you have applied your most attentive consideration upon these questions, I do assure myself your resolution will be affirmative in the first, and negative in the second. And then the conclusion will be that you will approve and follow the way wherein I have had the happiness to enter before you, and should think it infinitely increased if it would please God to draw you after.

Soon after Chillingworth went to France. Some writers speak of Douay as his place of residence during his brief sojourn abroad ; but others, Antony à Wood, amongst them, state that it was at the Jesuit College at St. Omer that he spent the time of his absence from Oxford. And this was probably the case, though he may have been at Douay also, and there received the letters from Archbishop Laud, which the latter appealed to in his speech before the Lords on the first day of his trial, March 12, 1643, in order to defend himself from the charge of Popery. " Mr. Chillingworth's learning and abilities," he said, " are sufficiently known to all your lordships. He had gone and settled at Douay—my letters brought him back, and he lived and died a defender of the Church of England."

It is indeed true that after a very short sojourn in France, the new convert returned to his native country, and soon afterwards published a book called, *The Religion of Protestants a safe way to Salva-*

tion. The Rev. Mr. Lacy, a Jesuit, wrote thus on the subject :

Had he not been in so great haste to turn back from us, he might have acquainted himself better with the practice of the Holy Church in this very point of miracles and devotions concerning saints. Had the man but remained to have learnt his Catechism, he might have known the use and meaning of our cere- monies. Now having come into the Church, as Cato' came into the theatre, only to go out again, what marvel was it, if he returned a ridiculous censurer of what he only saw and understood not ? Such post- haste would have been scarcely tolerable in a spy, much less in one who came to see and judge. Would any one think that this man, who professes to know the Jesuits so well, was never a Catholic for two months together ?

Dr. Fuller says on this subject :

Chillingworth was an acute and subtle disputant, but unsettled in his judgment, which led him to go beyond seas, and get in some sort reconciled to the Church of Rome, but whether because he found not there the respect which he expected, which some shrewdly suspect, or because his conscience could not close with all the Romish corruptions, which some more charitably believe, he returned into England.

Antony à Wood's version of the same facts is as follows :

Chillingworth being much unsettled in his thoughts, he became acquainted with one who went by the name of John Fisher, a learned Jesuit and sophistical disputant, who was often in Oxford. At length by his persuasions and the satisfaction of some doubts of his which our great men at home had not solved, he went to the Jesuits' College at St. Omer, forsook his religion and became a Roman Catholic. But not finding satisfaction with them, on various points of religion, or, as some say, not that respect which he expected, he returned to the Church of England. The common report among his contemporaries at Trinity College was, that the Jesuits, to try his temper, had put upon him servile duties far below him. Be that as it may, he left them. The Presbyterians say that he always continued a Papist at heart, or as we now call it, in masquerade. He was kindly received on his return by his godfather, Dr. Laud, Bishop of London, and with his consent went again to Oxford.

Then began that long course of contradictions, recantations, counter-statements, and endless tergiversations through which he made himself during the remainder of his life, in the wrong sense of the words, "all things to all men." Whether he was a complete hypocrite and deceiver, or, to use a foreign word, impressionable to such a degree that he changed almost from day to day his own opinions, for real faith he never seems to have possessed, and spoke or wrote according to the fancy of the hour, it is probably impossible at this distance of time to discern.   Antony à Wood tells us[1] that after his second settlement at Oxford,

He persued his inquiries into religion, and after some time declared for the Protestant religion, and about the year 1634, published a paper to confute the arguments which had drawn him from it. He also wrote to Dr. Sheldon, detailing some scruples he had about leaving the Church of Rome and returning to the Church of England, which led to a report that he had returned to Rome a second time, and then again re-embraced the English Church. So far from seeming to think these changes sinful or disreputable, he gloried in them. [In another place the same writer says:] One of his most intimate friends was Master of the Horse to Lord Montague of Cowdrey. This gentleman, who heard all the world extolling Chillingworth for his great learning and skill in controversy, asked him as a true and sincere friend to tell him his opinion freely and candidly which was the true religion, to which he answered briefly that the inquirer, who was a Roman Catholic, should keep in the religion in which he was, for if there were any true religion that it was the right one, and if there were none, that the worst that could happen to him would be to have lost his pains. I don't say, [the writer adds,] these were his precise words, but I remember they were much to this purpose. Now it is plain by this letter (which I don't doubt you will say is feigned) that this great champion of your religion was at best but a sceptic.

[1] In his letter to Bulstrode.

We shall have occasion later on to speak of Mr. Chillingworth's unhappy intimacy with Lord Falkland and the influence he gained over him, and further extracts will support our view of the real tendency of that singular man's writings and conversation.

In the meantime we must revert to his conduct with regard to the Miss Carys. There can be no doubt that he must have given himself out as still a Catholic, at any rate in heart, when in 1634, previously to their reception into the Church, he began to frequent Lady Falkland's house. The whole account of the consummate skill and cunning with which he strove to undermine the faith of her daughters, is given in such detail and so graphically, as greatly to conduce to the belief that there was neither truth, honour, or real religion in him.

By a sentence in Dr. Laud's letter to the King, which we shall give further on, it may almost be inferred that he was employed by him in this unholy mission. It appears that Chillingworth contrived to impress Lady Falkland with a conviction that he was faithful to the Church, though not openly professing adherence to it. For it is only thus that we can reconcile the statements, that she encouraged him to converse much with her daughters for the sake of making them Catholics, and on the other hand, that "he was one of those for whose own conversion she thirsted." He had also succeeded in persuading her of his sanctity, chiefly by a bold way

L

he had of reproving her for her defects, which in her eyes was a great merit. The writer of these details adds: "He was the while most apprehensive of anything that seemed to derogate from esteem of himself in all respects, and ever complaining of some fancied neglect, or of not being considered equal to those in the very highest repute." Lady Falkland, guileless and unsuspecting as she was, listened to him with the greatest respect, and sought to inspire her daughters with the same feeling, fully convinced all the time that his object was to draw them to the Church, and after they had made their abjuration, to confirm them in it. We are told "that he was indeed busy with them unto troublesomeness, but God effected these ends by means of a more true servant of His—one that intended His glory only and the good of their souls. That man of whom it is hard to know when he began really to change, if indeed he ever was a sound Catholic—used to brag of his own charity in having dissembled for six months for their sakes that he was one. And yet it was not so much as half a year after they were reconciled that he openly fell from the Church!"

The writer of these reminiscences attributes the change in Chillingworth's tactics, with regard to herself and her sisters after their conversion, to the circumstance that it had been brought about by another agency than his own, "who could hardly think anything well done that was not done by himself." "Now," she goes on to say, "that he saw what he had offered to effect performed, without his having any knowledge of or hand in it, accomplished by one who meddled not in the matter, except by his prayers, until he was resorted to, he began to show signs of dislike to what had taken place, and from that time appeared to seek to draw them back again, with so much closeness, subtlety, and so many deceits, as it may well be thought none but the devil could have invented, and certainly none but God delivered them from." It would appear that having failed to lay Lady Falkland under obligation to him as the instrument of her daughters' conversion, he undertook this in order to win favour from their Protestant friends, "and that this was the reason that made him condescend to make these young converts his business." It is probable that he availed himself of their mention of some difficulties such as often occur to recent converts, and conveyed to Dr. Laud the impression "that they met with some things they could not digest, and were willing to be taken off again (from the Catholic Church) by any fair means."

We shall close this chapter with Laud's letter to the King, which seems to have been written some little time after the conversion of the Miss Carys.

May it please your sacred Majesty,—The Lord Newburgh lately acquainted me that Mrs. Anne and Mrs. Elisabeth Cary, two daughters of the late Lord

Falkland, are reconciled to the Church of Rome, not without the practice of the lady their mother. Your Majesty, I presume, remembers what suit the Lord. Newburgh made to you at Greenwich, and what command you sent by Mr. Secretary Coke to the lady, that she should forbear working upon her daughters' consciences and suffer them to go to my lord their brother, or any other safe place, where they might receive such instructions as was fit for them. The lady trifled out of all these commands, pretended her daughters' sickness, till they are now sick indeed, yet not without hope of recovery. For (as my lord informs me) they meet with some things there which they cannot digest, and are willing to be taken off again by any fair way. I have taken hold of this, and according to my duty, done what I could think fittest for the present. But the greatest thing I fear, is, that the mother will still be practising, and do all she can to hinder. These are humbly to pray your Majesty to give me leave to call the old lady into the High Commission if I find cause to do so. And further, as I was, so am I still an earnest suitor, that she might be commanded from Court, where if she lives she is as likely to breed inconvenience to yourself as to any other. I write without passion in this, but with the knowledge I have of her mischievous practices. And now I have once again performed my duty, and acquainted your Majesty with her dangerous disposition, I leave it to your piety and wisdom. Your Majesty's most obliged and faithful servant,

Croydon, July 20, 1634.   W. CANT.

In the next chapter will be found a minute account of the insidious manner in which the author of the famous statement that "the Bible is the only true religion of Protestants," promoted his treacherous plans with regard to the girls whose mother he believed he was confirming in her own faith. The picture one of them gives of Chillingworth's character has in it a vivid appearance of reality which makes it worth preserving.

CHAPTER X.

A traitor in the camp.

IN order to understand the part which William Chillingworth acted in Lady Falkland's family, it is necessary to consider a little the state of things in England with regard to religion, at the time we are writing of. From the time of Charles the First's marriage with a Catholic princess, full of zeal for her religion, and the establishment of a Catholic church for her use, served for a while by priests of the French Oratory and afterwards by Capuchin Fathers, a new era had opened for the English professors or secret adherents of the ancient faith. The penal laws against them were not repealed ; the Parliament as adverse as ever to Catholicism ; the mass of the people as prejudiced against it ; but the Court, a great portion of the aristocracy, and the scholars of the time, were more or less favourable or tolerant on the subject. The King's opinion seems to have been that people could safely profess either Roman Catholicism or Anglicanism. Charles adhered himself to the latter and brought up his children members of the Church of England, contrary, indeed, to the pledge given to his wife's relatives and to the Pope when the dispensation for his marriage was granted, because his position as King of England and Scotland would have been untenable had he acted otherwise. Archbishop Laud and the High Church party of that day were violent against converts to the Church of Rome, like many Anglicans of our own time, not so much on account of difference in faith and worship, but because each such act was a protest against the assumed Catholicity of the State Church. Meanwhile controversy was actively carried on, conversions numerous, and the services of the Queen's chapel crowded, not only by Catholics but by wavering or curious Protestants. Now and then remonstrances and complaints on the subject occasioned orders to restrict or prevent this attendance on Popish worship, but on the whole there was that amount of persecution which rather stimulates inquiry than precludes it.

At the Universities there had been many remarkable conversions. Religion, and especially controversy as to the claims of the Church of Rome and the State Church, formed a continual subject of argument and disputation, especially at Oxford. Lady Falkland, with her great abilities and knowledge and her vehement zeal, no doubt took a leading part in the Catholic movement of those days. Dr. Laud's earnest recommendations that she should be sent away from the Court and from London prove this, but, as is almost always the case with converts, she shrunk, and wisely so, from arguing with her own children, and Mr. Chillingworth's practised skill in disputation, always in her presence on the side of the Church, impressed her with a conviction, that what he said would strike them more than anything urged by professed Catholics. Most of us have known in our day persons who delight in proving to others the truth of what they do not act upon themselves, and who give occasion to hopes on the part of their Catholic friends which are never realized. This explains Lady Falkland's infatuation about this dangerous man, whose tactics are thus described by one of those whose faith he so sedulously laboured to undermine, and " who heard him with an open ear, as one who would instruct and confirm them in the Catholic religion. He with much diligence sought to gain knowledge of their thoughts and power over their spirits. He insinuated to them reasons for looking back a little, hinting, not so much that they had not arrived at the right place, as that they had not arrived there by the right way. He proposed himself to them as a most proper assistant, having been long himself a waverer, and they, too speedy resolvers. He questioned them much as to the motives which had induced them to become Catholics, and professed to furnish them with others more reliable, so that he might more easily destroy what he had himself built. He offered to assist them in the performance of their devotions, and sought to make them leave their ghostly Father, for his own, who," the writer adds, " had a higher opinion of him than the former." From this last sentence it may be inferred, that he secretly at that time practised the Catholic religion, though outwardly he had returned to the Church of England.

In pursuance of his plan of drawing the recent converts either to apostacy, or at least to the wavering state of mind he himself was in, he urged them to learn some things, for which he offered to be their master, and pressed them to open their hearts to him as to any doubts or difficulties they might have. This, as the sequel showed, was in order to arrive at something he might lay hold of. " He knew by experience, that those who are proud are more easily deceived by thoughts which seem to arise out of their own heads than by any directly proposed to them by others." The young girls he thus dealt with were, however, more inclined to listen to him than to communicate to him their own impressions, " for he never seemed so dead to the world in their eyes as to inspire them with confidence." But at length, " having on one occasion discovered that there was some little point about which they had difficulty, or rather that they did not know what to think on the subject, he explained it to their satisfaction, with the view of leading them to go on with him, and to have full confidence in the simplicity and sincerity of his proceedings, having had at the first so good a proof of his impartiality." To others, however he stated, that the difficulties mentioned by these young persons had given him himself the first occasion to doubt. Again we are led to wonder, whether this strange man's versatility of mind was such, that he could not hear anything said on either side of the controversy that did not impress him so much, that he could never fix himself in belief or disbelief as to any point of doctrine. If his brother had the same unfortunate constitution of mind, it would explain what has been asserted as to the correspondence, carried on between them on the subject of religion, having ended, by each adopting the other's opinions. Certainly in William Chillingworth's case, faith could never have been the principle of his actions or the basis of his belief. But to return to the graphic account of his tactics in Lady Falkland's family. "At first he only showed some little dislike of what he perceived that they, as recent converts, did not adopt or use quite readily, and whilst he condemned the senselessness of Protestants, at the same time he would tell them what it would be most reasonable to think, were it not for the authority of the Church, and then laid before them what he himself practised on that point. By degrees he spoke with stronger dislike of what was a difficulty to them, but not charging the Church with being any way concerned in it. Then he would point out other things somewhat blameable, attributing them to private men's irregular devotions, till little by little he made these things appear to them of more consequence and greater in number?" What he did not venture to assert himself, as sounding too harsh for one who professed to be Catholic, he brought before them by means of counterfeited letters—one, for instance purporting to be from a friend of his who was inclined to join the Church of Rome, but was diverted from it by some things he found practised in matters of devotion, and who advised him not to strain at a gnat in the Protestant religion and swallow a camel in the Catholic. This he showed to the Miss Carys, and afterwards boasted of the deceit. Also another from the Archbishop of Canterbury, "with a paper of motives for the further consideration of religion," which, he said, "was a matter not so soon to be resolved on." This letter of the Archbishop's, the Miss Carys concluded to have been also a feigned one, because some time afterwards they found the rough copy of it written in Mr. Chillingworth's hand. In this, however, they were probably mistaken. There is reason to believe that it had been at any rate seen and approved by Dr. Laud. After a while Chillingworth became more open in his attacks on various points of Catholic belief and practice; he began to say "that he saw not how fully to excuse the Church, yet always ended his discourse by professing himself a Catholic, and to prevent their speaking to others of the language he held on these points, he complained that the eldest

Miss Cary, the one who had led her sisters to become Catholics," had already done so to those who would think worse of him on that account. He blamed her for it as a breach of trust and sign of a suspicious character. The others, who were still confident of his sincerity, were thus placed on their guard against making people judge him wrongfully and more severely, they thought than he deserved."

By imperceptible degrees, day by day, he arrived at the point of at last affirming "those things to be impious which at first he had only insinuated might be doubtful, and that the Church was guilty in allowing and approving of such practices." Still he maintained that what the Church pretended to teach was good, but that it approved and used the practice of things inconsistent with her own doctrines. He also expressed a great desire to be satisfied with regard to these points, and a hope that when he spoke of them to learned men such would be the case, but still he charged them not to mention his doubts to any one, as he would be blamed for speaking thus freely to those who had but recently become Catholics. Sometimes he would come to them with great joy at having received a plausible answer to his difficulties, but very soon returned with a fresh discovery that such answers were unsound.

The poor girls kept urging him to speak as fully to others as he did to them, so that they might hear the answers to his objections. He delayed this, "pretending not to be ready, and that to receive more entire satisfaction he wished to furnish himself with all the arguments he could use. He had no doubt he should then receive entire satisfaction, but in case he should not, and that, going fully into the matter, he should find those things as condemnable as they seemed to him, and the Church committed to them, and so its authority overthrown, whose chief foundation was its infallibility, for on it all its doctrine rested, would they, the Miss Carys, then consent to withdraw from their mother's house and go to their brother's, there, by his help, to begin a new inquiry into religion, they two, Lord Falkland, a Protestant, and himself a Catholic, debating between them and then informing them of all that passed in their disquisitions?"

This wily proposition for a moment prevailed with one of the sisters, Elisabeth Cary, "who did not perceive what it was to admit such an *if*." She was induced to give this consent, from his assuring her that he did not really doubt the Church's doctrine nor its authority, and made no question but that the inquiry would end in full conviction on that point; but that having hastily arrived at it, they should go back, and by a more thorough examination arrive at an immovable resolution, for did not St. Peter say, that every one ought to be able to give a reason of his faith? It was not enough to believe the right, unless one could defend the reasonableness of it.

This sophistry puzzled the young converts; they could not see at once how easily they might and how many things they did know to be certain, which they were not capable of proving. But in his absence, when left for a time to themselves and quietly reflecting on what he had said, they did discern innumerable contradictions in his words, and that all he asserted was only founded on suppositions. Some insincere dealings also they detected in him. He affirmed one day to Elisabeth Cary that all reasonable Protestants, as well as Catholics believed something which she had expressed her own conviction of, and professed his own to be similar to hers. But on comparing notes with one of her sisters, she found out, that the very same day he had given the latter two sheets of paper, containing (as he asserted) quotations from St. Augustine against the very same point of belief, " and in some other things they at last plainly saw that he had juggled, and told them if not formal lies, at least used most large equivocations, which they might well wonder at in one, who pretended to such high truthfulness, as to reprehend the least departure from it most sharply, and who was always alleging St. Augustine's saying, that one is not to tell the least officious lie to save the whole world." Yet when this man's whole life was afterwards found to be one long deception, and duplicities of every sort were manifested in it, he ventured to justify himself by saying, that like St. Paul he was all to all to gain all—a Catholic to a Catholic, a Puritan to a Puritan. The Miss Carys, with the exception perhaps of Elisabeth, wished to see and hear him no more, but this was not so easily executed. They were still afraid of judging him too harshly, or of defaming him in the opinion of others. It was so difficult for these ingenuous and simple-hearted girls to believe in hypocrisy and double dealing. In the meantime others became aware of the part he was playing.

CHAPTER XI.

Mr. Chillingworth's tergiversations and apostasy.

WHILST all was going on in the way described in the last chapter, in Lady Falkland's own house, almost under her own eyes, though not in her hearing, she conceived no doubts as to Mr. Chillingworth's honesty, and was greatly surprised, when one day, a Protestant friend of hers, Lord Craven, warned her that he was not a Catholic and that he had been playing false with a brother of his, whom he had led on to the point of resolving on becoming a Catholic; then he had stopped him and drawn him back; but that when he saw him ready to remain a Protestant, he had again filled his mind with doubts.

Lady Falkland even then was not at once convinced, and thought Lord Craven had been misinformed. By the desire of the latter, she told Mr. Chillingworth what he had said and conveyed to him a message from that nobleman forbidding him to approach his house. This communication was received with much patience by Mr. Chillingworth, who treated it as a calumny brought upon him by his zeal for God's cause.

In the meantime, though he had told the Miss

Carys that he was not acquainted with their uncle,
Lord Newburgh, he went secretly to him and suggested that he should again urge his nieces to remove
to their brother's house. Three of the young ladies
at once refused to agree to this, but Elisabeth, the
one who had been induced to give a sort of condi-
tional consent to this plan, acknowledged that she
was somewhat shaken as to her religion. She had
no idea that it was at Chillingworth's suggestion
that Lord Newburgh had renewed his solicitations
on the subject, and she professed herself willing to
go to her brother's, provided she might have a
Catholic with her, naming Mr. Chillingworth for
that purpose; he having previously offered to
accompany her. He had insisted much that it was
false shame and want of courage that were withhold-
ing her from drawing back, and this had somewhat
influenced her. But when once she had in this
conversation with her uncle, done what had seemed
to her most hard, by admitting she had some doubts,
and the fear of being thought cowardly having disap-
peared, she began to see that she had been deceived
and surprised by Mr. Chillingworth. The proofs of
his double dealing became apparent to her; she saw
clearly that her misgivings were all based on his
unproved assertions, and recollecting herself, she
absolutely refused to go until the proofs he had
promised should be forthcoming and laid before her.
Having by this time all grown suspicious of him, the
sisters urged him to delay no longer what he had

M

promised to do, and not to keep them in suspense. He was "most crafty in excusing himself and in trying to regain their good opinion, but at last he saw that to put them off any longer was impossible." He afterwards chose to assert that it was their indiscreet urgency which had thrust him out of the Church.

To leave the Church of Rome and still remain on good terms with Catholics, and especially retain his footing in Lady Falkland's house, where, if unsuccessful with her daughters, he was establishing an intimacy with her eldest son, and gaining an influence over him which effectually destroyed his inclination towards Catholicism, he carried on a deception which would seem incredible, were it not related in such detail and with so much simplicity by the writer of Lady Falkland's life, that it can hardly be called in question.

He announced one day that he had been summoned to an interview with the Bishop of London, "feigned much apprehension of what should be the matter, commended himself to every one's prayers and encouraged himself as if in fear of some conflict."

We can well believe, from what he said took place at that interview, that our authoress is justified in the assertion "that my Lord of London never sent for him, nor that he was ever with him, as one of the Bishop's chaplains affirmed from his own knowledge."

But returning to Lady Falkland's house after this

pretended interview, "he seemed sad and full of thoughts, but would not tell why. However the next morning he appeared better resolved and more cheerful, and then declared openly, that my Lord of London, on examining him, as to what he had done hitherto in matters of religion, and also of his further intentions, had proposed to him in case he were writing a book of inquiry into religion, which he had expressed his intention of doing, which was to serve as a guide to others, that he should separate himself for the time being from the Catholic Church, so that by this impartial proceeding it would be of more weight and authority towards all, as being written by one disengaged on all sides; and that to this end he had proposed to him, to take an oath to forbear all communion with either Church for the space of two years, which was the time he had said would be required for the writing of this book. The Bishop adding that if he should refuse this, he would suspect his sincerity and proceed with him as he should think fit." Having made this statement, Mr. Chillingworth told them that on the previous evening he had felt very sad, fearing what would follow if he refused to act as the Bishop proposed, and indeed he was loth to decline what appeared to him so reasonable a proposal and one so greatly to the advantage of his intended work, but that now his mind was made up on the subject, on account of the hope that great fruit would follow from it and he had taken the oath.

Father Cuthbert and Mr. Clayton, the pious
Catholic layman already mentioned in this history,
appear to have been present when this announcement
was made, for we are told that they exclaimed at the
unlawfulness of such an oath and declared it could
not be binding.   Upon which to stop their condem-
nation of it, Chillingworth alleged that Fathèr
Leander had approved of this act.   It so happened
that this good Father had gone out of town early that
morning and therefore could not be appealed to.
For several days his Catholic friends disputed with
Chillingworth on the point, but could only obtain
that he should add a clause to the oath he had said
he had taken, and that was, that it should not hold
good in case of danger of death, but he did not even
pretend that he asked the Bishop of London's consent to this proviso, and within less than three
months he communicated in the Protestant Church.
Two days before doing so, for the better satisfaction
of his friends as to the uprightness of his intentions,
he wrote a paper which he gave them, in which he
declared that all he did was only out of a desire for
the advancement and glory of the Catholic Church
and faith, and this he signed with his name.   And
only five days afterwards he publicly made the pre-
posterous assertion, sometimes put forward in these
days by Anglican clergymen, " that Roman Catholics
are held for heretics in the Church of England," and
added " that they are so shall be proved by William
Chillingworth."

During the week which he had spent disputing in defence of his oath, and though they had seen him write and sign the paper expressing his fidelity to the Catholic faith, he began speaking more freely than he had ever done before to the Miss Carys of his abandonment of the Church, and pressing upon them the obligation of doing the same.

What follows indicates, that Chillingworth's object was the formation of a sect of which he aspired to be the originator and leader. "He told them that the cause of so many persons turning Catholics was the discovery of the unsoundness of the Protestant religion, which he confessed was easily made, and not the truth of Catholicism. That people took it for granted that they must be either Protestant or Catholic, and finding that Protestantism was false, they at once concluded that Catholicism was true. Whereas if a third way was opened, the Catholics would have as much trouble to defend themselves as the Protestants. The title that he desired to give to this third way was Christian." He never seems to have taken up the Laudian High Anglican theories. A mind so impatient of difficulties and argumentative to excess, would probably have been unable even for a moment to entertain such utterly illogical views. Besides, to have merged his conception of a *via media* within the lines of the Established Church would not have made his own name conspicuous enough. He bragged that thirty persons depended on his resolution for the choice of a religion, and whilst still professing himself a Catholic, he pressed these disciples of his to communicate with the Protestant Church, no doubt with the view of first detaching them from the Church of Rome, and then leading them wherever he chose to point the way. Our authoress is of opinion that he deceived himself as to the number of these followers. Perhaps he reckoned at that time on herself and her sisters being of that number.

Father Leander returned to London just at the time when Mr. Chillingworth had begun decidedly to urge Lady Falkland's daughters to apostatize, and was of course asked by their mother and the Catholics who frequented her house, whether he had approved of his taking the oath he said had been proposed to him by the Bishop of London. Father Leander utterly denied it. He had been asked by him before he left town whether for the attainment of a great good, a Catholic might for a time deprive himself of the sacraments. That he had inquired what length of time was meant, and Chillingworth answered, whether truly or not it would be hard to say, that a friend of his, inclined to be a Catholic, wished for his company in his house in the country for three weeks or a month, in order to come to a resolution on that point, but that his unwillingness to lose Mass and the frequentation of the sacraments, even for so short a time, made him refuse to go. This led to his giving an opinion, which, during his absence, Chillingworth had entirely misrepresented, by the assertion that he had sanctioned his taking the monstrous oath in question.

This led to Lady Falkland's holding a conversation with Father Leander and Mr. Chillingworth, at which no one else was present. On the evening of that day, as she was walking behind them, she overheard him giving her daughters his own version of this conversation, ending with an exclamation against Catholics, whose religion, he said, was founded and maintained by lies. She instantly confronted him, and charged this zealous lover of truth, of falsehood in his report of what had passed at the above-mentioned conference, and of dissimulation in having contrived up to that time to seem to her a Catholic. So indignant was she at the discovery thus made, that she would have instantly forbidden him her house, had she not seen that some of her children were not wholly disenchanted with him, and that there was danger of their taking his part if she turned him out. We cannot but admire the self-command, exercised by one whose character was so impulsive and so vehement, in controlling her natural and righteous indignation, from the fear of driving her daughters, whose spiritual condition was most critical, to an advocacy, that might have led them further than they had hitherto gone in the direction she most dreaded. The difficulty of forbearance was great. She was hardly able to endure the presence of that man, whose apparent doubts and struggles when he first

returned from Douay, and afterwards regarding his
oath, she had, with her trustful and unsuspecting
nature, sincerely compassionated and desired to
assist, but whom clear evidence had now shown her
to be " a deceiver and seducer."   During the four
days which ensued, she did not dine at her own
table in order to avoid him, but seems to have been
present when he was arguing on the subject of
religion, for it is related that: " The next two
days were spent in a confused discourse of divers
things with several different persons, such as herself, Father Cuthbert, Mr. Clayton and another
Catholic gentleman, Mr. Chaperlin.   These were
all very earnest, being touched with the danger in
which they saw her daughters ; she herself (who can
wonder at it ?) was sometimes somewhat bitter, and
Mr. Chaperlin, a zealous Catholic and a very good
man, but violent, was so fierce, that the uttermost
of what he could do was to keep his hands from
having their part in the dispute ; whilst Mr. Chillingworth received all that was said with so calm a
serenity as if his peace and patience were immovable.
He took care not to lose the advantage of this
supportation, and continually did call on the Miss
Carys to take notice with what mildness, he bore
all ; and by this his behaviour, at the end of two
days, their esteem of him was greatly increased."

He then complained of the confused manner of
these discourses ; of the speaking of several things,
and the passing from one to another in a disorderly

fashion. To remedy this, he was to choose the person with whom, and the manner in which, he would dispute. He did not care to have to do with Father Cuthbert, for he had often experienced that his work had been overthrown by him, when the Miss Carys had had recourse to him in the perplexities which he had placed them in, and that though they had not divulged who it was had suggested to them these doubts, they always returned satisfied with his answers. He also knew in what respect they held Father Cuthbert, and was not willing to have such odds against him. So he chose a stranger to them, yet for his own credit a superior man—a Father of the Society of Jesus—Mr. Holland, whom they had never seen before, nor any one of his Order.

He first made this Father take an oath on the Bible not to say anything in the heat of dispute which he was not most certain was true, and which he did not in his conscience take to be a full and sound answer to what he should say, and he himself took the same oath. He forbade all school terms and methods as improper, and not understood by those to whom they spoke, but that in long discourses and plain terms they should object and answer ; not interrupting one another, nor removing from one topic to another till by common consent it had been fully discussed. This seemed fair, but he soon showed that it was his own advantage he sought, not the clearer understanding of those who listened. The Jesuit was most accustomed to the other mode of disputation, and he himself hoped to dazzle them by the multiplication of words. But the Father, stripping his arguments of all the exaggerations and exclamations with which he disguised and adorned them, so easily and clearly answered them, that he was forced himself to transgress his last regulation. For having failed to prove what he had undertaken, and having left it to his opponent to prove the contrary, which he had clearly done, and the difficulty which had been first started, and on which he had built all and which had most troubled the young converts, having been plainly confuted, he was constrained to run from one thing to another, till at length he went so far from the matter that he seemed only aiming to prove something, though it had no relation to anything that had been said, and in no way concerned those they spoke for."

Whether Mr, Chillingworth's apparent mildness had proceeded from the double satisfaction of thinking that the irritation of his adversaries indicated a fear of his ability and sense of his superiority, which supposition flattered his pride, or the thought that his composure advanced him in the opinion of those he was so anxious to influence, it failed entirely when he found himself engaged in disputation with one, who dealt with him not uncivilly but slightly, as not attaching much importance to what he said, and like a man who wrestles with a child, not putting forward

his whole strength to defeat him. He lost so completely his affected serenity that he called his adver-
sary a knave and a fool, which being only answered by
smiles, "he fell into such a rage and fury as to swell
with it, and looked so terrible that one might have
thought him possessed." For two days this went on.
From morning to night he was with the Father, and
at last seemed quite to lose his senses with anger.
In spite of his long preparation which the Miss
Carys had witnessed, and the fact that Father
Holland had only been engaged to meet him the
night before they began to dispute, he seemed to have
nothing more to say, and was fain instead of proofs
to thunder out threats, with a confused heap of words
such as hell, damnation, devils, spoken in a tone
capable of frightening those he knew well were
inclined enough to fear. Then the veil completely
fell from the eyes of Lady Falkland's daughters, and
with the consent and good will of all of them he
was banished from the house. He went away in a
fury, " saying that of his knowledge, the wily Jesuit
had been told that the Miss Carys had been struck
with his own serenity and mildness on previous
occasions, and that they much disliked all earnest-
ness, so that he had resolved at all costs to keep his
temper."

He came afterwards twice to Lady Falkland's
house; once to speak in private with Father Fisher,
of the Society of Jesus, who had desired to meet
him with the hope of doing him some good, but the

effort failed; and once in order to hold a disputation with Father Francis of Santa Clara, of the Order of Recollects, which was to be carried on in the presence of the eldest of the Miss Carys, the Maid of honour. By a new request of Mr. Chillingworth's, it was this time to be in writing instead of speaking. But no result ensued. Thus ended his intercourse with Lady Falkland's daughters, who ever since that time seem to have remained firm in their faith and affectionately attached to their mother. But his baleful influence was still working evil of a most dangerous nature in her family, for he had obtained the esteem and confidence of her son, Lord Falkland, and when he ceased to frequent her society was invited by him to lodge at his house.

Not only did she grieve that this double-faced individual should be befriended and cherished by her eldest and most loved son, who at one time had seemed so well inclined towards the Catholic Church, but she had an additional reason for lamenting his residence in his house. Her two youngest sons, Patrick and Placid, who were very young then, had come from school to stay with her in London, and "conceived great inclinations for the Catholic religion." This was probably the cause of their removal to their elder brother's house. It may have been even then at the instigation of Mr. Chillingworth, who had, however, always laughed at her talking of religion to such young children; be that as it may, he was now appointed their tutor by Lord Falkland

We may well imagine how keenly their mother must have felt their being committed to such an instructor. Humanly speaking, no hope seemed left to her of making them Catholics, but we shall see that Providence assisted her in a wonderful manner for that end. These children never wholly lost their predilection for their mother's religion even whilst absent from her, though Lord Falkland took great pains with Patrick Cary, the eldest of the two, which would naturally flatter a boy, and one whose nature was singularly affectionate. He used to show him his own writings on religion, "as considering him capable of understanding them." If Lord Falkland's sister describes accurately their drift, what she says may well account for the slight impression they made on his little brother. Children are never inclined towards what is vague and uncertain, and would not understand the frame of mind of one "who always rather pretended to be an inquirer than an absolute defender of anything; who confessed there were few truths so clear that it was not more hard to prove them, than to find something to object to against them. And that to one who would deny what he himself held, he would not be able to prove plainly what nevertheless he did think to be so, though he always seemed to require fresh proof of it." No wonder that the reasonings of their talented brother and their learned tutor, who gave them for a first principle that there was nothing certain in religion, failed to make Patrick and Placid Protestants; it might have easily made them unbelievers, but their mother's and their sisters', prayers were pleading for these innocent souls, and God was preparing a means of escape from the dangerous snares besetting them.

This happy consummation was brought about by a singular series of Providential circumstances, some of which arose from what, at the time, appeared a great misfortune, but in the end, turned out to be one of those blessings in disguise, afterwards recognized as such, and looked back to with wondering gratitude.

Relieved from her apprehension regarding her daughters' steadfastness in the Catholic faith, and at the same time, Mr. Chillingworth's presence in her house, and the religious disputes and controversies, which had embittered her life, for several months, Lady Falkland; "being now free from her fears, and all things settled in quiet," would have been comparatively happy, had it not been, for the difficulty of maintaining the children, whom she had so earnestly laboured to keep with her.

Not only had she to support them out of her own most inadequate means, but one of them, who had been a Maid of honour, continued to go a great deal to Court, and into society. Being now out of mourning, a number of things had to be provided for her equipment and dress, which her mother could ill afford, yet, she did not venture, until God Himself inspired her to withdraw from the world, in any way to thwart the tastes and inclinations of this young lady.

Each day these pecuniary embarassments increased and so did also, the number of persons dependent upon her assistance, "for she was ever ready to charge herself with all those who knew not how to bestow themselves, especially if she had seen and known them ever so little, and, on that account, filled her house with many unuseful servants."

The following description of her disposition in this respect, is worth transcribing in its original form.

She was always glad to find those whose wants, being reduced to a lower degree than hers, she was able to help. When she was not able to do much it was a joy to her to meet with those that a little would succour. Never in her greatest scarcity, did she refuse a little when she had it, to those whom it would relieve, saying with St. Paula, that should she refuse it to those who applied to her, they might not find any who would give it them, whereas she was confident that if she herself was in their place she should never fail to find somebody to help her. But as this confidence was partly human, built as it was on her many friends and acquaintances, God permitted her to be in some sort deceived in it before she died. She never reckoned how often the same persons came to her for assistance. If they came when she had anything that she could spare from present necessities, never being

much given to provide for the future, it was not with-
held at a time when she had herself little ènough.   One
Sir William Essex, whom she had known when he had
a very great estate, frequently resorted to her in his
need.   He was a lone man, and that would be something to him, which did not seem to her anything to
give, if it so happened she had it, and in this way he
received from her, in about a year, thirty pounds, by
crowns and halfcrowns at a time, as his occasion
required, or her store permitted.   At the year's end he
brought her a note of these alms as a grateful acknowledgement, which did much encourage her to continue,
seeing how considerable had been to him in his pressing
case what she had never perceived the want of.
Indeed, whatsoever she may have had in the morning,
there would be nothing left of it at night, unless she
had met with none that did need, or did ask.   She was
almost certain to go to bed without money unless
some friend of hers had got it out of her hands to
keep it for her.   Yet she was careful (in such a degree
as she could be) not to give frequently, nor any considerable matter, but to such as would use it well.

No wonder that having continued for two years
since the death of her husband, maintaining her
family with totally inadequate means and assisting
all who applied to her, in the spirit of the highest
Christian charity, but also with some degree of that
imprudence which belonged to her character, Lady
Falkland should have found herself "at the last
extremity and not able to hold on any longer."   She

had reckoned on Providence, and on the experience of all those who have tested the Scriptural promise, that alms deeds will never impoverish them, but without, perhaps, remembering that in persons like herself by nature lavish as to expenditure, the conditions may be wanting which constitute, if we may so speak, a claim on that Divine pledge. But God is a loving Father and if there had been a slight admixture of human frailty in His servant's boundless generosity, He ordained that the conse· quent suffering it entailed should be the very means of her obtaining what seemed an all but impossible answer to her prayers.

From her children she had concealed as long as possible, the urgency of her position. They were the very last who knew of it. For, "having disfurnished her own chamber wholly, even of her bed, being fain to sleep on a chair, she kept the door of it locked, that they, who were not disaccommodated in anything, might not perceive it." But matters at last came to a crisis. Grief and apprehension of the step she saw herself compelled to take, caused her a severe illness, and no alternative remained but to ask her eldest son, to come and break up her establishment, and fetch away his sisters. This it was that most went to her heart. She could hardly bear to break it to them.

Lord Falkland had ever been a more than ordinarily good son and brother, and his wife, far from hindering, encouraged him in the performance

N

of his filial duties.   He accordingly hastened to provide means to settle his mother's affairs, and in the meantime, she, and all her family, were sustained by the charity of those, who became aware of their necessities.

Sir William Spencer, a cousin of hers, especially befriended her at that moment.   He paid part of her debts, and assisted her with ready money.

For the first time, Lady Falkland seemed overcome with grief and distrust of the future, but, as her daughter remarks, God was preparing to teach her a greater and stronger confidence than ever in what He ordained, by the happy results of what she looked upon with despondency.   "God's Almighty Providence showed itself in the fact, that the absence of every one of her children continued no longer than seemed absolutely necessary for some good it was to effect."

Three of her daughters, Anne, Lucy, and Mary, went to reside with their brother, "to be again tormented, but—by the grace of God—not hurt, by Mr. Chillingworth."   She had been much afraid that they would complain bitterly, especially the eldest, "who loved the Court," of having to go and stay with their brother, who did not, at that time, reside in London.   Yet he was the only one of their relatives and friends who would receive them whilst they remained Catholics.   They took it, however, much better than she expected, and this anxiety being removed, she soon recovered her health and new courage as well as her habitual confidence in God.

As soon as she was well enough, she went to visit them and promised as speedily as possible to arrange for their return to her. But as our authoress says, "That was not yet done for which God had sent them thither." The first of these unforeseen results was that, "whereas the loss of their faith had been feared for all these her daughters, one of them was to find there her vocation to Religion."[1] Their little brothers—after having their dispositions to Catholicism confirmed by intercourse with their sisters, were to be delivered through their means from Mr. Chillingworth's tuition. And a young Catholic gentleman, Mr. Harry Slingsby, who was in danger of being affected by that dangerous man's artifices, warned of his peril, and his faith preserved."

As the history of this young man and of his family, affords an interesting picture of those times, and his own friendship with Lady Falkland and her daughters connects him with her life, a sketch of may well find place in these pages.

[1] How this came about we are not told.

CHAPTER XII.

The two Slingsbys.[1]

HENRY, or Harry Slingsby, was the second son of Sir Francis Slingsby—a Yorkshire gentleman—who settled in Ireland about the beginning of the seventeenth century, acquired estates in Connaught and near Cork, and became Constable of the Castle of Haulbowline and a member of the Royal Council of Munster. His eldest son, Francis, was born in Ireland and educated there up to his thirteenth year, when he was sent to Oxford, where he remained about five years, "learning philosophy without making much progress, but succeeding a little better in mathematics," according to his own account of his studies. At the age of eighteen, he returned to Ireland and after coming of age, went abroad to accomplish the tour, which it was the fashion in those days, for young men of a certain rank to make, before taking up their position in society.

During his stay in France, a young lady fell so deeply in love with the young Englishman, that she

[1] This chapter is an abridgment of a memoir of Father Francis Slingsby, appended by the Editor to the original life of Lady Falkland.

asked him to marry her. He appears to have consented to this unexpected proposal and to have been
for some time engaged to her. This marriage was on
the point of taking place when, in consequence of
an opportunity occurring for completing his travels,
it was put off, and in the end given up.

Francis Slingsby's visit to Italy wrought an entire
change in his views, his desires, and the whole
current of his life. On his arrival in Rome he made
acquaintance with Father John Gerard, Superior of
the English Jesuits, by whom he was converted to
the Catholic faith. His first act after his reception
into the Church was to make the Spiritual Exercises
of St. Ignatius, and soon afterwards he made up his
mind that he was called to enter the Society of Jesus.
Family affairs prevented for a long time the actual
fulfilment of his vocation. He broke off, however,
his engagement to his French *fiancée*, and returned
at once to his own country.

In July 1634, Francis Slingsby reached London,
from whence he wrote the following letter to Father
Gerard. In it he speaks of himself under the
feigned name of Lewis Newman, and designates the
General of the Jesuits, Muzio Vitelleschi, under
that of Scævola, one of his uncles, as Mr. English,
and his own father as Mr. Irish.

I am now, thanks be to God, safely arrived in London,
where, for a welcome into these parts, the searchers
coming aboard found a little packet wherein were my
books, papers, and letters, and took it away with them,

but by good luck Scævola's letter to me had been sent before unto Manners.[2] I was glad to swallow that misfortune and say not a word, lest that by seeking to recover them I might have lost myself. The Lords of the Privy Council were informed that Newman was pensioner under the Governor of your town (the Pope), by reason whereof he is obliged to keep close. He is now going into the country to visit Mr. English, and from thence speedily into Ireland. I send you the copy of a letter which Newman has received from his father, whereby you may perceive how the matter stands between them. If a Saint said '*Quoties inter homines fui minor homo redii,*'[3] in what danger then, think you, stands he whom necessity doth constrain to be almost continually amongst them? He hopes his poverty will plead for pity and that you will bestow a spiritual alms upon him. Farewell.

Sir Francis Slingsby's letter—a copy of which was enclosed within the preceding one—seems that of an earnest and affectionate father, and to refer rather to the command he had apparently laid on his son to come home immediately, than to the subject of his change of religion.

My Son—If ever you thought I loved you and did not take always more care for your soul than your body, and if you do not think I have not given you sufficient motive for your return by means of which you can do your parents so good service, in the first

---

[2] Father Manners, S.J. then in London.
[3] The more I converse with men the less man I find myself.

case, you judge uncharitably of me, and in the second, you deal uncharitably with me. I must needs acknowledge, I have much offended God in trusting too much to an arm of flesh and blood, as though by mine own endeavour I could attain my desire. But now I find my fault and feel my punishment. Our hearts are in the hands of God to dispose of as He pleaseth, yet are we allowed and commanded to use all lawful means and then refer the success to Him. These arguments might call forth many good, feeling motives. You know my education has not been such as to give my pen effectual persuasions, yet what I now write might be sufficient to give you a sensible compunction in disesteeming my loving advice. If the defect I found in myself made me seek to redeem it in you, that might be a sufficient motive for you to think how dearly I loved you. And shall I be thus requited for all my care, travail, and cost? My time, in the course of nature, cannot continue long, and will you shorten it by an unkind requital? Take this for your theme, and comment upon it with such moving reasonings as yourself can furnish and your own thoughts would dictate to you if your case were mine, and be not partial. Let not this undue style make you either disesteem, or deride it. I have said enough if it prevail, if not, too much, and till I shall either see, or have a good answer to this my letter, you shall neither hear from me, or of me. Sincerity is the best policy. Deal as plainly with me as I with you. And if you give me not great cause to the contrary, I shall ever remai your unfeigned loving Father.

Francis Slingsby after receiving this letter, went to his uncle, probably in Yorkshire, and met with a far kinder reception than he had looked for. Writing again, after his return to London, to Father Gerard, he says:

Newman hath now been with Mr. English, where, contrary to all expectation, he was received with such joy as cannot be expressed. They will give him all kind of liberty for his mind, make greater show of love to him than ever, and to conclude, will deny him nothing, so that he will stay with them and not become a journeyman, (a Priest) but live quietly without moving others to be of his opinions.

He adds that his relatives urge him continually to a bargain, which probably means that if he agreed to these conditions, the settlement of property, which had been assured to him in a legal form long before, though he did not know of it, would not be interfered with.

This drives him into a difficulty how to come away and yet retain what had been assured to him. To stay on there "he neither can, or will. If he comes away it must be secretly, or publicly with the consent of Mr. Irish (his father) and a pass from superior powers. If secretly, then all will be confiscated and, in the other way, it can never be hoped for." In this doubt he asks for counsel.

In the meantime he is with Mr. Hebden (S.J.) daily, and adds that " by the grace of God, he stands fast, and by His grace obtained by prayer, hopes to persevere."

He encloses, this time, a letter from Lady Slingsby addressed to him abroad but apparently only just received, and says "I send a letter Newman has had from his mother, that you may see, that as he told you, he shall have a greater contest with love than with fear." This sentence, and the affectionate pleadings of that afflicted mother, will come home to the feelings of many, in these days, who have known the acute pain of such contests with the hearts most tenderly devoted to them. It is curious to find Slingsby's mother begging him to consider "that our laws do not enforce men's conscience," which would have been a singularly bold assertion were it not that she evidently meant that people might think as they pleased, provided they conformed outwardly to the Established Church. It is impossible not to be touched by the gentle, earnest, tone of this loving letter, and to help being interested in the writer, who subsequently became a Catholic.

My dearest Son,—I have seen, read, and considered with the best of my poor judgment, all your letters, written to your father and myself, both before and since your sickness, especially that long one of two sheets of paper signed with your own hand, but written by another, whereby I perceive the great pains you took to be resolved, which zeal I trust the Lord will favour, howsoever you may be misled. But although I cannot judge of controversy, yet I think you ought not to forsake your old father and me, to enjoy that liberty of conscience which (if there be no remedy) you may enjoy here at home as many other good subjects do. But you fear your father will be offended —much better can you bear that than we your longer absence, which I can assure you would bring us both with sorrow to the grave. My dear son, consider that our laws do not enforce mens' consciences, and therefore what cause can there be for you to absent yourself? If ever you took pity on my sorrows, add not unto them, but return to comfort me, whose eyes have failed with expectation of it. Oh! my son, you, who ought not to turn your ears away from the prayer of the poor, are much more bound to regard the tears and supplications of your mother. I do beseech you, with heaved up hands, to return by the nearest way and not to think of passing through Spain. The infinite proofs I have had of your piety and obedience to both of us assures me, that you will be grieved that I cannot know the haste with which you will make home, but my dear child, let not that trouble you for I am consoled in the confidence of it and so are all your sisters. Your sister Willoughby is the mother of three children, and your sister Betty is married, but in all this I can take no true content till I see you. And, if it please the Lord of Mercy, to permit that, then shall I say I have had one joyous day before my death. Farewell, and all the good a mother's blessing can add unto you, be heaped upon your head, my dearest child.

Francis Slingsby did not remain long in London, but hastened to Ireland, and on his arrival there went immediately to seek the Superior of the Irish Jesuits, Father Nugent, who was residing at that time in the house of the Countess of Kildare.

This lady was one of those noble-hearted, thoroughly Christian, and Catholic women, who, in the days of persecution in England and in Ireland, devoted themselves heart and soul to the cause of religion, and the consolation and support of their afflicted brethren. It might be almost said that from her very birth she was a confessor of the faith, for it was in the Tower of London, where her friends were incarcerated, on account of their adherence to the Catholic Church, that she was born, and spent the period of her infancy. At an early age, she was married to the Earl of Kildare, who died a year after their marriage, leaving her a widow with one boy.

From the first hour of her widowhood, she employed her time and her means in works of charity, protecting and relieving all those who suffered on account of their religion, and affording shelter and support to the Priests of the Catholic Church. Her only son died when nine years of age. She did not falter under this terrible blow. With wonderful generosity she accepted this bereavement as a sign that God called her to a still more complete consecration of her life, her fortune, and her time to His service and that of His afflicted servants. Henceforward her castle became not only a place of refuge for Catholics and a home for Priests, but the centre of a religious movement which extended all over Ireland. The name Catholics gave it was the House of Holiness, (Sanctificater Domus) whereas by the Protestants it was called, "the sink of Hell."

From thence Francis Slingby, by the advice of Father Nugent, proceeded to visit his mother, who in consequence of domestic disagreements had long been separated from his father, and likewise his sisters, and his only brother Henry. So successful were his efforts, his arguments, and the effect of his example on his relatives, that he soon brought them to Kildare Castle, fully convinced of the truth of the Catholic religion and eager to be received into the Church in spite of sacrifices of every sort which this step was certain to involve.

Sir Francis made his wife, as it was, a very slender allowance, and even that pittance he was likely to withdraw on her joining the Church of Rome. One of her daughters was married to a man bitterly opposed to Catholics, and as to Henry Slingsby, he had not a shilling of his own. It was whilst he was still at Oxford that a letter from Francis had informed him of his conversion. The news took him entirely by surprise, and he at once gave up all study but that of theology, and employed himself in reading books of Anglican divinity in order to prepare for controversial encounters with his brother, whom he both wished and expected to induce to retrace his steps. But when they did meet, the story of Francis's conversion, made so great an impression upon him that he soon resolved to " go and do likewise." After a course of instruction from Father Malone at Dublin, he was received into the Church at Kildare by Father Nugent.

It took more time to prepare his mother and sisters for this important step, and their reception was, in consequence, deferred a while.

Sir Francis Slingsby was, of course exasperated at the results of his eldest son's action in the conversion of so many members of his family and especially Henry's. "My father," Francis writes, " was so incensed against me that with extreme passion he used the words that " I had broken his heart snd almost murthered him."

His intercourse with Lady Slingsby—by what means we are not told—was put a stop to, and measures taken to prevent his visits to his sisters, one of whom, especially, seemed determined to be a Catholic. Nor did the matter end there. Both the brothers were kept prisoners for eight days in their lodgings in Dublin, and during that time Archbishop Usher held a conference with Francis which the latter says, " by the grace of God took no such effect as he looked for."

Sir Francis Slingsby and one of his friends were awaiting the result of the conference. They were much astonished at the Archbishop's discomfiture, and the affair was hushed up. The Catholics soon got wind of it and the Marquis of Westmeath gave an account of the incident to the Pope and Cardinal Barberini.

In the course of this disputation, Francis Slingsby, tired of the trouble of arguing, suddenly asked the Protestant Prelate, whether he would consent to do in behalf of his religion what he was prepared to do with regard to the Catholic faith.   Usher asked what this was, upon which Francis knelt down and prayed as follows, "I humbly beseech the Almighty God, before Whom I stand, that if the Roman Catholic faith which I profess be not the only true one, the earth may presently swallow me up alive."

Usher became dreadfully pale.   "Desperate wretch," he exclaimed, "to dare to tempt God in this wise. Hence, away with you, I will have nothing to do with you," and he hurried into the next room, where the irritated father filled up a dozen sheets of paper with complaints and accusations against his son and addressed them to the Lord Deputy, who instantly issued a warrant for his arrest and imprisoned him in Dublin Castle.

The charges laid to him were, "the seduction—as it was called—of a young gentleman coming out of England, and also of his own brother and others."

Whilst he was awaiting his trial, Sir Francis, not discouraged by Archbishop Usher's ill success, took advantage of the presence in Dublin of the famous controversialist, Bramhall, Bishop of Derry and Chancellor of Ireland.⁴ At his request this Anglican

---

⁴ Bramhall, Bishop cf Derry and Chancellor of Ireland, was ordered by the Lord Deputy to enquire into the state of the Established Church in Ireland. The following extracts are taken

dignitary proposed several times to Francis Slingsby to confer with him about religion; who answered that he had no doubt whatever as to the truth of any of the dogmas taught by the Catholic Church, and that it would therefore be superfluous to argue about them. But at last Bramhall gained his point, and came with several other Protestants to hold a disputation with the young convert.

The result was of course what might have been anticipated. The Anglican Bishop's brief account of the state of the Protestant Church of Ireland, which he was charged to report upon, inclines one

from his "Brief account of the present state of the poor Church of Ireland."

"First, for the fabrics, it is hard to say whether the churches be the more ruinous and sordid, or the people irreverent; even in Dublin, the metropolis of this kingdom, and the seat of justice, we find one parochial church converted to the Lord Deputy's stable, a second to a nobleman's dwelling-house, the choir of a third to a tennis-court, and the vicar acts the keeper. In Christ's Church, the principal church in Ireland, whither the Lord Deputy and Council repair every Sunday, the vaults, from one end of the minster to the other, are made into tippling-rooms for beer, wine, and tobacco, demised all to Popish recusants, and by them and others so much frequented in time of Divine service, that though there is no danger of blowing up the assembly about their heads, yet there is of poisoning them with the fumes. The table used for the administration of the Blessed Sacrament, in the midst of the choir, made an ordinary seat for maids and apprentices. . . . . . . Next, for the clergy; I find few footsteps yet of foreign differences, so I hope it will be an easier task not to admit them, than to have them ejected. But I doubt much whether the clergy be very orthodox, and could wish both the articles and canons of the Church of England were established here by Act of Parliament, or State, and that as we live all under one King, so we might both in doctrine and discipline observe an uniformity. The inferior to wonder that he could face a Catholic at all. He, indeed, appeared to have had strong misgivings as to the success of his mission, for he would not allow a gentleman who was inclined to become a Catholic, to be present at the conference.

Meantime Francis was plied by his father with every imaginable work of controversy, which he refused to look at, unless Sir Francis consented to read those he sent him in return. The aged knight agreed to the condition, but does not appear to have been impressed by their contents.

After spending some weeks in prison, Slingsby was examined before the members of the council on the

sort of ministers are below all degrees of contempt, in respect of their poverty and ignorance; the boundless heaping together of benefices by commendams and dispensations in the superiors is but too apparent ; yea, even often by plain usurpation, and indirect compositions made between the patrons (as well ecclesiastic as lay) and the incumbents; by which the least part, many not above forty shillings, rarely £10, in the year, is reserved for him that should serve at the altar, insomuch, that it is affirmed that by all, or some, of these means one bishop in the remoter parts of the kingdom doth hold three and thirty benefices, with cure. Generally their residence is as little as their livings. Seldom any suitor petitions for less than three vicarages at a time. And it is a main prejudice to his Majesty's service, and a hindrance to the right establishment of the Church, that the clergy have, in a manner no dependence on the Lord Deputy, nor he any means left to prefer those who are deserving amongst them; for besides all those advowsons which were given by that great patron of the Church, King James, of happy memory, to Bishops and the College here, many also were conferred upon the *plantations* (never was so good a gift so infinitely abused) and I know not how, or by what order, even in these blessed days of his sacred Majesty, all the rest of any note had been given, or passed away in the time of the late Lord Deputy."

crime and misdemeanour he was charged with, the head and front of which was having persuaded others to profess the Catholic faith. He confessed that he had endeavoured, and with some success, to induce others to follow the way of salvation. Upon which one of the councillors inferred that he had been guilty of high treason. Francis's reply was, " If it be so, I cannot help it."

There were at that time a number of Irish and English noblemen and gentlemen at Dublin Castle, imprisoned, some of them for their faith, and others on political grounds. The Lord Deputy Wentworth was carrying matters with a high hand, and transferring all who opposed him to the strong walls of the old fortress. It does not appear that they were treated with great severity; at any rate they seemed to have formed a society amongst themselves, and Francis Slingsby was, by this means, introduced to a very aristocratic set. By this means he became acquainted with the Earl of Castlehaven, who often visited the prisoner, supplied him with everything he wanted, obtained his liberation, and, at last, permission to remove him to his house, on condition that he was never to go more than three miles distance from this agreeable prison.

The Earl's family derived great benefit, we are told, from his example and conversation, especially one of Lord Castlemain's sisters, who afterwards married Richard Butler, Lord Ormond's brother, and probably became a Catholic. We

o

find Francis writing at that time to his spiritual
father :

When I went into the country to my father, he
received me with tears and much love, but since the
conversion of my dear and hopeful brother, he hath
almost quite withdrawn his affection from me and
procured my imprisonment in the Castle of Dublin.
My mother and one of my sisters are not far from the
Kingdom of Heaven, but there is little probability of
gaining my father. I expect with longing desire to
know how you will dispose of me, for if you say but
Veni, by the grace of God, nothing but violence will
keep me.

Dublin Castle, Jan. 1, 1634.

From Lord Castlehaven's house a few months
later, he again writes to his director at Rome :

The Superior in these parts [the Father Provincial
in Ireland] labours to procure my stay in this country,
but if you would know my own affection, or inclination
on this point, I must confess that I esteem Rome a
Paradise and this my Purgatory. But yet, as well in
this as in all other things, obedience shall be my rule
of action. . . . . My brother to my great comfort
remains still a constant Catholic. My eldest sister,
who was my father's chiefest joy, is lately dead. My
mother on her part, is well disposed to be reconciled
unto my father but he remains obstinate.

In the meantime Henry was subjected to many
trials by his father. Every attempt was made to

shake him in his new faith. Francis writes on the 24th of November, 1635 :

Mr. Young, [feigned name of his brother] remained with me in these parts only six weeks after his conversion, and then was sent to England where he hath been strongly and dangerously assaulted. But by God's help, and the industry of Mr. Manners, he remaineth still constant in his resolutions though all means have been used to divert him from it.

We can imagine how great were the dangers that Henry Slingsby was running at that time, when we hear of him at Lord Falkland's house in Oxfordshire, exposed to the fascination of his host's conversation and attractive manners, witnessing in him and in his wife many virtues and merits, and a prey to Mr. Chillingworth's subtle and invidious tactics. Francis wrote at that time to Father Blake ;

I understand, to my great grief, that my dear and only brother is in danger of falling away from the Catholic Faith. I beseech you to use some means in England for the preventing of so great an evil and here, to beg of God his perseverance by all the prayers you can procure.

At this critical moment, three of the Miss Carys arrived at Few, and became, under God, the means of opening the eyes of the young convert to Mr. Chillingworth's true character, and irrevocably confirming him in the resolution of living and dying in the Catholic faith. A great friendship sprang up in consequence between him and these young ladies, who introduced him to their mother, whose house in London he ever after frequented; not, however, to the entire satisfaction of his brother, who seems to have been afraid that Henry might fall in love with one of the Miss Carys, and thus lose a vocation for the Religious life, of which he thought there had been signs at the time of his conversion.

Lady Falkland's daughters still lived much in the world at that time, and her house was the centre of an animated, though pious society. All this, Francis dreaded. Moreover, though we have seen that she invited a Jesuit Father to dispute in her presence, with Mr. Chillingworth, her knowledge of the Society was slight, her sympathies with the Religious Orders, centred in the Benedictines, and, as Francis says in one of his letters, "She and her daughters, liked the Secular as well as they did the Regular Clergy."

The spirit of rivalry between those two great forces of the Church, of which there is always some danger, prevailed even in those days of persecution, when it would have seemed natural that it should have merged, in the presence of common enemies and common dangers. Even in the best men on both sides, it exerted an influence.

Meanwhile, Francis Slingsby was released from his mild imprisonment and reconciled to his father, of which fact he apprises "his ever dearest friend," Father Gerard.

Your well known friend, having for a long time sued in vain for his liberty, after the space of a full year, obtained it unsought for, it being entirely granted to him, he knows not by what means, but he conjectures, by some mediation of our Queen. . . . [Then writing in the first person, he adds,] My father and I are now good friends, he loveth me exceedingly, and I am as careful to please him. I know not what to say about my mother and my sisters for I have not seen them for a year and more, only this I can certify, that they still retain a great affection towards me and are not far from being of the same mind with me, but I know not how to proceed any further herein, by reason I am so watched, that the least thing I do in this kind is observed.

Francis does not seem ever to have relaxed in his fervour during those trying years. When he lived at the Earl of Castlehaven's, his servant used to grumble at his master's long prayers. He and George, the Earl's brother, used, he said, to try which could keep on his knees the longest, and his conclusion was that "those two young men were ruining each other."

After leaving Lord Castlehaven's house (unspoilt by the comforts of that abode) Francis Slingsby refused to live at Dublin with his father, "who kept up great state and splendour," but took up his residence in a private citizen's house, observing there the rule of St Ignatius as strictly as if he had been in one of the houses of the Society.

In spite of this, Sir Francis became more and more attached to his son, and employed him in the management of his suits and law affairs. Later on, he took him with him to his estates in Munster, where he was received with great demonstrations of joy by the Catholic peasantry. He, in his turn, became exceedingly attached to these good people and spent a great deal of his time with them, leaving to his father the care of the Protestant tenants. He used to give his friends books, rosaries, and tobacco, and, it is said, even smoked with them himself, for the sake of good fellowship.

At that time he wrote to Rome, that though his property was entailed, his father had the power to cut off the entail and disinherit him, but that as long as he remained with him he did not think he would do so, nor did he despair of obtaining his consent to his departure, "*when I shall be sent for to his Majesty's Service.*" "And now," he adds, "I am ready to do and also to think that best which Scævola by you shall command me." Further on he mentions, that his brother had several times written to his father to obtain means to join a Pilgrimage to St. Winefrid's Well, with Lady Falkland and her daughters, which he had been as constantly refused, and Francis says, "I hope for his greater good." For he had also expressed a desire "to go to Rome." But neither to that would his father consent, "therefore," he adds, "I have endeavoured to get him back to Ireland. My mother and sister" he goes on to say, "are in good estate though not yet reconciled, yet not through any backwardness on their part, but for good reasons. They still profess themselves Catholics and both they and myself are threatened to be brought into the High Commission Court . . . ."

Nothing came, however, of these threats, and at the end of the letter Francis adds: "My sister was reconciled, and heard her first mass on St. Xaverius' Day."

Discussions were going on at that time relative to the settlement of Sir Francis Slingsby's property. His eldest son had long ago made up his mind to become a Jesuit. As to Henry, he seems to have inclined to the same course, but he told his brother that if he persevered in his intention, he would not do so, "because one of the two ought to remain in the world and continue the family. And, in that case, he expected their father's estates to be settled upon himself." But this line of argument Francis met by a distinct refusal. He probably thought that the expectation of wealth would only tempt his brother to remain in the world, and he wrote accordingly, "that he considered the world was already sufficiently peopled, that he had no wish to see his family continued in a race of children whose fidelity (to the Church) was uncertain; that he thought it would be much more to the glory of God that the property should go to found a Seminary in Belgium, and the memory of the family far better preserved

by a monument of this kind than by children,
if, indeed, it was desirable that the memory of the
family should be preserved at all."

The Jesuit Fathers in Ireland, moved by the consideration of the good Francis might effect in his
native land by means of the wealth and position
which, if he returned to Rome, he would forego,
were anxious for him to remain at home, and laid
their views before the General, who did not, however, concur in this opinion.   Father Nugent had
written, " The young man is of our opinion, yet most
ready to do what he shall be directed." And Francis
himself thus states the case :

If I come away now, I am morally certain to lose
my property here.   If I stay five or six months longer
there is great probability of making it sure to me.

But Vitelleschi, the General, and Father Gerard
were not to be moved by these considerations.   The
former wrote :

Though doubtless, your Honour is sufficiently aware,
from my letters to Father Nugent, of my opinion
concerning your further procrastinating and putting
off your coming hither, and of my one wish that you
would come to Rome at the first opportunity, yet since
you may possibly think, that the reasons which you
and Father Nugent have written caused me to change
my opinion and advice, I write these few lines to
inform you, that all those things which you tell me
about putting off your journey, or, as I gather, giving

it up, seem to me unsound. I do not think them of sufficient importance to prevent your throwing them all aside and flying hither to the Cross of Christ, that so coming out of your father's house and from your friends, you may give yourself entirely to the service of your Creator. This is my full conviction after considering the matter in the Lord, that this course will be for the greater glory of God and the salvation of your soul. May the most sweet Jesus, Who has cast the chains of His love about you, bring you hither, and may He mercifully perfect the work which of His great kindness He hath begun in you.

In a long letter Father Gerard wrote to the same effect. We extract the following passages from his letter :

Scævola perseveres in his former opinion, and makes choice of your speedily coming hither as the means of your much greater good, which is far to be preferred before the temporal means, which by your staying where you are, you might give unto us, with the loss of yourself which would speedily follow. He will be much better pleased with my friend alone and the internal riches which he will bring with him and which cannot be taken from him, and which will be so much the greater by this act of renunciation than if with less measure of internal goods he brought with him a far greater proportion of exterior wealth. . . . . God has clothes enough for His servants, and He that giveth feathers to the birds of the air, and fur to the beasts that live upon the earth, will not be wanting to

His chosen servants whom He loves so dearly, who labour for Him and to further whose provision is to set forward His own work. Besides, my dearest in Christ Jesus, you lose not what you leave behind you. First, you will ever enjoy yourself, the comfort of that Apostolic testimony of your love to Christ by which you may say with St. Peter, 'We have left all things.' And although the chief part of this consists in the will to renounce the desire of having, (which St. Peter had, and therefore truly left all things, who otherwise had but little to leave) yet the greater the quantity is, which one doth actually leave for the love of God, the greater is the perpetual comfort of the treasure he hath laid up in Heaven, and I dare boldly say, that this will be a far greater and more persevering contentment to you, than you could ever have received from your father's estate, if you had enjoyed it in this world. Your companions also, and those whom you would pleasure with it, do not lose thereby, as they have yourself, much enriched by what you have renounced, and the example of that renunciation will do much greater good amongst them, than your estate would ever have done. Lastly, the body of which you are to be a member, shall not lose by the loss of what you leave behind, because you bring with you the credit of a hundred times as much to be paid to you, even in this world. For this they have better assurance than any merchant's bond, yea, more assured than the standing of Heaven and earth—'Heaven and earth shall pass away but My word shall not pass away.' . . . . . I have written at large to Mr. Nugent in answer to all the reasons he set down for your stay. To those therefore I refer you, they are too long for my shaking hand to repeat and are not needful for you to whom a *Veni* is sufficient, as St. Ignatius justly presumed of the known entirely resigned mind of the Apostle of India, whose imitator I doubt not you desire to be.

Further on, Father Gerard recommends his friend to imitate the example of our Saviour, in leaving His Blessed Mother to St. John, and says that Father Nugent will be to his mother and sister, in his absence, what he was in his presence.

The struggle was an arduous one, and many a battle had Francis Slingsby to fight with the natural affections and inclinations of his heart, before he finally made up his mind, to the abandonment of parents, relatives, fortune, and home, to which his vocation called him. Vitelleschi wrote to him once again in a less imperative tone, but one which perhaps, by leaving the decision to himself, alarmed his conscience, and determined his will more effectually.

What has been, and still is, my opinion about your Honour's return to us, you will have easily seen by my numerous letters, for where the salvation, or the perfection, of a soul is in question all other things must be despised in comparison, and certainly I have abundant reason for congratulating your Honour that you have hitherto discerned the precious from the vile, and in thinking that no riches, but those of Heaven, are worth seeking. The only thing I could have wished is, that, after triumphing over so many difficulties, and so nearly reached the harbour, you had not been unexpectedly carried into new dangers of wind and wave. I know indeed that it was the salvation of your father and relatives which made you retrace your steps when you had got almost half way, and I pray God that your laudable wishes may be fulfilled. But I think you should anxiously consider, whether for the uncertain hope of saving other people you lose the opportunity of certainly saving yourself. But since you are good enough, and wise enough, to determine fairly what you owe to your parents, and what to God and your own soul, I will add no more, for I am fully persuaded that your dearest hope is to overcome every difficulty, and then lose no time in flying to the loved Tabernacle of the Lord of Hosts and the Father of all.

At last grace triumphed, and Francis Slingsby, breaking through all the shackles which detained him, departed for Rome, accompanied by his brother Henry. On his arrival there, he wrote to his father, the following letter, in which we find an incidental mention of Lady Falkland's ever generous hospitality.

Now that Henry had, as it would appear, made up his mind to remain a layman, and to become his father's heir, Francis was probably less afraid of the influence, which at one time he had feared would interfere with what he had, perhaps without just grounds, believed to be his vocation.

Most dear and honoured Father,—Being now by
the assistance of my good God arrived at the place
where He showed so great mercy unto me as to make
me a member of the Holy Catholic Church, which of
all places ought to be most dear unto me, and best
deserves the name of my country, wherein I was born
unto Christ, I am resolved here to spend some years
in the service of God, and prosecution of my studies.
And since that, considering your age, my intended
stay in these parts, and the dangers in so long a
voyage, when I return it is most probable I shall never
see you more, the love and duty I owe you induce me
to bid you farewell. And first of all, I most humbly
crave your pardon if, at any time, in the heat of
discourse, about matters of religion, I have forgot the
duty I owe unto a father by being more earnestly vehement than modesty allows. Yet have I this consolation,
that my intentions were pure and that I sought you
and not yours. For He that shall be my judge is also
my witness, that if I had in my possession all that
estate wherein God and nature gives me a right, I
would most willingly leave both it and my life too for
that your soul—so dear unto me—might enjoy that
happiness for which it was created. My dear father,
it is not in your power to hinder my love: all the
persecutions you can rise against me, all the afflictions
and wants you can make me suffer, nay, your refusing
to love me (which to me is more than all the rest) are
not able to blot out my love towards you. For when
I consider how good a father you once have been, how
careful of my education, how tender in your affection,

how liberal towards me for my expenses, these former benefits do prevail; and if I put them in the balance with your latter unkindness, yet, in my own judgment, they weigh them down to the ground, especially since the troubles you make me undergo proceed not originally from any evil will but from a deceived judgment. Now that you may see how good a Master I serve, I will declare unto you how the Providence of God hath so disposed things, that I was never brought to extreme necessity though I were indeed constrained to sell some clothes and books. For first, I had, when I was first at Rome, lent unto an English gentleman £80 sterling, which I could never get paid till my last being in England, so that it seemed God had laid it up in store till I should stand in need thereof. For our diet, we had it, for the most, gratis at my Lady Falkland's. When I came into France, my lord of Castlehaven maintained me, in all things gratis for the space of a year, wherein he made no difference betwixt himself and me, to use his purse as my own, and when I came away into Italy, leaving him in France, he lent me fifty pounds for my expenses by the way, which, only, I desire you to repay. When I came into Italy, the Cardinal Barberini, hearing thereof, had given orders, before my arrival at Rome, that lodging should be provided for me in his own palace; but when I came to kiss his hands I told his Eminence that if it pleased him I would rather follow my studies in the English college, which he willingly consented unto, giving present orders for my main- tainance, offering me the privilege of keeping a servant, which I refused. Thus I may truly say, *pater meus et amici mei dereliquerunt me sed Dominus suscepit me.* His goodness hath a care of me and suffers nothing to be wanting unto me, one thing alone I except, that we two are not one, yet whilst I have a tongue to speak I will never cease to beg and say, Lord, if Thou wilt, Thou canst grant me what my soul so much thirsteth after. O my father, give me a blessing! you know what my heart would say, *sapienti pauca.*

My brother hath refused certain maintenance here that hath been offered him by the Cardinal, out of the desire he hath to return to you; and chooseth rather to hazard the suffering of wants in your presence, than to want nothing, being absent from you. Receive him, therefore, I most humbly beseech you, despise not your own bowels, since in all things (yourself being judge) except matters of religion, he hath been a dutiful and loving son unto you. And as you tender the favour of Him, of Whose favour we shall one day stand so much in need, reject not my mother, since He commands you to receive her, and assures you, by His own mouth, that unless you forgive, you cannot be forgiven.

As indicated in this touching letter, Henry Slingsby returned to his father, and soon afterwards his brother — even before entering the Jesuit Noviciate at St. Andrea—made, in his behalf, a total renunciation of all his right to the paternal inheritance, their friend, Lord Castlehaven, having, out of interest for the family, negociated this affair. On this subject, Francis writes as follows:

My most dear brother,—You are exceedingly bound
unto the Earl of Castlehaven for the love he bears you,
and the care he has of preserving our house and family.
He has dealt with me about yielding you my birth-right,
as earnestly as if you had been his own brother, and
his reasons have prevailed with me, though there were
no small motives to the contrary.   First, it is the
common custom of Father General not to permit any
to make this act of renunciation till they be *de facto*
religious, which I am sure not to be this four and a
half years, and if, in the mean time, God should permit
my mind to change (as there are too many sad examples
of those who desired it with greater fervour than I,)
then should I be, in all men's judgment, most miserable
to be deprived of both.   Secondly, if, in the mean
time, I should become blind, fall into a consumption,
or contract any other infirmity, whereby I should be
made incapable of being received, what then should
become of me?   I know many youths, eminent both
in learning and virtue, who for these causes alone
cannot be admitted.   But the love I bear you makes
me pass over these difficulties; for my firm hope is
that the God of mercy, Who sought me when I thought
not upon Him, will not now forsake me when, by His
grace, I have some desire to please Him.   For the
second point, if God should permit any of these
impediments to happen to me, whereby I should be
disenabled to enter into religion, yet my comfort is,
that He will never disenable me to do His will, nor of
doing that which is most perfect.   For He requires no
impossibilities at my hands, and voluntary poverty in

a secular habit wherein there are commonly more incommodities, would not be unto God less grateful.

To this letter was joined the act of renunciation.

I, Francis Slingsby, do by this, my deed, renounce mine inheritance, and do resign unto my most dear brother, Mr. Henry Slingsby, my birthright, for ever disenabling myself of pretending any title, or interest, in my father and mother's estate. Provided that my said brother, so soon as he shall be in possession thereof, do make over a portion of land, of the value of £100, sterling, per annum, to some one that I shall appoint, for my use in perpetuum, and likewise pay unto me yearly the sum of £25, sterling, during my own life only. In witness whereof, I set my hand and seal.

F. Slingsby, *manu propriâ.*

Rome, April 21, 1639.

It does not appear that what seemed so likely to benefit Henry Slingsby's destiny had that effect. His troubles deepened more and more, to the degree that we find him writing to Francis in 1639:

I am in expectation of being shortly in prison for my debts, nor do I dare hope for any assistance from my father, but my dear sister tells me that she will rather lie in prison with me than I shall suffer by it, and that as long as she has credit, or money, I shall never be brought to such extremities.

His intimacy with Lady Falkland's family was still maintained, for he goes on to say:

P

I received letters lately from Mr. Patrick Cary, I pray present my thanks and service to him, let me know where he lives and how, you can invent no better news than this for your letters.   If Latin, or Italian, be not more difficult to you, I would rather you would exercise yourself and me in those languages, than in English.   And if Mr. Cary knows Italian I should be glad if he would use it too, the affection to the language would beget in me stronger desires and hasten my resolution of seeing Italy again.

I pray you forget not to feed my father with letters, if you cannot with news.   For myself, it is one of the greatest contents I have in this world to receive your most dearly welcome lines.   My mother sends you her blessing, and my dear sister remembers her most cordial affection to you.

The property which had been the occasion of such anxious thought—of struggles between expediency and grace, of generous surrender on one side and care and trouble on the other—did not eventually benefit any of those concerned.   The part which Sir Francis, in his old age, took in the Civil war, utterly ruined his fortune, and Henry's inheritance dwindled almost to nothing.

Meanwhile Francis had been received into the Roman College, and was quietly pursuing his studies; the climate, however, after awhile affected his health, and he had to spend two successive summers at Tivoli.   In July, 1641, he was ordained priest, and began his novitiate at St. Andrea, on the

10th of October of the same year—the Feast of St. Francis Borgia. He went through it successfully, and had the happiness of making his vows. But soon his health entirely broke down, and he died in 1643 or 1644, at Naples, "in the opinion of sanctity."

One of the Society—Father Ward—who had followed him to Rome, and often saw him at St. Andrea, writes of him as follows :

By the unanimous consent of all good men, he is esteemed a young saint; nor, perhaps, can any testimony be stronger than the voice of such a multitude; since Mother Church, herself, has always esteemed this as one of the modes of recognizing the great servants of God. It is not easy for so many to be mistaken, especially when the object of their remark is no solitary hermit, or enclosed monk, but one living a public life, easily accessible, and familiarly known to many, as Francis was.

We close this long chapter with Henry Slingsby's tribute to the memory of his brother. It was written at Kilkenny, May 17th, 1644.

No one can blame me for my extraordinary grief for the loss of such a brother, who, next to God and the Saints, was the chief author and helper of whatever in my life I can call happiness. From him I got my second and better birth to God and to the Catholic Church, to his care and prayers I ascribe it that I have hitherto constantly persevered in the Church, to

the astonishment of many persons. By his words and
example I was mightily drawn to profess a life in
accordance with the faith I had received, and I wish I
could say that since I was separated from him I had
not grown too, too, lukewarm!   If the honour we
receive from men is to be reckoned happiness, all that
I have of this I owe solely to him, and I am most
honoured where he was most known and I least.   If
the opinion of virtue and probity is of any use, wherever he lived, or wherever he was even heard of, in
this kingdom, there I am quite sure I shall never want
anything that a good name is sure to bring.   I have
his estate, I have everything of his but his virtue.

CHAPTER XIII.

Patrick and Placid Cary's escape from Few.

AFTER the crisis in her affairs which obliged Lady Falkland momentarily to part with her daughters, she reduced her household to a very small compass, and from that time forward, gave up what the writer of her life calls "those entangling businesses in which she had dealt, and always been a loser." These were evidently speculations, in which she had constantly embarked, in order to obtain means for the support of an establishment, which her large-heartedness had increased to a degree far beyond her means, and which at last ended in ruin. She now plainly saw that this system was a bad one, and finally renounced it, and in order to keep out of debt, resorted instead to a system of strict economy. This change relieved her from the necessity of seeing numbers of people, and carrying on suits at Court, and henceforward, she lived either in the country, or in a much more retired manner in London, giving up keeping or hiring a coach, and almost always going on foot. This she had refrained from during her husband's lifetime, for fear of annoying him, and also when her daughters were staying with her before, and in the early days of their conversion. When they went into company, she did not wish to impose upon them this sacrifice, "not being willing to put upon them, more than they could endure." Some time afterwards, she resumed for a while the use of a carriage, whilst one of her eldest sons was in London, as he could not bear to see her do without it. We are told of another luxury, she renounced at that time, the nature of which does not seem clear; this was the use of *chopins*. Whatever they may have been, she had always worn them, her daughter tells us, "being low in stature, and for a long time very fat," but it appears they were expensive, and made it more difficult to walk on foot. The absence of her children also enabled her to make alterations in her attire, such as leaving off wearing nothing but black, which she had done since her widowhood, and making use indifferently of anything that was cheapest, and would last longest. The horror of debt she then conceived, and a strong sense of the injustice of borrowing, without a prospect of being able to repay, made her resolve never again to ask friends to lend her money. When she was in pressing difficulties, she applied to them for assistance, which was more humbling to herself, but fairer towards them.

Her society became much more restricted, and her life more private from that time forward. It was principally her Catholic intimate friends, who now frequented her house, and priests for whom she had a particular esteem and regard. "If any less remarkable for virtue and holiness, were still invited by her at times, it was as a charitable duty. She entertained them willingly and civilly, but did not retain them with such earnest and importunate solicitation, as she had formerly done." Her spare time was now almost entirely spent in reading.

As soon, however, as she was able to breathe, her anxious desire was to have her daughters back again. Anne, the eldest, soon returned. The Duchess of Buckingham, who was a Catholic at heart, had been the intimate friend of Miss Cary, from the earliest childhood. She begged Lady Falkland to recall her to London, and offered to provide for her maintenance. Elisabeth also returned to her. The two others were still at Few, and for the sake of their brothers, it was well that they stayed on there. They wrote to their mother, that these children "had an extraordinary desire to see themselves Catholics, and would have desired to refuse to go to Church, though they should be ever so much whipped for it, if it would not have caused them to be taken away from their sisters and cut off from all possibility of becoming Catholic." Moreover, "that with great diligence and art, they used to observe the fasting-days without being observed, enduring for it, especially one of them, extremity of hunger, not being allowed to eat most fasting meats, as unwholesome for children." Lady Falkland, on hearing these details, felt of course the most ardent desire to assist her boys, in achieving what had been the constant object of her prayers. She had barely enough to support her little household as it was, her means being reduced to a small weekly allowance, but in such a case as this she was willing to run any risk, and perhaps had friends willing to assist her in securing the conversion of her little sons. She began by writing to Lord Falkland, and urging him to send his brothers to some school abroad, naming several for that purpose, and telling him, that she could not endure the thought of their remaining under Mr. Chilling-worth's government. If he would not agree to this, she warned and assured him, "that she would steal them away."

This was no surprise to Lord Falkland. Mr. Chillingworth had informed him of what he had observed in London, when the children were at home, and since the Miss Carys had been at Few he " had been skilfully inquisitive, and spied out all they said or wrote, how secretly soever " and reported it to his patron, who refused to allow the boys to be sent abroad, and though he did not think it likely that his mother would be able to accomplish her purpose whilst they were in his house, still, to make it yet more impossible, he resolved to send them off under the care of Puritans, where they would be narrowly looked after. This intention on his part, only made Lady Falkland more solicitous to effect their removal. She gave up neither the hope nor the expectation of it, though for the time being, it appeared almost impracticable. As her means were not improved, she knew that Lord Falkland would be annoyed at her recalling to London all his sisters, whom at her request, and on account of her inability to support them, he had taken charge of. They were most anxious to return to her, and declared that they would be willing to do so on any conditions, and suffer any hardships, for the sake of the exercise of their religion, and deliverance from Mr. Chillingworth's importunities, which, though by God's mercy, now no longer dangerous to them, were unspeakably wearisome. We find his proceedings, thus described in the forcible language of the time.[1]

They (the Miss Carys) knowing him better, heard him, for heard he would be, no more as a saint, but as a procurator of the devil. Whilst they were at Few with him, they arrived at such an acquaintance with this gentleman that, if they had retained any doubt as to there being truth in him, he quickly would have resolved it, for now he declared to them his opinions in their true colours, which he had not done absolutely before, never letting them know of his actual misbelief of the Trinity, though pressing upon them doctrine as much as he durst. To a young handmaid

[1] We quote the whole of this account, as a curious illustration of the religious confusion and fluctuations produced by the so-called Reformation.

of one of them, named Camilla, who had been reconciled at the same time as her mistress, he had dared to do more, and used force to make her listen to him, holding her in spite of her teeth when she wished to go, and keeping down her hands when she would stop her ears, into which he bawled his blasphemies. After all he had said to them, they saw him pretend to be a Puritan to those that were so, and their sister-in-law and her mother[2] esteem him for a kind of saint, though indeed they hardly believed they did so really, but thought they were rather desirous to maintain his credit before Catholics, in hopes he might work upon them, for these ladies kept very secret some proceedings of his which they judged would make him appear in their eyes unsaintlike and ridiculous. He was so good at denying his own words, that before Protestants he often did asseverate with horrible oaths and execrations, which made those that heard him tremble till use made it familiar, that he never had said those things he spoke to Catholics in their absence—so that those who had heard him were sometimes ready to doubt whether they had been deceived or not, or to think he must have forgotten his own words—until by accusing him of them immediately whilst he was yet speaking, they found even then he would not immediately forswear them, and afterwards returning to them repeat the same things he had said before, making strange equivocations to account for his oaths to the Protestants, and reproving them for discrediting him, alleging as his excuse for swearing

[2] Lettice, Lady Falkland, and her mother, Lady Morrison.

to do one thing when he meant another, the words of St. Paul, and our Lord's example, when He feigned to go further to the two disciples at Emmaus. They could not find words with which to question him before Protestants, for which he did not make some strained equivocation, yet such as served his turn, though no better one sometimes than what he made use of in disputing with Father Dunstan, who charged him with his denial of the Trinity. This being before Protestants, fearing to lose his credit with them, he professed the contrary. Father Dunstan, knowing his practices, questioned him more precisely, and asked did he believe in the Trinity, Three Persons and One God? He affirmed he did. Then the Father, who was certain he did not, as was then generally well known, desired he would write down his answer, thinking he durst not have done that for fear of disgracing himself with so many who would know it to be false; yet he did as he was asked, but afterwards said to those who questioned him, that it was true that he believed that there was One God *and* Three Persons, just as there were three or one hundred or one thousand or ten thousand persons, men or angels, and thus he meant what he had said; but that he had never said he believed One God *in* Three Persons, nor that the Three Persons were One God, nor that they had anything to do with one another. Yet for all these denials and forswearings, when his patron's sisters had left his house, he professed himself openly a Socinian, God not permitting any doubt to remain on whose side the lie had been, for at the table before all he bade the Protestants accept Transubstantiation or deny the Trinity, he having as good and as many arguments, against the one as against the other. It was no less admirable to hear those who, if they would not acknowledge the name of Puritans, were at the least rigid Calvinists, dispute with him. One would have thought that the endeavour on each side was to make the other Catholic. They objected to him his most high and intolerable pride in thinking the whole world to be in error, and that he alone was able to discern the truth which no one else had been able to do. Had there been none (they said) in so long a time of a capacity equal to his to find it, or as much in God's favour to be helped by His grace to see the right? Had God no care of all Christians to permit them to err till *he* came? When he answered that there had been, and were many of the same opinion, though they made not profession of it, which he would not have done had he not been constrained to it by the urgings and questioning of others, they would then ask him how he knew there had been such if they had not professed it, and when he did assert that there were many in Transylvania and Poland of his religion, since the break with Rome, they would continue to wonder that God should so neglect the rest of Christendom, as to confine the truth to that remote corner of the world, all which arguments, with many more of the like, he would turn back against Luther and Calvin, and their followers, and he would highly èxalt to them the Church of Rome, and affirm that whoever would make account of authority in matters of religion must necessarily submit to it, and that its authority and the belief of the Trinity were so inseparable, that none who had any reason would divide them.

These disputes had sometimes taken place before the Miss Carys, in whose presence to see themselves constrained to make use against one another of arguments to the advantage of the Church, was, we are told, "a torment to both sides." Lord Falkland, whom his sister says "had like opinions in religion to Mr. Chillingworth," was wont to say, "that the great convenience there seemed to be, according to human understanding in an infallible guide, and the great aptness every one had to wish there were such a thing, did make them readily assent to believe it, and that indeed it would be most reasonable to believe, that if God has any care or Providence over mankind, He should have provided such a guide, were it not that the only Church that pretends to this authority, teaches things so contrary to reason, the chief of which he counted to be the Trinity, that this argument is overweighted. The believing of those things being more against reason, than that other belief was according to it."

The writer of this statement concerning Mr. Chillingworth concludes by saying: Yet "abstracting *truth* and *religion*, he seemed to be in other matters *a kind of an honest man*, and good-natured, never seeking to do anybody any kind of temporal hurt, and ready to do courtesies to every one, which perhaps was much to his purpose."

With this last little bit of sarcasm ends her account of this strange man, from whose hands we cannot wonder that Lady Falkland was ardently desirous to withdraw her poor little boys, so great was the danger to which his tuition exposed their moral and religious principles. She had no doubt shed many bitter tears over the baleful influence Chillingworth had acquired over her noble-hearted and high-minded eldest son, "the one of all her children who loved her best," and it must have been an effort to her to act in a manner likely deeply to offend and estrange him from her : but the souls of Placid and Patrick were at stake, and she could not hesitate an instant upon the course she had to pursue.

Some business with his Majesty made it necessary for Lucy Cary to come to London, and as Lord Falkland's wife had also some affairs of her own which required her presence in or near town, her mother-in-law begged her to bring both her daughters with her, fully intending in that case to keep them in London. But her son, suspecting this design, was desirous to retain at Few the youngest of his sisters, knowing well that in that case Lucy would return, in order not to leave her alone with Protestants. He made objections, therefore, to Mary's departure, but the girls undertook to remove all difficulties, and hoped to succeed. At the same time they wrote to their mother, that if it was ever to be done, she must now at once contrive to get her little sons away, for if this was not accomplished before their departure, fixed as it was for the following week, it would be impossible.

The difficulties in Lady Falkland's way appeared insuperable, even supposing she could get hold of the boys. She had no money wherewith to make them travel to London in the usual way, nor to maintain them when there, nor to send them abroad, which would be necessary, for she knew that their relations would never allow her to keep them. No one encouraged her to undertake so difficult an enterprise as to steal them out of their brother's house and watchful Mr. Chillingworth's hands, for they were on their guard against her design, and bent on defeating it. She had no one to employ fit to be intrusted with such a matter; yet for all that she did not despair, but hired two horses and sent down two men with them. One of these was a poor fellow that got his living by going on errands and who at that time was not even a Catholic. The other was a servant of her own, "a stupid heavy creature, whose honesty turned out to be even less than his wit." This man only knew one servant in her son's house; the other knew them all, and on that account the former was to go up to the door, whilst the other remained concealed from sight, and give a letter from herself to one of her daughters, a strange hand having written the address. It was to be presented as coming from a lady, her friend, of whom he should be supposed to be the servant.   In this letter Lady Falkland directed her daughters to deliver their brothers into these men's hands.   She had traced a plan capable of success, supposing everybody in the house would stand still in the places she expected. The whole scheme was founded on possibilities only, without any appearance of probability.   These men were directed to carry the boys to Abington, a distance of about fifteen miles from her son's house, the children riding and the men going on foot by their side, which was but a slow pace for such an occasion.   Ten or twelve miles they would have to travel on the plain road to London, along which they would be sure as soon as they were missed to be pursued ; but to hire more horses, and so procure greater speed, she could not possibly afford.   At Abington they were to be met by a young gentleman named Alexander, who had once served Lady Falkland, " and from thence, with a pair of boatmen, he was to bring the boys to London by water, a thing unusual enough.   The money she had been able to obtain to furnish these two companies was so short that if they did not happen to despatch their business on the day appointed, they would want money to bring them up ; besides, the hired horses were to come back at a fixed time.   Howsoever, the Providence of God seemed extraordinarily to guide the matter—there was not the least circumstance that did not concur to advance it."   The man charged with the letter delivered it to Miss Cary. If her cousin, Mr. Thomas Hinton, had been at home, he would have taken it and discovered the man to be a messenger of Lady Falkland's. In the meantime,

The many arguments which had been going on as to the youngest of the two sisters remaining behind, and their conversations upon it, gave them excuses for whispering much, and for walking out often alone with their little brothers. In so doing that day they met their mother's man, whom they charged to come no more in sight of the house. They walked abroad several times in this manner, showing the men to their brothers that they might know one another, and also led them to the place where they should meet at the appointed time, when they should have resolved upon it. This was about one mile from the house. So far were the children to come alone and on foot. The two sisters thought that for many reasons no day would suit so well for the execution of this design as that of their own departure, when some bustle in the house would better hide it. They therefore stayed the men two or three days longer than had been planned for that purpose. One day more they could not have remained, because of the word that had been given for the return of the horses. That gentleman of their brother's, Mr. Hinton, who had been absent when his being so was necessary to their plan, returned that very night, without which their sister-in-law must needs have delayed her journey. It so happened, likewise, that just then one of the sisters received some money due to her, which should have been paid a quarter of a year before, which had

Q

it arrived then would have been spent and gone. This greatly advantaged their business, helping to further it in many ways, besides giving the two men their charges for the time they had delayed them, and also for Mr. Alexander at Abington, who had been waiting with the boat, and would be like to have no money now to bring them to London.

The eyes of those interested in stopping these designs seemed to be blinded, for they who at other times were most watchful, suspected nothing. Mr. Chillingworth, who always pried very narrowly, was just behind her who received the letter, and looked over her shoulder when she opened it, yet did not know the hand, though within it was her mother's writing, which he was well acquainted with. Though the children themselves kept all very secret, still their packing up their things and giving away many, which they did in the house, might well have been enough to make one less vigilant than him suspicious. Nor, on the morning of her departure, did their sister-in-law or any one with her, miss them—only when the coach was gone so far that it was too late, they remembered them, and lamented that they had not taken leave of them.

The night before they were to go away, the boys' sisters conveyed their cloaks to the men, with an advertisement to meet them in the place that had been appointed, by four or five of the clock. Then making a show of having themselves much business to do in the morning, before their departure, they expressed a desire to be called very early, which their little brothers, as previously agreed upon between them, undertook to do at three o'clock—so that they might have occasion to do openly what, considering the wakefulness of Mr. Chillingworth, which they were well aware of, and their sleeping in his chamber, they could not possibly have done by stealth. The desire of the boys to go was so great that it gave them not leave to oversleep themselves, but rising at three with as much noise as they could, they went to call their sisters, and played about the house for an hour, showing themselves to all who were up at that time. Then one of their sisters took them down, and saw them safe out of all the courts of the house without being descried by any one. It was not yet light, and all alone they ran for the space of a mile to meet men entirely strangers, and whose persons were not suited to encourage children to have confidence in them. Passing a little village on their way to the appointed place, they had to hide themselves behind bushes, the barking of the dogs having made the people come forth. After meeting the men they were obliged to leave the highway at the sight of every coach or horse, there being great fear that their sister-in-law's coach and company might overtake them, as they travelled along the same way at least as far as Oxford. When they arrived there, which was far in the day, knowing they were likely to be followed with a hue and cry, the men bethought themselves so to divide company as not to be seen in the town like any description that might be made of them. So they took the boys off their horses, one of the men passed first through the town leading one horse, the children following him on foot some space after, without hats or cloaks to look less like strangers, and lastly came the other man. on horseback. They came to Abington after noon, where they found the gentleman and his two watermen without money as they expected, but, which they did not expect, the latter so drunk that Mr. Alexander dared not remove the boys that night, and so the others tarried too. Howsoever, after supper, those that had brought them so far and he who was to take them on to London fell out, and by their disputing made it known in the house that they were stolen children, at which the town was raised, and the constable came to seize them. But this man happening to be an old acquaintance and gossip of the poor Protestant fellow, one of the two who had charge of the boys, was by him satisfied that they were his mistress's children, and that they were going to their mother, who had sent for them. Having so escaped, they did not venture to stay till the next day, lest some report of this inquiry having been made, should reach the ears of a friend of Lord Falkland's, who lived near this town, and the suspicion be renewed, so they were fain to take water at ten o'clock on a dark night with boatmen, not only not able to row, but every minute ready to overturn the boat with reeling and nodding.

Lady Falkland, whose anxiety we can well imagine, heard the news of the danger in which they had left her little s ns from the two men, who reached London before they did. The moments which intervened between this announcement and their arrival, must have been amongst the most trying of her life, and equal to that anguish, the joy and gratitude with which soon afterwards she received them safe and sound. But her troubles regarding her boys were by no means at an end. After her joyful meeting with them, her first care was to place them out of the reach of their Protestant relatives, which she succeeded in doing by paying for their lodging and board at the houses of Catholics in obscure parts of London. In order to meet this expense, she and the rest of her family, for now her daughters were all at home, were obliged, to use the expression of the writer of her life, " to keep more Fridays in the week than one." Meanwhile great was the agitation at Few, when at dinner the day of their departure Patrick and Placid were missed. After a diligent but vain search the truth was suspected; and when none of their books and things were found in their room, the doubts changed into certainty. Some of those concerned said, that the thought of their flight that day had never occurred to any of them, but that all had been arranged for the removal of the boys, during the absence of their sisters, to a place where it would have been impossible for their mother to communicate with them. Lord Falkland instantly sent to scour the country in search of his brothers, but soon came to the conclusion that it was too late to overtake the boys, and dispatched a messenger to his wife in London, charging her to use every endeavour to discover them there.

She instantly informed Lord Newburgh of their flight, and he announced the fact to the Privy Council, of which he was a member. Their lordships summoned the children's mother to appear before them, and whilst she was in attendance gave orders to search her house. In answer to the questions addressed to her, Lady Falkland admitted that she had sent for her sons and had placed them where she had thought proper. Though obliged to have them fetched away secretly from their brother's house, she pleaded that there had been in this nothing contrary to law, her son having no pretence or right to keep them from her against her will and theirs, seeing that they had never been committed to his charge either by the State or their own father; that she had often warned him, that if he did not remove them from under Mr. Chillingworth's care she would be forced thus to act, for she was determined not to let him have the guidance of her children. If my Lord of Canterbury wished to hear the reason why, she would make it clear to him whenever he chose to demand it. The persons she sent to fetch away the children were her servants, and the boys came alone a whole mile to meet them, which plainly proved they were not brought away by force.

The lords told her in reply that it was against the law to send her sons to seminaries abroad. She defied them to prove that she had done any such thing, and indeed the children, as we have said,

were for the moment in London, but she was not
sorry that their lordships should be under the impression that they had already crossed the sea, as
this would make it easier to contrive their passage
to France when an opportunity occurred; and she
went on to argue that it was not illegal to have them
brought up in a foreign country. Their lordships
rejoined that to send them out of England was
against the law, and showed her orders to officers at
various ports to let no one of tender age embark
without a licence. She alleged, that this did not
concern her; she was not one of the officers to
whom these orders were addressed; that there was
nothing said in them about sending children, only
commands not to let them pass, which if these
persons had done, let them be questioned, not her.
Somewhat nettled by her tone, one of the lords asked
if she meant to teach them law? " No," she answered,
" I only desire your lordships to remember what I
make no doubt you knew before, and which I, being
the daughter of a lawyer, am not wholly ignorant
of." They demanded the name of the person who
had conveyed her sons to France. She could assure
them with truth that she did not know it herself.
" It was not likely," they said, " she would trust her
sons in the hands of persons whose names she did
not know." Then they referred her to the Lord Chief
Justice Bramston, and in case he was not satisfied
with her statements, she was to be committed to the
Tower.

In compliance with this mandate, Lady Falkland presented herself to the Chief Justice, and " after being examined by him with much civility, and making the same answers, she was dismissed, though not in express terms acquitted. Wishing to bring the matter to a point, she asked how she was to be conveyed to the Tower, to which she was to be committed, in case he was not satisfied. He said he knew not what more he had to say to her, unless he could persuade her to recall her sons to England, and confessed himself satisfied with her replies. He even offered her his coach to take her home."

Some days afterwards, being pressed by the importunities of others, he summoned before him the two Miss Carys, who had assisted in their little brothers' flight, but had no interview with them. He was too busy to see them, he said, when they came; and when the young ladies showed no desire to wait, one of his gentlemen told them to go home if they pleased, and that his lordship's coach would carry them. The servants concerned in the affair, were examined and answered as their mistress had done. One of them, however, the false Catholic, turned against her, did all he could to betray the whereabouts of the children, and denounced his companion, who was put in prison, but as this was done on the sole responsibility of the officers who arrested him, and not by command of the Chief Justice, he was soon released.

Meanwhile, there was not a house where Lady

Falkland or her daughters had acquaintances, which was not searched. To put an end, to the danger and anxiety of delay, a scheme was formed, by which the boys were to be placed in the hands of a lady of the name of Mullins, who would have arranged for their departure, and entrusted them to some one unknown to their mother, so that, if again examined, she should have been able to affirm that she knew not who had taken them abroad. But this was not found to be necessary. Father Holland, S.J., the same Father who had once held a disputation with Mr. Chillingworth at her house, undertook to send Lady Falkland's children to France, under the guidance of another Father of the Society, and procured the money for their journey, which had been the chief difficulty in the way of their departure. On the road to Paris, when near Rouen, the young travellers and their protector seem to have been in some danger from robbers, but having escaped this peril, they reached Paris in safety. The boys were placed there in the Convent of the Benedictine Fathers, and placed under the care of the Prior, Father Gabriel, who showed them every kindness. Placid Cary became later on a religious in that monastery. Patrick when he left it went to Rome. There he found in Father Wilfred, probably of the same Order, a zealous and true friend. Moreover, Henrietta Maria recommended him strongly to Cardinal Barberini, who in consequence showed him great favour. After his mother's death the good Queen renewed on several occasions, her expressions of interest in the young convert. Out of what the King allowed her, Lady Falkland contributed something yearly to the support of her absent sons. This was even continued some time after her death by the kind hearted monarch, and when "the extremity of the times" necessitated the cessation of this subsidy, Father Philip, Father Watt, and other Catholics, came to the assistance of Patrick Cary. It appears that at one time, he wished to become a priest and a religious, but on account of his eldest brother, having no children, and Placid, the youngest, being a monk, he was dissuaded from it; so important did the existence of titled and influential Catholic families in England, appear to their persecuted co-religionists. Later on, probably when the Commonwealth had reduced such considerations to insignificance, he made a trial of the religious life at Douay, but was forced to give it up, "his constitution not being able to bear the kind of diet which the rules enjoined." After the Restoration, we find him applying to Sir Edward Hyde, afterwards Lord Clarendon, his elder brother's most intimate friend, for assistance in obtaining a military position in the Spanish service. Lord Clarendon advised him strongly not to pursue this plan, and "to bide a little while, in expectation of some favourable change in his fortunes." There is no evidence, however, that his worldly affairs ever

materially improved. All we know in other respects of Patrick Cary, is, that he revised the
manuscript life of his mother, written by one of his
sisters, and struck out of it some passages he
evidently considered as too familiar and homely in
style. He appears to have inherited some of his
mother's talent, at any rate he had some facility
in writing verses, for in 1819, Sir Walter Scott,
published a small quarto volume of " Trivial poems
and triolets, composed in obedience to a lady's
commands by Patrick Cary, in August, 1651." At
the end of the book, is a collection of hymns,
which show the author to have been a Catholic and
a cavalier. The escutcheon prefixed to the arms,
a red cross on a white shield, with the motto, *Tant
que je puis*, is not that of the Carys, but the design
probably meant, that he henceforth gave up all
thoughts of a military and secular life, and devoted
himself to the furtherance of the religion of the
Cross. We may therefore conclude, that Lady
Falkland's prayers and efforts with regard to the
·two little boys at Few, attained their object.
Their lives indeed were not, according to worldly
ideas, prosperous or brilliant ; but Placid, in the
peaceful retirement of the cloister, and Patrick, in
an existence of comparative poverty, preserved the
pearl of great price, the precious faith which their
mother, at all costs, had secured for them.

CHAPTER XIV.

The last years of Lady Falkland's life.

AFTER she had brought to a safe conclusion her children's removal to France, Lady Falkland found herself in another pressing difficulty. The plague broke out in London, and without any place to go to, or any money wherewith to hire a house elsewhere, she was sadly distressed about her daughters and her little household. In this extremity assistance came to her from an unexpected quarter. Young Henry Slingsby, full of gratitude for all he had gained from his acquaintanceship with the Miss Carys at Few, and the hospitality their mother had shown to him and his holy brother, volunteered, though poor himself, to lend Lady Falkland a sum which enabled her to remove her family to a little village at some distance from London. She took up her abode in two poor thatched cottages, and remained there about six months. At the end of that time, Lord Falkland having business to transact with his mother regarding the sale he had effected of estates which were to have been her jointure, but which he had redeemed, it became important for them to meet. Ever since she had stolen away, as he called it, his brothers, there had been estrangement and coldness between the mother and son. Letters written on both sides in a tone of anger, had increased this unpleasant feeling. But seizing on this occasion, she went to his house, "using no other ceremony than sending to him for his coach." He took this so well, we are told, that on her arrival they were soon good friends. He brought her back himself to the place where she lived, and settled her in a more convenient and better house, which she inhabited for three years, occupying herself as usual with literary pursuits and charitable exertions; completing during that time her translation of Cardinal Perrone's writings, and teaching poor people to work with yarn and wool, "which entertained her time and thoughts." In 1637, she returned to London, and spent there the two last years of her life.

For twenty-two years, Lady Falkland had suffered from a cough, which, from repeated colds and constant neglect, had become chronic and ended in consumption. From the time of her last removal to London, she began visibly to decline in health, and she was obliged to confine herself almost entirely to the house. In poverty and solitude this active and agitated existence closed, but not in gloom and sorrow. She was alone, for her six Catholic children had left England. We have seen that her two youngest sons each followed in the path which she had opened to them, and one after another the four daughters she so dearly loved departed from her, God, in answer to their mother's prayers and tears, having granted to all of them a religious vocation. Aspiring to the habit of St. Benedict, the Saint to whom Lady Falkland had always had the greatest devotion, "she much rejoicing to have them the children of such a father," they responded to the Divine call, and carried away with them to their religious house in France the blessing of the lonely but not forsaken mother, who was awaiting day by day her own summons to Heaven.

She had been far from taking npon herself, [her daughter tells us] to suggest a religious vocation to her children, knowing well that this only belonged to God, nor was she a mother who desired to be rid of them, how much care whatsoever their being at home might cost her, nor did she seek to oversway them in their choice of an Order. She honoured very much all the Orders in God's Church, and most welcome were they all to her house, but her especial devotion was to the Benedictine Fathers, who most did her the honour to frequent it. From them it was she had received the highest and greatest obligations, for besides that which she had in common with all those of her country, the English nation having received its Christianity from Benedictine apostleship, she had many others particular to herself, for she was in great measure satisfied as to religion and reconciled by a Benedictine; and to one of the same Order she owed under God the conversion of her children. Her ghostly Fathers were, from first to last, of that Order, and, a little more than a year before her death, she was admitted into the Confraternity of St. Benedict by the Father Prior of Douay, receiving from his hands the little scapular.

It was therefore not only with resignation, but with a joy that is compatible with the deepest human sorrow, that, in the course of the year 1638, she saw three of her daughters depart for Cambray, and felt that they were at last removed from the snares, the miseries, and the temptations of an heretical country, where to be a firm Catholic required the spirit of a martyr. But her eldest daughter—the one whom at her birth her mother, whilst yet a Protestant, had offered to our Blessed Lady, promising in her heart never to oppose her being a nun, if such should be hereafter her desire—up to that time, and after her sisters' departure, had never showed or felt the least inclination to the religious life, though she had attained the age of twenty-four. It was no doubt a consolation to the poor mother to retain near her this one child, this darling of her heart, who, in the midst of all her trials at the time of her conversion, had always remained devotedly attached to her. Though it is but a conjecture, we cannot but think that it is this daughter who was the author of the life we have been modernizing, and that in the account of the last sacrifice Lady Falkland was called upon to make, it is of her own vocation the writer speaks.

"Not having the least idea," she says, "that this daughter had any thought of becoming a nun, she had set her heart on a scheme for placing her where she would have the most free exercise of her religion under the greatest and most powerful protection in the kingdom." This evidently meant at Court. Steps had been taken for that purpose and seemed likely to succeed. We may well imagine then that Lady Falkland, " whom it was always more hard to divert from any design she had once conceived, than to make her quit the possession of anything she had," clung to this project with great tenacity. It promised for her child a pleasant and congenial existence, and secured for her the consolation of retaining in England one of her Catholic children. But in the meantime, Miss Cary had been for some time deliberating with herself, and, though tardily, compared with her younger sisters, had found that God was calling her also to the religious life, and was turning over in her mind how to break this to her mother. She had recourse for this purpose to some friends, who called on her for that purpose, but felt much embarrassed how to broach the subject. Lady Falkland, however, strangely enough began to speak of the vow and oblation she had made of this particular child to our Blessed Lady, adding that on this account, should she have happened to have had a religious vocation, it would have been more difficult for her to oppose it than in the case of the others.

Seizing on this opportunity, those who were charged with the disclosure proceeded to make it to the astonished mother, who, although this intelligence took her entirely by surprise, yet

Being taken in the instant when the memory and fervour of her vow were fresh, she consented without saying one word against it, albeit not without signs of inward strife; for, as she afterwards confessed, had she not been caught with those words in her mouth, she would have thought of many reasons against it, and had with much difficulty foregone a design she liked so well and had been so near effecting, and agreed to one so different from it, and which after all was only a trial, for the resolution did appear sudden and subject to change before execution, and indeed she saw no appearance of means to bring it about, for it sounded strangely to propose to Protestants to furnish her child with what was necessary to enter into religion. But when once she had consented and resolved on it, though all these thoughts were in her mind, she set herself, after her ordinary manner, with confidence and diligence, to bring it about, and reproached herself heartily for the momentary reluctance she had felt at the first hearing of it, as never so small a resistance to God's mercy in the acceptance of her vow, had been she considered a great ingratitude.

Contrary to her expectations, she found that her son, when once assured, and of this there could be no doubt, that it was his sister's own unbiassed desire to become a nun, was ready to do all she

R

asked, "and all the more speedily and willingly, as the Queen had done him the honour and his sister the charity to urge him on that point." Henrietta Maria also obtained from the King the payment to the convent of Cambray of a dowry due to it on behalf of another of the Miss Carys.

In the register of that convent we find the names of Lady Falkland's four daughters. Lucy Cary was called in religion Dame Magdalena, Elisabeth, Dame Augustina, and Anne, Dame Clementina; Mary's religious name is not mentioned.

In 1650, Anne was selected to lead a colony of the nuns to Paris, and was accompanied by her own sister Mary. There Henrietta Maria, to whom Dame Clementina had once been Maid of honour, received them with great kindness. The French Court followed her example. Five more nuns soon joined them from Cambray, and Dame Bridget Moore was appointed Superioress. "Mother Clementina," the record says, "could never be prevailed upon, from her great humility, to accept any office of distinction." Mary afterwards returned to Cambray, but Anne died in Paris. Of Lucy Cary (Dame Magdalena) there is a panegyric in the obituary of her convent which does honour not only to the memory of a holy nun, but also to her mother; on that account we give it here.

On November 1, 1650, died Lucy Magdalen Cary, daughter of Lord Viscount Falkland, sometime Viceroy of Ireland. She had been brought up and lived some years in heresy, during which period she was carried away by the vanities of the world ; but we have reason to believe that Almighty God had regard to the prayers and tears of the Lady, her mother, who never ceased to implore Heaven for the conversion of her children, for she was a woman of extraordinary piety, as appears from the relation of her life, written by one who knew her well. In fine our dear Magdalena cheerfully abjured her heresy after she had been convinced of her errors by a Reverend Father of our congregation, a great friend of the Lady, her mother, and she cast herself into the bosom of the holy Catholic Church, wherein she lived even during her secular state, a very obedient, pious, and zealous member, quitting the vanities of the world, and exercising even in her mother's house more than ordinary mortifications, indeed such as were rather to be admired than imitated in such a state of life. But as for her obedience to her mother after her conversion, she may be a pattern to all children towards parents, which shows the efficacy of Divine grace in her soul, for of an obstinate jeering lady, whose own mother did not escape her affronts, she became, when a convert to our holy faith, a dutiful, obedient child to her who was the best of mothers, and the most charitable of Christian ladies to her neighbours.

She was accustomed to frequent the Court of King James the First, when very young, and afterwards that of King Charles the First. She was highly thought of at that Court, but immediately after her conversion retired thence to live with her mother, contemning what the world might think of her sudden and extraordinary change; leaving her vain attire and dressing, about which she had been used to spend daily several hours, she now clothed herself in a decent but very homely dress, giving herself to the practice of many virtues. At length Almighty God very forcibly inviting her to seek and labour after perfection, she entered into religion, wherein for the space of eleven years she lived an infirm, sickly, and suffering life, God leading her by the way of the Cross to the end of her days, which she concluded with a most truly humble and sincere acknowledgement of her own nothingness, and of God's infinite goodness and Providence towards her, as also with a total abandonment and resignation of herself into the arms of His Fatherly pity, having led an obedient and humble life all the time she had been in religion, without any regard to what she had been or might have been in the world, which she never would speak of, except of such passages as might humble and confound her, being in a particular manner very sensible of the many faults her jeering wit had made her fall into before her conversion, and for which afterwards she did endeavour to satisfy. In fine, worn out with infirmities, patiently borne for the love of God, through which we have cause to hope she has by His mercy purchased a great crown, she peaceably departed this life, leaving us her religious sisters, a good example of humility, patience, and obedience.—R.I.P."

It seems probable that the support of her sons

abroad and the expenses incurred in the entrance of her daughters into religion, swallowed up all Lady Falkland's slender resources, for she appears during the last period of her life, and after the departure of her children, to have again been often in the utmost need. Her daughter describes her position as follows :

" She had more than ever to seek supply in her occasions from others, and use may have made it easier to her, who had passed through so many changes, and allayed that inclination to pride that would abhor such a proceeding, yet no doubt she could never have brought herself to do it, had she not offered it to God as a humiliation, and from a sense of the much greater justice there is in begging than in borrowing, and as a willing submission to His dispositions. She never did anything against her will, but if once she conceived a thing to be right and resolved upon it, however contrary to her nature, she set herself to perform it with a good will. Her own experience of the torture and slavery of debt, made her so loathe it, that her greatest fear was to occasion this misery to her son, whose estate barely supplied his necessities. Albeit some consider that asking where civility scarce leaves a liberty of refusing, might be some sort of extortion, yet she was freed from this apprehension by thinking all others to be of her own humour, who always had sincerely rejoiced to find that what she could at any time spare would be beneficial and acceptable to others, for she took the greatest delight in the world to be able to do a pleasure to any one.

" But with time, the willingness and the amount of her friends' help decreased, and the petitions which had at first been received with readiness and much civility, were soon not welcomely entertained, and before long, brought on nothing but contempt, which she did bear contentedly, if not gladly. Half a year before her death, being far gone in a consumption, she was wholly neglected by those who, by worldly title or relationship, might have been expected to relieve her. Yet God provided that she should not want, for she was faithfully assisted to the last by her intimate private Catholic friends. And very near her death, her eldest son, then for the first time informed how matters stood—for she had foreborne letting him know of her extremity of need for fear of oppressing him, and also because her doings were not like to have been very pleasing to him [1]—came to town with his wife on purpose to remedy it, which he did for the moment as far as he knew, for she, out of a great sense of his decreasing estate and great charges, did not make known to him what was further necessary. So he left her much as he found her, until, being further advertized by others, he took order with his mother-in-law, intreating her to see all provided his sick parent

---

[1] In withdrawing his brothers from his care, and sending his sisters abroad to be nuns.

should need, which she did, being most kindly careful of her."

Lady Falkland died about the beginning of the Rebellion, and was thus spared, by a merciful dispensation of Providence, the grievous suffering of beholding the ruin of all those she most loved, honoured and esteemed; the cruel fate of the King and Queen who had been such generous friends to her; the triumph of the religious and political party she abhorred; the deaths in battle of her two noble-hearted sons "whose lives indeed she would have thought could not have been better lost, than in the service of his Majesty, unless it had been in the immediate service of God," but as to whose spiritual condition she would have had at best great misgivings. As it was "a large time was granted her, with all means and commodity, to prepare herself for her last passage, to which she did most seriously apply herself. The Lord having discharged her of the care of her children, who by His Providence were settled out of England and the occasion of heresy, she took better order during the last half year of her life, for the payment of her debts, than could have been thought possible, and, then, by much exercise of contrition, resignation, and confidence, disposed herself for death, which she expected and accepted willingly, with great acknowledgment of God's mercy towards her in all, and particularly in her last sickness, in which she was very quiet and pliable and easy to be ruled, which qualities were not very natural to her.

All her life before, she had suffered a most dreadful apprehension of death, yet, being questioned on her death-bed, by Father John Mentisse, Prior of Douay, as to the dispositions she was in as to resignation on its approach, she affirmed that she was desirous of it, but being told by him that she ought to be content to remain as she was, as it should please God, leaving herself in His hands in perfect indifference, she said that if it were best and God's will that she should so continue, she resigned herself entirely to live and die, as it should best please Him. Having ever since her conversion, made glad profession of the Catholic faith, so at her death she was most careful to avoid' making the least show to the contrary. Being often visited by her son's mother-in-law, a most earnest Protestant, she was afraid that in some sort of trance she used to lie in, not being perfectly herself, Lady Morrison might urge her on that point, and she should answer unconsciously somewhat not so Catholic, as she should have wished. For that reason, she did entreat a Catholic friend of hers, Mrs Platt, who carefully and painstakingly assisted her to the last, not to leave her at any time alone with Lady Morrison."

In the month of October of the year 1639, having received all the Sacraments of the Church, from the hands of Father Placid Gascoyne, her ghostly father, and assisted in her last moments by the visits and prayers of her Benedictine friends, and other Catholics, Lady Falkland died, at the age of fifty-four, "without any agony, quietly as a child, wholly spent by her disease." Her weary pilgrimage was ended; her eager spirit found its rest with God. She was buried, by the Queen's permission, in her chapel, and the Capuchin Fathers, "out of their charity," performed the funeral service. Though she had no Catholic child able to procure Masses for her departed soul, "yet she found those who freely of their own accord were mindful of her." Whilst in England the monks her friends privately offered up the Holy Sacrifice for their benefactress, in the convents of Douay and Cambray Mass was solemnly celebrated for one who, though not free from defects and weaknesses, had been a true and faithful servant of God, and turned many unto righteousness—one who, in the words of her loving and impartial biographer, "did most highly reverence all the precepts, ordinances, and even ceremonies of the Catholic Church; who made great account and most use of the prayers to which the Church hath given a particular worth, making them hers, and saying that she did thereby hope to be heard as a child of the Church, though, as she always acknowledged herself, a most imperfect one."

We close this chapter, with some supplementary details as to Lady Falkland's literary acquirements, and the peculiarities of her character, which have not found place in the course of this history. It is impossible not to be struck with the pains taken by the original writer of ᐱ this life, to adhere to the closest veracity in her estimate and description of her mother's natural virtues and faults, and in so doing, to enable us to judge of the work of grace effected in her soul, from her youth upwards, and especially after her conversion to the Catholic Church.

Of Lady Falkland's studies, information, and abilities, her daughter speaks as follows: " From the time of her childhood she had read much poetry of all sorts, ancient and modern, and in several languages—all that ever she could meet with. History very universally, especially ancient Greek and Roman historians. All chroniclers whatsoever of her own country, and the French writers of that sort very thoroughly; of most other countries something, though not so universally. Of the ecclesiastical history very much, and especially concerning the chief Pastors of the Church. O books treating of moral virtue and wisdom, such as Seneca, Plutarch's morals, and natural knowledge, as Pliny. Montaigne's works in French, and Bacon's in English she had read when young, and made her profit of them. With the Fathers' writings she was conversant, particularly with the works of Justin Martyr, St. Jerome, St. Gregory, and St. Augustine, and of very many others, as she could meet with them, most of what she read of these being translations in Spanish, Italian, and French, at least for many years. Of controversy, it may be said she had read most that has been written.

having, before she was a Catholic, studied the writings of all kinds of Protestant authors, such as the works of Luther and Calvin, all English writers of name—Latimer, Jewel, and divers others; also of newer divines of note, whatsoever came forth, and much French of the same matter. After she was a Catholic, she read some Catholic works of that sort, especially Sir Thomas More's works.

"Besides her translations of the writings of Cardinal Perrone, Louis de Blois, and many other French divines, and many other innumerable slight things in verse, she wrote an essay which was thought the best thing she ever penned. Mr. Montague, a Catholic friend of hers, had published a *Defence of the Church of Rome*, to which Lord Falkland, her son, wrote a reply, in which he charged Catholics with the divisions occasioned in families by the conversions they procured. She made a reply, in which notice was drawn to the fulfilling of His prophecy, Who said He came not 'to bring peace but the sword; the son herein being against his father, and the mother against her son, when faith was in question.' This paper was acknowledged by her son, to be a sufficient answer to his arguments, though not satisfactory to him; and that it was certainly enough clearly to confute a Protestant. For himself to answer it again, it would be necessary to go further and deny more[2] than he had done in his.

[2] Of the dogmas of Christianity, we may presume.

"She had conversed much, and with those that were very capable of several conditions and qualities, ` the conversation of her friends being the greatest delight of her life, yet she was never much over afflicted by the death or absence of any one.

"Though she was most forgetful and heedless in small ordinary things, which had no relation to one another, and about which she was apt to confound time strangely; for what she had read, her memory was good and sure. She spake very much and earnestly. Her heart was very open and she was easily moved; nor was it hard for those near about her, to get some power over her. Her manners were not in any fashion graceful, and her neglect, through forgetfulness, of customary civilities, was so notable, that it had grown into a privilege. Her heedlessness in this was so great, that she at divers times would come to see those she respected most, and having entered the room where they were, so wholly forgot them and the intention she came for, as to go forth again without saying to them a word. She rarely heeded whomsoever she met, and scarcely knew any but those she conversed with daily, when she met them in places where she was not used to see them. A short absence made her quite forget the faces of those she knew exceedingly well, though not themselves. It seemed not possible for her to help this, yet in two instances, respect had so great a power over her mind, as to overcome this heedlessness. She was so desirous at all times, to show her esteem of priests, and made so great account of their blessings, that negligent as she was of worldly customs and ceremonies, she never did omit to ask them for it, though she did forget sometimes, where she did it, kneeling for that purpose in public places, before she was aware. Nor did she when at Court, lose the thought of the high duty she owed to the King, nor the recollection of his presence, though his Majesty to try her, gave her often on purpose, occasions to make such mistakes.

" She had faults, but they seemed greater at some distance, than to those nearest at hand—what she truly had, was a hearty goodwill to God and His service. She was a most sound, sincere Catholic, greatly desiring the conversion of others, in order to which she cared nothing that she had to endure. For what may yet be wanting to her, to set her soul free from suffering in Purgatory, may it please God to inspire His servants to assist her with their prayers and sacrifices, and of His mercy give rest to her soul."

www.ingramcontent.com/pod-product-compliance
Lightning Source LLC
Chambersburg PA
CBHW030630030726
47497CB00006B/1714